INVADERS

KENNETH PASSAN

SEVERED PRESS
HOBART TASMANIA

INVADERS

Copyright © 2021 Kenneth Passan

WWW.SEVEREDPRESS.COM

ISBN: 978-1-922551-77-1

PROLOGUE

It was slightly breezy on a warm September day in the northwest forests, but also a sunny one. A good day for studying and collecting. Their location was about six hundred miles from Tokyo. It was like a different world from the hustle and bustle of the concrete and steel jungle that was the city. Here one could enjoy the peace and tranquility that the wilderness could offer. Although the forest was not a tourist attraction, it did attract those who loved to explore the wilderness as well as those who liked to hunt small game. And there was plenty of that around.

A small group of scientists were, at the time, the only group of people around for many miles. It included specialists in entomology from the Japanese government research facility for herpetology and entomology. On this particular day, its focus was on only one kind of insect species which could be found only in their country and nowhere else on earth.

Accordingly, they were dressed in protective suits to the hilt. But they weren't just any kind of protective suits. They had to be more than one quarter inch thick. That thickness included the gloves and face masks as well. This amount of thickness gave them the full protection that they needed. But it had the disadvantage of making the suits very heavy, so they couldn't spend very much time in them. Regardless, it was a necessary requirement that would save their lives.

They gathered themselves around the nest. Their nets and containers would hold the fierce, deadly creatures. Each group member had to move slowly and carefully. Any movement that was quick could trigger an attack by the swarm. Extreme care was the primary rule.

Before each movement, each of the three scientists would discuss their next move before making it. It was vital they complete this mission successfully. What they were doing to collect the specimens was not only for the Japanese government, it was also for their agency which had contracted with an agency in the United States in the research of this particular insect species and how it impacted the environment here and how it might in the US.

A mission of this kind would not be publicized, of course. There was no need to do that. Some people, if they found out, might panic unnecessarily, while others in the animal activist groups might cry "animal cruelty", also unnecessarily. There was nothing cruel about what they were doing.

As they gathered around the nest and goaded circling fliers into the nets, they were agonizingly careful not to leave any openings between the hoop where the net was attached to and the solid containers the specimens would be put into. The containers had small enough holes to provide air to the specimens for breathing while not allowing any of them to escape.

Although it seemed simple enough, it was not. The most important element and requirement of this whole mission was to capture the queen. Without her, there would be multiple phases of the research that could not be completed: phases such as determination of the reproductive cycles and growth phases of the larva into adults in two different climactic environments.

Because of this, they had to make sure that they obtained and enclosed the entire hive. "Her majesty" was somewhere in there along with hundreds of her personal caretakers and bodyguards. Not one could they leave to chance, especially if it could be her. If one regular worker escaped, so be it. Or even a few. That would be fine. It was their leader they had to worry about.

Not surprisingly, the buzzing was loud and continuous. The fliers were angry at this intrusion of their territory and they wanted nothing more than to attack the intruders. The scientists were well aware of this, knowing also that this was quite normal and expected behavior for insects of this kind.

Once they got what they believed to be the entire hive in their vented containers, they sealed them up in preparation for transport to the laboratory. Before they left the location, they checked as best as they could to ensure all nest residents were captured. Any that were already out in the forest somewhere they couldn't worry about. They also knew that this was not the initial introduction of them to the US. Some were already seen up in the northwestern corner of the US and into Canada.

Once they arrived at the lab, the specimens would be brought inside into an enclosed area where they would search for the queen. They believed she was in the hive because she rarely left it. Only if a new hive had to be established would she venture out.

Her life lasted only a year. It was during winter when she would mate and then hibernate. When spring arrived, she would wake up and lay her eggs. Sometime after that, before the following winter, she would die.

The scientists didn't know what part of her life cycle she was in. Regardless, they had to make sure she was in there and then somehow extract her along with some of her workers or "servants", place them in another special container and ready it for shipment to the US. They were successful.

The shipment was labeled "Hazardous Material" and required special handling. It could not be placed on just any flight, but one that would be privately contracted and paid for by the US agency ordering it.

These species of insects were not migratory. They had never been in the United States before. That is, until recently. If one regular worker or drone were to escape, it would be neither good nor disastrous. If, however, the queen were to escape, that would be quite a different matter. In that situation, the area's ecosystem could be thrown into complete chaos and the beginning of the end for honeybees everywhere could commence. Because if she were to lay eggs out in the American wilderness, that end could potentially begin sooner than later. The Americans had to pull out all the stops to ensure no escape would ever occur on their soil.

When killer bees first invaded the US, it was thought that they would take over and destroy the normalcy of the ecosystems in those areas they affected. It was always possible that any of them could mate with our normal honeybees, or European bees, which are far less aggressive. Even so, the ecosystems were not negatively affected so much as the increased fears of disturbing one of the killer bee hives. That in itself was enough to prevent anyone from disturbing any kind of bee hive unless they knew for sure what kind of bees they were. Only their level of aggressiveness betrayed their true identity. Otherwise they looked exactly the same as the other.

This, however, was different. So much so that they kept the transfer of the specimens to US scientists under heavy wraps and from the public eye and ear. The intention of the American scientists was to study the queen and her few court members as much as they could, obtain as much information as possible, and destroy them afterwards. That was the plan.

Because the work would be quite dangerous, far more so than working with killer bees, they would have to work under heavy protection from them.

The transfer to the cargo area of the special flight was completed successfully. Soon the flight took off. Its destination was to a lab on the coast of California, where a lab crew would be waiting for it with a special van at a private airport, far from the view of prying eyes. One would think they were transferring a bomb. In a sense they were. All were dressed in special suits, heavy gloves, and helmets with face coverings.

Unknown to them, there was an unseen hole on the bottom of the crate. It was not noticed back in Japan because it hadn't been there at the time. Japanese scientists made sure the container was not compromised. It was heavy cardboard. However, inside of it was a large, very thick and hard plastic container which contained the insects. They could never have bored through that. But the crate had been placed on something which somehow compromised that part of it. No one could have foreseen that or become aware of it unless by pure chance. In fact, no one did.

What they also hadn't noticed was that just before they put the locking lid on the container itself, a larger specimen had managed to escape from the other side of the lid unseen. The lid was then locked, and the top of the box closed and sealed heavily with a special packing tape.

When the Americans took possession of it, all seemed well. But they would soon find out that was not the case. Once they eventually noticed the anomaly, the search for what they feared had escaped would blossom into something far worse than that of the killer bees years ago.

They looked at the packing invoice that was inside a small plastic compartment on the outside of the container to make sure it was the right shipment. It was. After checking the item identification, they prepared to return to the lab. The ID was correct. It was Vespa Mandarinia: the Japanese Giant Hornet. The van was soon on its way.

1

August in southern California was not like Florida or any of the eastern southern states. Especially around San Diego, where it was a mostly Mediterranean climate all year round. It rarely got cold even in the winter. A little chilly at times maybe, but mostly at night. During the day, one could go swimming nearly all year round.

In Lemon Grove, just a few miles north of San Diego, residents of this small quiet bedroom community were enjoying the warm sunshine and dry air that made the climate so relaxing and pleasurable. In one neighborhood, a little boy was playing in his backyard. His home had a decent-sized swimming pool. The eleven-year-old assumed most homes had one. To a certain extent he was right. Many did have one, but not necessarily most. For most residents, swimming pool owners or not, the beach and the ocean weren't far away. So no one was deprived of swimming and therefore no one complained.

"Billy, come on in for a minute. Time for your medicine." Sandra Jansen was his mother and a housewife for some ten years. It was 4:00pm and her husband Henry hadn't yet come home from his civil engineering job. In the meantime, Billy needed to take his afternoon antibiotic which she had forgotten to give him earlier. But it wasn't too late even at this time. He was getting over a throat infection and was nearly done with his medicine. Only two more to go.

"Mommy, I want to go in the pool now."

"Honey you can go in. Come and take this and you can go right in. C'mon now."

The boy ran to the back door where his mother waited with the pill and a small glass of juice in her hand. After downing both, he ran back

to the inground pool and jumped in. Sandy watched her son having a good time and thought maybe she'd go in and take a dip later, perhaps after supper.

Their home was a large, raised ranch style, with two bathrooms and three bedrooms. It was the kind of home for a nice, mid to upper middle-class family and was in a quiet neighborhood that, so far, hadn't seen any crime or other kinds of trouble. Most people that lived there had jobs either as semi or full professionals or other high skill professions. The cost of living there, as in many other parts of southern California, was a little on the pricey side. Still, there were decent benefits there that one really couldn't complain of.

The Jansens had lived there for four years and loved the area. They got along well with all their neighbors. When Henry got transferred there from the northern part of the state, it had been a promotion for him. Working for the state as a civil engineer certainly had its broad array of benefits, not to mention the good pay. His six-figure salary was enough for them to afford the modestly affluent neighborhood.

Although Sandra had proven herself to be an excellent saleswoman with Mary Kay, she decided to break from it for a while and concentrate instead on taking care of the house and her family. That was enough work anyway.

Billy was a typical little boy but a good son. Although he had his moments of anger or pouting when he couldn't have what he wanted at times, he never went so far as to defy his parents. Fortunately, he would calm down quickly and move on to focus on something else he enjoyed, like swimming in the pool or playing with his friends. And he had quite a few of them.

One of them had come over from next door and saw Billy playing in the pool. His name was Stevie and was just a year younger but seemed equally smart if you saw them talking to each other. They both went to

Harris Middle School and had just started there this year. Both had done well in school as average students.

"Hey Billy, want to come over later? My dad bought us a netball kit and we have it set up in our back yard."

Billy looked at him over the pool edge. "Sure. After supper maybe?" he asked Stevie.

His friend nodded, followed by a 'yeah'.

"I'll check with my mom to make sure it's ok with her."

"Ok."

Billy then decided he wanted some company. "Hey Stevie, want to come in the pool here?"

Stevie looked back. "Naw. Not today. But see ya later." Billy's friend then turned and walked back to his house.

Billy dove underwater again. Sometimes he would grab the Styrofoam pool stick, as he called it and use it to float on. He would have invited Stevie to play with him there, but they had a pool of their own. Besides, it was getting too close to suppertime and his mom limited his pool time with friends to no later than 4pm.

A slight breeze gently shook the small branch that hung about ten feet above the pool. It was part of a still-young elm tree that had been there for umpteen number of years. No one really paid much attention to it. Why should they anyway?

On that branch near the trunk, it watched Billy. Its wings made a loud buzzing sound as they flapped quicker than the eye could see, but it didn't fly off. Having left the newly established hive about half a mile away in a small woodsy area, it was sent out to do some scouting.

Humans were not its prey. Other insects, especially honeybees, were its favorite meal. It would soon go on the hunt. It decided this was a good territory to include for the colony. Consequently, it now regarded this human as an intruder. It was a scout so it would take no action on its own. This problem would require the troops. Before it called them out, it would scout and hunt for the presence of honeybees.

Suddenly it flew off and started its own patrol of the back yard of the Jansen's and the Woodruff's house next door. Once it detected the presence of bees, it would home in on their hive. It knew it wouldn't be far away. After that, it would emit pheromones which would signal the troops to come in. They would smell it and know that it was the call that they instinctively responded to.

***

At 4:45pm, the front door opened and in walked Henry.

"Anybody home?" he asked in his usual cheerful voice. He was always happy when he got home, despite having worked whatever hours he had done. Sometimes it was eight, other times it was ten or twelve.

Sandy came out from the kitchen. "Hi hon. Rough day?" She went up and gave him a brief kiss.

"No more than usual. Hmm, something smells good. Almost as good as you. What is it?" he asked.

"Just getting supper started now. Want a quick taste? I made my own version of chicken ala king. Homemade."

"Hmm. Yummy. Sounds divine. I'll pass on the quick taste. Might be difficult for me to stop." He pulled off his tie. "Might as well get out of these glad rags." He left to go upstairs.

After supper, Billy was able to go to Stevie's house to play for a while. He had to get back by 7:30 the latest, before it got dark. After Sandy finished the dishes, she went to join Henry on the sofa. They watched the news on the living room TV.

As they talked, Sandy asked how his day had gone. On the news, the anchor mentioned day to day current events throughout the state, with a little on what was going on in the world. In the Middle East, tensions were rising between Israelis and a group of Palestinians who seemed to be trying to stir up some trouble. So far it wasn't a major issue. Henry knew the Middle East was and always would be the great hotspot of the world.

"Oh, not bad," he answered. "The usual stuff. Had to do a little surveying for a potential project down in Escondido. Nothing else out of the ordinary. They are talking about putting me in charge of the project if it comes to fruition. More money if it happens."

Sandy looked at him and smiled. "That would be great. Good for you career-wise. Hope it works out."

"Yea, me too. You never know though. Some people have changed their minds at the last minute. So it's never a sure thing until the final decision is made." She knew that to be quite true. Both continued to watch the TV.

More news of police gunning down a suspect who was shooting back at them. It seemed like the news was nothing but violence or potential violence. *Isn't there ever any good news that could catch people's interest?* thought Sandy.

Although they didn't hear some of what followed, when their attention focused back on the news story, their eyebrows raised. They heard *"anaphylactic shock from the deadly insects but dangerous to everyone, including those not allergic. The venom is far more toxic than from bees or normal wasps. These were found to have escaped from a scientific research facility and now for the first time in history have found their way deeper into the state of California."*

"What the hell are these things they are talking about?" exclaimed Henry.

The two looked at each other, then focused again on the TV, which revealed a close-up picture of the deadly hornet, positively identifying it as the Asian or Japanese Giant Hornet. Just its appearance alone was terrifying.

The broadcaster stated they were last seen north of Los Angeles. Entomologists from the California Department of Wildlife's entomology section were assigned to hunt down and either capture or destroy the hive.

"In other news…"

"Oh my God," said Sandy. "I have heard of them. I saw a documentary about them on TV not too long ago. They are supposed to be only in Japan and nowhere else on earth. They are so scary. They can kill people!" Her voice was revved up a bit. Her long-time fear of insects was well-known to Henry.

"Now honey, let's not get worked up about this," he said as he tried to reassure her. "They are way up north. I don't think we will have any-thing to worry about down here. Besides, what are the odds? A thousand to one, maybe?"

That seemed to calm her down. But having seen a photo of one on TV made her continue to have the heebie-jeebies about it in her mind. As the news continued with other stories, it took her mind off of it and soon she was back to her near-normal self. Having now seen it and knowing it was around kept her a little nervous. Her fright of nasty things, like stinging bugs and spiders, always kept her a little on edge.

***

San Luis Obispo

In the state department of entomology lab, Doctors Maria Hernandez and Calvin Kablinski had found out about the escape of the queen. Initially it seemed that their entire research and study plans went out the window. It wasn't just a devastating blow to their plans; it was becoming a worst-case scenario situation, not unlike the start of an epidemic. This could be equally deadly. Unlike a contagious disease which is insidious in its spread, this kind of epidemic could cause panic and even greater fear because people would be able to see and feel the threat immediately.

Where to begin the search was like trying to find a particular planet in the entire galaxy without a telescope. They would need to wait to hear a first report of a sighting and its location before they could spring into action. They needed a starting point and wherever that turned out would be that point.

The good thing was that the year was approaching hibernation time for the queen. Two or three months more, or sooner if they were lucky. Still, the sooner they could find the newly established hive, and there would have to be one, the sooner they could prevent their spread into other areas. Once it spread, it would be like a cancer: nearly impossible to stop. The only thing is, that timetable was in Japan. This was America. Would it be the same?

They would be leading the hunt for the hive when the approximate location was established. They were not responsible, of course, for the escape. They had only just heard about it. It had been an unforeseen and unseen occurrence at the receiving transfer point. They would need to see if the queen was still in the container in their lab here in San Luis Obispo. The scientists didn't have the time to look now. They had to work fast on a plan that could be put into action the moment any escapees were spotted. Not much different than looking for a needle in a haystack.

"Cal, are the containers packed and ready?" asked Maria.

He looked over to the corner of the room and said they were all packed and ready. "Also," he added, "the nets and traps are being packed right now in the other lab."

"What about the suits?" she asked.

"They are ready to go. I think we are all set."

"Wonderful. Ok, Cal. Thanks so much for taking care of that. I have to get back to my office to work on some other stuff. In the meantime, if you hear anything, let me know."

"Ok. You too."

Back in her office, she looked through some paperwork on other studies they were following up on. And there were more than enough of those to keep them busy for the next year. Yet she couldn't help thinking about this latest. In fact, she couldn't get it out of her mind. How in the world could that escape have happened? The reports stated that all the hornets were contained, including the queen. Perhaps the queen had escaped at the shipping source. After all, no one knows when or where it left.

The scary thing was the not knowing. Did it escape and if so, where did it escape: here or in Japan? If it was here, they'd know soon enough. They had to be prepared to act immediately after the first report-if there was one.

2

In the small patch of woods not far from the Jansens' and Woodruffs', she found a large hole in the trunk of a tree, about twenty-five feet off the ground. In there is where she decided to establish her new "palace". For unknown reasons she hadn't yet laid her eggs. She was late and that wasn't good. Was it possible she knew she was in a different environment?

Fortunately for her, two of the workers had flown out close to her when she flew out the container. It was open just enough and long enough for the three of them to get out. Once they were out, their vanishing was never noticed.

The workers set in right away to make up some kind of instant hive. They knew somehow that she had to lay the eggs quickly or they might die inside her. So they worked as fast as they could to build some kind of nesting area for her. Their instinctive efficiency and stubborn determination paid off. In a matter of hours, the temporary nesting spot was ready for her to settle down in. The cubicles around the spot were numerous enough-more than enough in fact-to accommodate the large number of eggs she was expected to lay.

As she laid her eggs, they tended to her and the eggs with their protective coating. The larvae themselves were the source of an energy-producing substance that the workers would ingest, and they would go out to attack the beehive colony that the scout located and where it left its pheromones. The hornets primarily kill and eat honeybees, as well as other types of wasps and insects. In the flying insect world, they are at the top of the food chain. One giant hornet can kill up to forty honeybees. The bees stand no chance against them. The hornets tear apart and decapitate the bees, bringing pieces of them back to their nest to feed their larvae.

The exception to this is in Japan. Honeybees there have become adapted to the presence of these giant insects and have developed a strong defense system that is not only quite effective, but also reveals their intelligence level. When a scout shows up at their hive "doorway", they are already prepared.

Before the hornet could leave, they attack in great numbers, surrounding it and preventing it from escaping. They beat their wings continuously until heat builds up to make it more difficult for the hornet to survive. When the temperature reaches a whopping one hundred seventeen degrees Fahrenheit, the hornet dies. Thus, it never gets to release its pheromones and the hornet colony as a result never gets the scent to bring them to the beehive.

Because European honeybees, those in the US, have never encountered these ferocious insects, they have virtually no defense against them except for their standard general defense tactics which are useless against these new enemies. In this new situation and invasion, the honeybee population will be devastated and wiped out within months if not weeks.

Once a new hive is set up and a hornet queen makes preparations to lay her eggs, the workers send out a scout to search for honeybee hives. The two-inch killer leaves the new nest. It can smell pheromones from bees if any hive is in the area. This is typical of any Vespa Mandarina.

Then it flies on a path where it eventually picks up a faint scent. The direction it is flying toward is where humans live. The scent is not of them but of bees. It now knows it is flying in the right direction. It picks up speed and soon notices the human habitats. The scent is becoming stronger and luring it toward a particular house. The closer it gets, the more pungent the scent becomes. Now a tree is ahead of it and the scout is led toward the lower branch where it now sees its target. It ignores the house and focuses only on the beehive.

The bees at first pay little attention, then soon realize there is an intruder in their territory. They don't know how to react because they've never seen anything like this before. Confusion takes over.

The scout enters the doorway of the hive where bees are swirling around, angry at this intruder. They try to attack it the only way they know how. The scout reacts by attacking and decapitating several of the bees as part of its defense. As other bees continue to attack it and try to get it to leave, the scout continues to violently react and kill more bees in the process. It soon decides it's time to call in reinforcements.

It escapes by first leaving its pheromones at the doorway and then flies off, emitting more of its scent markers. This is a guarantee that the troops will detect it, find the hive, and destroy it and all its inhabitants. The beehive is now marked for destruction. The bees don't know it yet, but their time is coming far sooner than what would be natural. Once the hornet warriors show up, the bees stand no chance, even if they outnumber their attackers. They will be annihilated, and their queen will be quickly killed. Soon, the deadly infestation and invasion will begin.

***

Wearing their covid masks, Maria and Calvin, along with some assistants, began their search for the hornet hive that they knew would be out there. They knew that the escapees would have to build a hive right away. Without reports of sightings, it was currently like looking for a needle in a haystack. They had to search in an organized pattern in woodsy areas. Despite the environment being mostly urban, there were countless numbers of those areas in the region. They had to make calculated guesses as to where the queen might go to start her colony; and that was based on the lab's location which is where they had to figure the initial direction they would start toward. It was pure educated guesswork, but they had to start somewhere.

They decided to start north, work eastward, and then move south. Other lab workers would start at the south and move opposite to where Maria and Cal would be going. It was a long shot and there was no guarantee of success. Until they got sighting reports, it was all they could do for now. It could take days, even weeks. This was barely just the beginning.

***

The next day brought cloudy skies with occasional peeks of sunshine through the thinner layers of clouds. The area didn't have an overabundance of rain and in fact went for somewhat lengthy periods of time with no rain at all. But it did get enough of it to avoid droughts. Most of the time.

School was still out but only for a couple more weeks. At least that's what the original plan was. With the pandemic, it was not too likely that it would begin again. Talk about online schooling was becoming more prevalent now. Homeschooling had been going on for a few months, which meant kids were home all the time.

This gave them more time to be outside and enjoy their outdoor play.

The hive in a backyard of a home was buzzing with activity. Bees constantly entered and left. Those leaving were on the hunt for more flowers to pollinate and to pick up pollen and nectar as well. They were hard workers which not only benefited themselves, but humans as well. People didn't see too many of them around. Their population in general seemed to be on the decrease. Most people either didn't know that was happening or didn't know the reason for that decrease was unclear.

Billy was out in the backyard, playing near the pool. He wasn't yet ready to go in, although he was wearing his bathing suit. Stevie Woodruff had come over and together they were playing with squirt guns, running all over the yard and basically having water-loaded fun. Each was trying to out-squirt the other in a "battle" for the water gun championship.

Mom Jansen came out just at the moment that Stevie was trying to hit Billy with the water squirt gun. He missed and got Billy's mom in the face.

Squealing for a moment as the water hit her face, Stevie was surprised to see she didn't get mad.

"Oh, I am sorry, Mrs. Jansen," yelled Stevie. "I didn't mean to do that."

"That's alright, Stevie," she replied cheerfully as she dried her face off. "It's only water. Tell you what. You give Billy an extra squirt and I'll forget about this completely."

Stevie screamed. "Yeah!"

He immediately ran after Billy who was trying to avoid him as he ran in the other direction. It was comical watching Stevie chase after Billy. Both were yelling, having fun. Every time Stevie got a little closer, he triggered the gun for a long squirt at his friend. He missed a few times, but he also got a few hits in there as well.

As they continued to have fun outside, Sandy went in and started to finish what she had been doing. It was midafternoon. The housework was nearly done, with just the laundry left. After throwing the dirty clothes in the washer, she decided to break out the food and start preparations for the evening meal. Tonight it would be baked lasagna, which was already prepped and ready to be completed in the oven, along with some mixed salad. Billy hated that but was told he had to eat at least a couple of forkfuls to provide his body some of the nutrients it required. He neither understood nor cared. But rather than giving his parents a hard time about it, he chose to eat those two forkfuls. Besides, he knew if he didn't eat them, he wouldn't be able to go in the pool after supper. That in itself was enough to get him to eat it.

It would be at least another hour and a half before they would be eating. While the two boys romped around outside still with their squirt guns, Sandy continued preparing the food in the kitchen.

When the phone rang, she dropped what she was doing to answer it. It was Barbara Newburg, a good friend from the church who kept in touch regularly.

"Oh, hi Barb. How are ya?"

"Not bad, girlfriend. Keeping the house standing?"

Sandy chuckled. "Naw. The roof is caving in and the walls are starting to crumble. Guess I'll build a new one tomorrow."

The two women laughed. "Got a minute?" asked Barbara.

"Sure. What's up?"

"A few of us are getting together next Tuesday for a Tupperware party. Thought you might like to know in case you're interested. There will be coffee and cookies."

Sandy enjoyed going to these events on occasion and her friend knew that.

"Hmm, sounds good, Barb. Where, at your place?"

"Yep. Will be at 7:00pm. Want to come?"

Before Sandy could answer, she thought she heard a yell outside.

"Hold on just a minute," Sandy told her friend. "I thought I heard some yelling outside." She put the phone down and walked to the back door in the kitchen to the outside.

The screaming was loud and obvious.

"Billy! Billy, where are you?" she yelled from the back landing. Stevie came around from the side of the house and ran up to her.

"Mrs. Jansen, Mrs. Jansen, Billy got bit!"

Her jaw dropped. "Bit? Bit by what?" She climbed down the steps from the landing and started running behind Stevie until she got to her son who was sitting on the ground, holding his right hand and screaming.

She took Billy's hand in her own and was shocked to see how incredibly swollen it was. She couldn't imagine what it was that had bitten or stung him.

"Stevie, did you see what it was?"

"No, I didn't. It happened so fast. Is he going to be ok?"

Billy's screaming was constant, with tears gushing down his face. His screaming from pain terrified Sandy and Stevie.

By now a redness had started spreading up his hand and onto his wrist, where it began to swell as well. Then his forearm. She was alarmed but did her best not to signal that to Stevie.

"Uh, he should be ok. Will probably have to see the doctor at the office and get it fixed, but he should be fine." As young as Stevie was, he found that difficult to believe. He saw the swelling increasing, now really frightened for his friend.

Then a woman came from next door. It was Brenda Woodruff, Stevie's mother. "Is everything all right, Sandy? What happened? I heard Billy screaming."

She explained what happened to her quickly and asked her to call 9-1-1. "Oh absolutely," she replied, then ran back into her house. Unfortunately, she had forgotten to bring her cell phone out with her, not realizing she would need it.

After the call was made, she ran back out and informed Sandy the ambulance was on its way.

"Brenda, could you do me a favor? Stay with him for a minute. I have to go inside and get some ice packs for the swelling."

"Sure, hon. I'll be right here. Go get 'em."

While Sandy ran inside, Brenda took a look at Billy's hand and was shocked at the appearance of his hand and arm. The swelling had spread quickly up to his elbow, and now the little boy was starting to shake and grimace and yell as the pain spread and intensified. She'd never seen anything like this before. Now *she* was scared for him.

Billy started becoming delirious and limp in her arms. Could this be an anaphylactic reaction to whatever stung him? She had looked for bite marks from an animal but did not see any. Besides, she didn't know of any animal, even from around here, which could cause this. Unless it had rabies!

Sandy came back out with two ice packs wrapped in a towel. As she applied them, sirens were heard in the distance. By this time Billy had gone limp and she said "Oh my God" out loud.

Stevie was looking on, scared and was in tears watching his friend suffer like that. She wrapped the ice packs around his hand and arm as best she could.

Brenda asked her son if he'd seen any kind of animal running around looking or acting strangely. He said no, he didn't see anything. No dog or cat, or coyote. The only thing he did spot was a squirrel, but he just happened to notice it in the tree. Brenda knew that if it had been any kind of animal, it certainly would not have been a squirrel that caused this.

The sirens were getting louder, which meant they would be here within a matter of minutes. "Is he allergic to bees, Sandy?"

"No, he's never shown any allergies to them. He's been stung once or twice. Other than the temporary pain and only slight swelling at its worst, he never had any kind of serious reaction to them."

"'Cause I'm thinking," Brenda continued, "that it could be a bee."

She wanted to ask more but with Billy in trouble right now and her friend frantic, she decided to wait for another time. For now, the only concern was to help Billy however they could until the ambulance got there. She, too, for that matter, was frantic with worry for little Billy. That could have been *her* son. She turned her face to him.

"Stevie, go inside the house."

"But mom…!"

"Go inside now. Do as I say. I don't want you getting stung!"

He turned and ran back to his house. He didn't want to get stung either.

Brenda noticed there were no dandelions or other flowers on the side of the house where they were. She was looking around for the culprits responsible.

Just then the ambulance arrived, and mask-garbed paramedics and EMT first responders approached the trio. After information was quickly given to them about the situation by Sandy, one of them immediately removed the ice packs to assess the affected areas, while the other EMT took his vital signs. They checked his pupils and response status. His pupils were equal and reactive. However, just his vitals alone indicated something serious was occurring within him. His blood pressure was very low, and his heart was beating abnormally fast. His breathing was rapid and shallow.

"We gotta get him to the ER stat." While the EMTs went to pull the stretcher out of the ambulance, the paramedic told the mother it appeared her son was going into shock, based on the vital signs and his sluggish response to stimuli. In addition, while the two women were looking on in fright for the little boy, the paramedics were checking the boy's level of conscious reading, known as the Glasgow-Coma scale. Right now, he appeared to be in a delirium state. That had them concerned.

Both women were horrified by what was happening. Sandy couldn't believe what was happening to her son. The paramedic knew it was a sting and, of course, asked her if he was allergic to bees.

"No, he was never allergic to them. He's been stung a couple of times. Not recently, though. This never happened to him before."

"Well, Mrs. Jansen, allergies could occur at any time when they had never existed before. He could have developed it. Did you see the site where he was stung?"

"I looked but I saw nothing except swelling and redness. Isn't it true that bees usually leave their stinger in the victim and then die?"

He nodded. "That's true." He looked at the hand and arm thoroughly, covering every area. He thought he saw at least three small puncture holes but wasn't sure because of the swollen redness. Yet he couldn't rule out something other than bees. He also had the presence of mind to look around the immediate grassy area looking for things that weren't there. Things that would attract bees. From what he saw, there would be no reason for bees to be in this particular spot.

They lifted the boy onto the readied stretcher, covered and strapped him in and took him away. Sandy talked briefly to the paramedic before he left, finding out Billy was going to San Diego Children's Medical Center.

Brenda stayed out there with her while Sandy called her husband on her cell. He would leave work immediately and meet her at the hospital.

She turned to her friend and neighbor. "Thanks so much for helping, Brenda. I better go. I'll keep you posted."

"Yes, please do that. Listen, just go! Don't forget your purse and keys. I'll lock up for you. Don't worry, hon. Everything will be ok." Sandy ran in, got her necessities and left. She trusted

Brenda to lock up for her. Besides, she had the life of her son to worry about. A house could be replaced. Her son couldn't. A couple of minutes later, she was gone.

After she locked up the Jansens' house, including checking the front door, Brenda started to walk back to her house but then stopped and turned around. Looking back to the tree in the Jansens' back yard, she noticed something a little odd.

Walking back slowly to the yard corner, she saw where the beehive was, careful not to get too close. She wasn't allergic to bees and didn't mind them that much. Unlike other times when she sensed the energy and business of the hive with its inhabitants constantly coming and going, this time there was the distinct absence of that. In fact, she sensed a deadness about it. *That's strange,* she thought. *Do bees normally abandon their hives?*

She looked around the surrounding area of the tree and the hive but saw not one bee anywhere. Her curiosity continued to get the best of her. She started walking around the yard to see if she could see any bees anywhere around the yard. She looked at whatever dandelions there were and any other wild flowers. In addition, she looked along the sides of the house for any flowers that might attract them. There still was an eerie absence of them.

"Oh, this is crazy," she said out loud. "Where the hell did they all go?"

Returning to the hive, she decided to do something she would never normally do because she knew she wasn't really crazy. Under the present circumstances, she felt justified in doing it. She found and picked up a broomstick that was leaning against the back of the Jansen house.

Back at the hive, she said a quick prayer under her breath, "Protect me Lord." If any were in there, she knew she might get stung. But these weren't the notorious killer bees, so she would survive a sting or two. But she had to find out. This was damn peculiar. For peace of mind, she *would* find out. Nerves or not.

Very gently she poked at it. It swung slightly and then stopped. There was no response from inside of it. She didn't have to be a bee expert to know that was a bad sign. Nothing flew out of it. To be sure, she poked a little harder this time. She jumped back when the hive came down. When it hit the ground, it broke apart. Nothing flew out of it, but what she then saw surprised her.

On some of the broken parts of the hive there were, what looked like, parts of bees. Not wanting to pick any up, she bent over to take a closer look. Despite the fact that they were only insects, still the sight was disturbing to her. As far as she was concerned, these were not natural deaths. Bees don't just die all at once for no apparent reason. Something killed them. But what? What could kill *all* the bees and leave no evidence behind? After deciding she'd mention this to Sandy at a later time, she stood up and returned back to her house. At the same time, she thought of Billy and prayed that he would be alright.

***

From the high branch, it looked at her with its multifaceted eyes. Staring. Despite the fact that the creature below was much bigger than itself, it wasn't afraid. If it had come at it, *it* would have attacked immediately, without hesitation. But the creature walked away. *It* had done its job, and now it was time to lead the colony to its new home here. Its wings went into motion and soon it had disappeared.

3

At the Children's Medical Center in San Diego, doctors and nurses in the ED were working on Billy to stabilize his vital signs and do everything they could to bring him out of his shock. Because no one knew for sure what had stung him but believed his stings to be from bees, they infused IV fluids into him to stabilize his pressure and keep him hydrated and injected epinephrine into him. He was hooked up to the vital signs monitor and an EKG monitor to keep track of his heart. He was also on oxygen to offset respiratory problems due to swelling in his airways.

Sandy could not get the worried look out of her face. Her son had never been this sick before. *She* had never been this sick. Thoughts that were trying to invade her mind were some of the worst and she was doing her best to keep them at bay. Could Billy die? It looked that way to her. Was he suffering more than he'd ever before? Absolutely. But she prayed that God would see him through this safely and that he would come out of it ok. He would just have to get through this terrible ordeal.

Minutes after she got there, Henry came in, instantly seeing his boy lying on the bed, grimacing in pain and delirious at the same time. He had left work the moment he hung up from Sandy's call. There was an oxygen nasal cannula in his son's nose. He was shocked at the swelling that now involved his entire arm up to the shoulder. He didn't have to ask how he was.

"What're they doing for him?" he asked Sandy softly. His frown said it all regarding what he was feeling.

"What they have going in him now. Fluids to hydrate. Other things for his blood pressure. Fluids for the swelling. His airways also had some swelling."

Henry rubbed the boy's head, trying to stifle the tears that began to flow. He rarely ever cried, but this was something he had a hard time dealing with.

He looked at Sandy and her eyes met his.

"Honey, what did this to him? He was stung you said? Bees?"

She shook her head. "I really don't know. I didn't see any around. Apparently he got stung by something when I was in the house. He was playing with Stevie when all of a sudden I heard this god-awful screaming. I didn't know who it was until I got outside and saw Billy on the ground, screaming and holding his hand and arm. I hadn't seen any bees around for a while as a matter of fact. So I don't know."

Henry looked at her and scratched his face. "Neither have I, although I'm not home during the day so naturally I won't see any. But he's not allergic to bee stings."

The nurse came in just then and greeted them. That's when the questions came out fast and furious from the couple. "What's going on? Will he be ok? What's being done for him? How long will he be here?"

"The doctor will be in very shortly and will explain. He will know more. Right now, I'm just checking his vitals and breathing."

She looked at the monitor and noticed the blood pressure was decreasing slightly still. Despite the IV med to bring it up, it was still going in the wrong direction. She did her best not to show concern on her face. The parents were already worried enough. His swelling had gone down slightly, but not enough to make anyone think he was out of the woods. The fact that the steroid hadn't brought it down more than it had worried her. The physician would know before he came in here. She left quickly, saying she would soon be back.

To Sandy, he didn't look much better than when he came in. He'd been there for almost an hour. Perhaps because it was her son, she might be feeling a little too impatient.

For now, Henry and Sandy didn't have too much to say to each other. Their focus and concerns were on Billy. The nurse hadn't said anything very optimistic. But then she was limited in what she could tell them. Although his screaming had stopped, his delirium continued. Occasionally his eyes would open briefly. That's when Sandy tried to get him to respond to her. She hoped he would look at her while his eyes were open. But then they would close again.

"God, I feel so helpless," Henry blurted out. "Why Billy? Why did this have to happen to him? And what the hell did this? I don't believe it was any bee that did this."

Sandy looked at him with the corresponding feelings of her husband. It showed in her teary eyes. She brushed back her hair from them.

"What do you think it was then?" she asked.

"I don't know, sweetheart. I wish I knew. But I damn well am going to find out."

"What makes you think it wasn't a bee sting?" She wanted to know his thoughts about it now. "Bees can do this to those who are allergic."

"You said he had gotten epinephrine here, right?"

"Yes."

"Yet, he doesn't seem to be responding too well to that. Not from what I'm seeing here." Sandy looked at her son. She didn't have an answer to that. His face was pale, and his breathing looked a little shallow. She figured the meds should be kicking in by now, if they hadn't before. Henry was right. There didn't seem to be much improvement in him. But then, she could only go by what she was seeing.

Yet she *knew* her son. Billy was a fighter. He wasn't one to give up easily. And she believed he was inwardly fighting this thing. Fighting the venom that had permeated his body and was trying, so it seemed, to destroy him.

There was a knock on the room glass door and a man in a white coat stepped in.

"Hi folks. I'm Doctor Herrera." He shook hands with each of them and thankfully wasn't one to beat around the bush. He got right to the point.

"So, looks like your son has had a serious run-in with something."

Henry quickly jumped in. "Doc, any idea what could have done this?"

The physician sighed. "Afraid not. So far. It's the venom from a sting. That we are pretty sure of right now. But as you may be thinking, we don't believe it's from a honeybee. The venom is pretty potent. In fact, it's much stronger and likely more toxic than from a bee."

Henry and Sandy's eyes met in an immediate response. Henry had been right.

The doctor continued with concern evident in his voice. "The fact that Billy's body is not responding as well as we'd like to the epinephrine we gave him which, in most cases has a very good response, has me concerned. His vitals aren't too bad right now, although they could be better. I'm concerned about the blood pressure. It's still too low, despite the anti-hypotensive medication we have given him. We're going to try another dose soon as well as another dose of the epinephrine and continue to keep him well hydrated. At the same time, his blood oxygen level is low as well, which means his body is not taking in enough oxygen, despite what we're giving him. That means we have to be careful with his fluid intake as well. Hydrated but not overly so."

Sandy eyes were now fully welled with tears, as fears for her son quickly grew.

"So what's the plan, doctor?" she asked with a shaky voice. "Is there any anti-venom that can be given to him?"

"Well, I'm afraid not, Mr. Jansen. For one thing, we don't have a positive ID of the culprit. Even if we did, we don't carry anti-venom here anyway. Epinephrine, or adrenaline as it's also called, is the drug of choice for bee sting allergic reactions. With Billy, there was no positive reaction to it. In other words, it's highly likely that he did not suffer a bee sting. It was something else. Something that was far worse than a bee sting or even normal wasp sting."

Sandy was shocked. "Doctor, what could be worse than a wasp sting other than a snakebite?"

Herrera shook his head. "Wish I could tell you, Mrs. Jansen. Spider or scorpion, I imagine. But we have no scorpions around here. Out in the desert, sure. And although we have plenty of spiders, the only ones I know of that live around here are the small ugly ones that are scary-looking but are actually quite harmless. I know because I hate spiders and am always on the lookout for them. But none I know has ever landed anyone in the hospital here.

"Our plan is to keep Billy in the hospital here because his condition right now is too unstable, and his prognosis is uncertain."

"How long will he be here?" asked Sandy.

"Hard to say. I would expect a few days. However, I don't want to get your hopes up. His body is going through a terrible trauma right now. It's fighting the venom which, in turn, is fighting back to destroy his body and his life. In other words, he's in a very serious condition right now which is on the brink of going critical. As terrible as that sounds, you need to know that."

He saw patients in trouble all the time. But seeing a child in distress was always particularly disturbing to him. That in itself would make him work harder to help that child.

Both parents were now in tears. Sandy ran around the bed to her husband and they hugged. The comfort they mutually needed from each other didn't seem to be enough to assure them about their son.

Sandy turned around, still in Henry's arms. She wiped the tears from her eyes and then turned back to her son. Her hand gently caressed his head and pale cheek. "What chance does he have?" She was afraid of his answer.

The doctor's face continued to solemnly express his seriousness. With a gentle shake of his head, he replied, "I'm not sure at this point. Right now, I can only give him a fifty-fifty chance. He's actually worsening right now, even with the medications. I'm going to give him more and maybe change something that might be a little better. We're working against an unknown cause at this point, so we can only hope that what we're going to continue to do will work and show improvement in him."

Just then Billy suddenly arched in his bed. His face was grimacing and turning blue. The alarm on the monitor went off and it showed his saturation blood oxygen level had decreased from ninety-one percent with continuous oxygen flow down to eighty-five percent, which was life-threatening. The doctor turned up the flow on the wall oxygen flowmeter to six ml per hour, then quickly yelled out for help and lifted the head of the bed to a forty-five-degree angle.

"Mrs. Jansen, can you please wait out in the hall."

Sandy now was losing it. "Doctor, what's happening to my little boy?" she yelled, nearly in hysterics.

"Will explain later. Right now we have to take care of him, and we need the room. Please." He pointed to outside the room, while ED code staff came in.

Several of the staff came rushing in as Billy's airways continued to swell and he was continued to turn blue. Because the steroids weren't working to reduce his airways fast enough, the doctor decided to insert an endotracheal tube attached to a ventilator until the swelling was reduced enough for Billy to breathe on his own. It was not an ideal situation but for the moment there was no choice.

The doctor had never known any allergic reaction to a sting to cause this much respiratory distress, although it could feasibly happen to anyone at any time-even in someone not having had such a reaction before.

While the team worked on Billy inside the curtain-covered room, Henry and Sandy were doing all they could to keep it together. They were determined not to make a scene and didn't. However, it was more difficult to maintain a calmness, considering what was going on with their son. All they could do was wait as patiently as they could.

One of the nurses came out and advised them to wait in the family waiting room and someone would come and speak to them as soon as Billy was stabilized. Without argument, Henry escorted his wife down to the room where they settled down to what would seem like the longest wait of their lives. Henry picked up his cell phone. He decided he better let Billy's grandparents on both sides know what was happening.

4

Los Angeles and San Diego counties

In their search so far, the team had stumbled across several honeybee hives. Even though their search was for something else, these sightings were equally essential. They had to assess them for any untoward anomalies which could indicate stress. Any kind of stress seen in the bees could, in turn, be a sign of danger from an outside source. Considering what they knew so far, that danger could be the beginning of the end for the bees.

With each hive they came to, they had to be absolutely sure there was no sign of anything unusual. At the same time, they had to be careful not to disturb the hive. Fortunately, these were European bees. If they had been killer Africans, the team would never have been able to get close to the hive without being viciously attacked first.

Maria led one team, Calvin the other. They had split up in their assigned area to cut down on the search time. The hornet hive was expected to be aerial, which meant it had to be up in the trees or another high place. But it could also be at ground level, so they couldn't exclude any possibilities. Sometimes other species of wasps would have their nests closer to the ground. These, however, were intelligent and used their size and barbaric behavior to their greatest advantage. But if they saw that advantage to be closer to the ground, that would be their choice.

As Maria combed through her area, she thought she saw something in one of the trees. Taking out her small binoculars, which were necessary on expeditions such as this, she scanned the upper part of the heavy tree until a large hive-like object came into view. Bingo. It was a hive, alright. Not a honeybee type. It was far too large. Her worst fears were confirmed when she saw a huge hornet fly around, land and then enter its dark opening.

Putting down her binocs, she picked up her radio and called Calvin.

"Calvin here. What's up, Maria?"

"Cal, unless you found a mark, you better get down here. I have located and positively identified one."

"Roger that. I found nothing in this area. On my way there now."

In a minute or so, he arrived and was shown the huge hive up in the tree.

"Oh my, that is a big one alright."

They studied it for a couple of minutes, observing any comings and goings of the insects. This was very bad news, not only for this area but for all others as well. If this was not contained and eliminated soon, the consequences for bees and people everywhere could be disastrous.

"Maria, hopefully this is the only one."

"I don't know. No way to be sure. Usually, where there's one, there will be more. I would almost bet on it. These things build and reproduce rapidly."

"It's pretty high up there. We'd have to get some proper equipment to reach it. Not to mention the chemicals and other things."

Maria looked around. "We'll have to get some people to clear all this thick shrubbery and small trees around our tree so we can get that equipment in here. This is not going to be so cut and dry."

They looked up at it and some of the hornets came out and flew away, while others entered. The activity was slowly increasing. Maria thought that the workers might have found a bee hive and attacked it, possibly bringing back pieces of bee bodies to eggs inside. If that was the case, the area was in serious trouble. For now, they had to leave it but would mark the area for when they returned. They knew it would still be here. Their concern was not so much for it still being here, but more for the possible presence of other hives. The fact that people's homes were nearby made this situation all the more urgent.

"We better get back and get things started, Maria. Don't have any time to waste."

After calling all the teams back to the same rendezvous point as when they arrived, the entire team headed on back to their vehicles. Luckily, the dirt road they had parked on within the woodsy area was far enough from the homes to be easily missed by residents, yet close enough for the team to see that they were on the periphery of the residential area. The fact that this hive was so close to people made the situation threatening. So far, they hadn't heard of any confrontations with people. Not yet.

***

In El Cajon, just a few miles northeast of San Diego, a woman was hanging her clothes out to dry. Even though she had a washer and dryer inside her ranch-style home, she believed her clothes always dried nicer and had a nice fresh smell to them when they hung outdoors. As long as the day was sunny and dry, not humid, she took advantage of this weather when she could.

Emma Compton was a fifty-year-old woman who'd been married to her husband for twenty-five years. They had two children; a seventeen-year-old son who was a senior in high school, and a daughter two years younger. They were both quite smart and were doing well academically. Her husband, Paul, was a salesman who spent two weeks away from home on the road about every six weeks. She didn't like it when he went away but realized that was a part of his job and it kept them living comfortably. He was a good husband, father and provider so she had no reason to complain, and she didn't. Right now, he was on his second week away from home.

She loved this Mediterranean type of weather. It was a kind of distraction for her from Paul being away. The warm, light, occasional breeze she was feeling seemed to give her a sense of safety and security.

As with most of her extended family, she'd lived in southern California all of her life and wouldn't want to live anywhere else. To her, this was her earthly paradise. Working outdoors was something she enjoyed and took advantage of when she could, whether it was gardening or hanging clothes out on the line. She realized she was one of few that still hung clothes out on the line, but she didn't care. Neither did anyone else for that matter.

As she finished hanging up another shirt on the line, the ringing in her pants pocket almost startled her. Digging in, she pulled her phone out and answered. It was Paul. He usually called every day or two to make sure she was ok. He figured if he had to be away that long, at least he should take the time to call her, even if it was only for a couple of minutes. He said he was just checking in.

"Yes, honey, it's gorgeous weather," she told him. "Hanging out the clothes. How is it up there in Frisco?"

"Not bad. Little cloudy. The meeting is kind of boring and it's not something I would have chosen voluntarily. But at least I'm getting paid for it."

Paul worked for Prescott Prosthetics Company, which made artificial limbs and other parts for those disabled who needed them, including artificial knees and other joints. He loved the sales work but hated some of the meetings he was required to attend.

"So when are you coming home?" she asked, hoping he would say now. But she knew better. He was only halfway through the two weeks.

"Well technically I have another week. But if I can get the deal nailed down sooner, then I can be home sooner." She started to smile.

But as he talked, Emma was startled to suddenly see two large insects land on her white sheet. They weren't just large-they were huge, the largest insects she'd ever seen. Shocked to see they were hornets they were none like she'd ever seen before. Her eyes widened from sudden fear. *Where the hell did they come from?*

"Oh my heavens. Oh Lord have mercy on me!" she said into the phone, keeping her eyes glued to the terrifying sight. As if that weren't bad enough, a third and then a fourth one landed next to the others.

"Sweetheart, what's the matter?" asked Paul worriedly.

"Bugs," she yelled out. "The clothes are being landed on by big hornets. I have to get out of this area now. I'm going back inside before I get stung."

While she got ready to get off the phone, they strangely turned with their heads in her direction as if on cue. The sight of them terrified her so much that she hadn't had the presence of mind to truly notice that. The only thing she noticed was that they looked like hornets on steroids. Why are they here? And why did they land there?

"Oh my God, Emma, ok go! Call me back when you get inside safely, ok? You have my number. Go!"

"Ok, I will," she replied, then hung up.

Emma had good reason to be frightened. She was allergic to bee venom. That was bad enough. Wasps and hornet stings could be potentially much worse and end her life even faster. She had to get away from these things.

***

They looked at her in their reddish-yellow vision, seeing a dark figure looking back at them. Their wings occasionally buzzed. The dark figure was not moving, and they didn't know if it was a threat to them or not. What they landed on didn't matter. What they were looking at did. Any movement by the dark figure could trigger their immediate response. The fact that they saw a blotch of red under the dark top of it was significant to them. They didn't like the color red, for reasons they would never know.

Their huge mandibles moved to open and shut, although they were not their primary weapons. What they mainly used to stun and kill were their half-inch stingers, the largest in the stinging insect kingdom and the largest of the vespa species of stinging insects. Their potent venom did not guarantee death; it merely increased the chances along with excruciating pain. In those that were allergic, it would almost always be a death sentence. They continued to stare at her, waiting for her to make the first move. These were the strongest and most fearless of the vespa species. They never surrendered or backed down from anything.

***

She was in the middle of the clothesline and she felt the breeze blow one of the clothes up against her side and back. The sheet with the hornets on it, just in front of where she was standing, was gently being lifted a little by the breeze. The hornets stayed as still as death on the sheet, moving up and down with it. The sheet's movement didn't seem to faze them. They remained looking at her instead of changing their positions.

They were at least three to four inches in length, with a proportionally thicker thorax than a regular hornet. She figured they were hornets because they weren't black like wasps. The combination of orange, yellow, and black stripes revealed what they were, generally speaking. She wasn't sure about the orange head. She'd seen regular hornets with black heads. These were certainly different, and not just in size.

Slowly she backed away, never taking her eyes off them. They continued to eye her. A breeze blew and the shirt behind her caressed her back. She felt a drop of sweat coming down into her eye and she was afraid to move to wipe it off. The further away she got, the smaller and less fearsome they looked to her. Like stained blotches on the sheet, they remained still on the gently flowing sheet. Their black, multi-faceted eyes remained glued on her.

As she neared the end of the clothesline closer to the house, a sudden gust of wind whipped the last piece of cloth against her and her arm reflexively swung up as if to stop it. The multiple movements of the clothes and sudden movement of her arm set them off in a burst of instantaneous violent motions.

She was attacked in three different places. Each of the stings caused immediate unrelenting pain. The hornets penetrated her flesh with their half-inch stingers, stabbing her repeatedly and viciously, injecting the toxic venom multiple times. Emma screamed as loud as she could as her fast beating heart was forcing her into a tachycardiac crisis. Her heart continued pumping her now venom-filled blood rapidly as the toxin spread its deadly effects throughout her entire body. Already it was beginning to damage her liver and respiratory system and would soon affect her kidneys.

Her pain was excruciating and not just in one area. In her mind, flashes of her life appeared seemingly on a timeline from when she was just a little girl. She caught brief glimpses of her parents, then their times on the beach they used to go to. Her high school friends quickly appeared and vanished and then the same with friends from church. It was all so brief and rapid, and yet so vivid and clear. Then she saw a hand reaching down for her from a cloudy source. She cried out but didn't know if it was for real or in the visions.

There wasn't any stopping them as they continued to sting her over and over. Her heart began to go into spams, her airways began to swell, and she collapsed to the ground. She was now having difficulty breathing and in serious respiratory distress. She flailed on the ground and tried desperately to call out for help. Her mouth was wide open but no sound came out. Her throat had swelled enough to prohibit her trachea from its normal functioning. She was, in effect, suffocating to death.

Large swollen red areas appeared around the sting sites which were on her left thigh, left arm and the right side of her neck. Those areas were rapidly reddening and ballooning. Before she collapsed, she tried again desperately to call for help, but no sounds could escape her and no one could respond from the house next door. When she tried to call her husband on her cell phone, her fingers refused to work and she dropped the phone. Delirium now overcame her. Her skin was beginning to turn blue as her body was depleted of much-needed oxygen.

Life around her continued as usual. The birds flew and paid her no mind. Traffic out on the street continued to pass by. The mailman dropped their mail in the box at the street and drove to the next house. The sun continued to shine and the occasional small cloud revealed its passing presence.

On the ground and approaching unconsciousness, her life started ebbing away. Her back arched as her body prepared to seize. Her skin and lips were pale-blue at first, but then started to turn purplish as her breaths became irregular and raspy with death rattles. Her body quivered and her muscles spasmed and cramped uncontrollably. The all-encompassing seizure, a grand mal, indicated the venom had attacked her brain. It had fatally damaged her insides and ability to breathe. Her lungs were ravaged by swelling.

Her death throes went unheard and unseen. Had she had help in time, she might have survived. Unconquerable pain could have been treated and she might have regained her normal breathing. Lots of things could have been done for her. If only someone, anyone, could have heard or seen.

In the middle of a bright sunny day and surrounded by other homes, there was no one that saw or heard anything. In a world full of people, for that moment…she was alone. Lying on the ground in her own yard.

In her final attempt to call out for help just before she became unconscious, Emma had made one final attempt to yell out "please!" but could only open her mouth. She could only mouth the words, "I'm sorry." No one but her would ever know that. And God.

Darkness enveloped her as her soul quietly left her body, leaving her with no more pain.

5

In the Children's Hospital, Billy had been transferred to the ICU after having been stabilized enough to be moved out of the ED. He was still far from being out of the woods and remained in critical condition. In addition to all the blood tests that had been done to check for any anomalies that might be present in the blood as well as his liver function tests, they checked for the presence of venom and, if present, what kind it was. They wanted to know if it was a hemotoxin or neurotoxin, or a combination of both. Both snakes and spiders, as well as poisonous marine life, have these.

Entomologists know that bees, strangely enough, have beneficial components in their venom. In most people, their sting is painful but not life threatening because of these relatively harmless components. For others, even bee venom can kill.

In this case, behind-the-scenes lab workers were checking out the blood components in Billy's blood. Chemical analysis on the printout showed an "unknown component" in his blood. Further deeper analysis would have to be made to determine what this component was. But to do that they would have to have some possibilities as a starting baseline. Many toxicology tests require a specific chemical to be checked for in order to conclude whether it's present or not. If present, the test will quantify the chemical that's present.

A lab worker coming to this discovery part of the analysis picked up the phone at that point.

In the ICU, Billy was hooked up to two IV solutions running into him. He was conscious now. Doctors had said his prognosis looked more promising, although he was not completely out of the woods yet. But they had to determine what, if anything, had been injected into him by some-thing unknown that had nearly killed him. And they wanted to know what that something was.

***

Two hours after she died, Emma's body was found by her neighbor who had gone out into her own back yard. She immediately ran over to her and saw the now grayish-yellow skin. Her mouth was frozen open as if in a silent scream. Although shocked, she kept her presence of mind and tried to see if she could revive her. She pumped her chest and gave her mouth to mouth but soon affirmed that her attempts were futile.

She ran back to her house and dialed 9-1-1. Unfortunately, she had no idea how to get hold of Paul. She knew he was on the road a lot with his job and figured he was out there somewhere. It wasn't long before she heard sirens in the distance and hoped it was the ambulance on its way.

About five minutes later, she saw the ambulance pull into the driveway. She ran to them and directed them to where Emma lay. After checking her vital signs and seeing there were none, they checked for other signs of life, such as the pupils and pulses. The pupils were fixed and non-reactive and there were no pulses anywhere. They hadn't yet realized that taking vital signs was no longer necessary for this patient.

The body was cool to the touch and rigor was beginning to set in to her face and neck. The combination of the warm air temperature and the sudden traumatic agonies and injuries causing her death would have accelerated the decomposition process, including rigor mortis. They radioed in to inform the trauma center of their findings. In response, they were advised to bring her to the ED for official pronouncement. After that, it would be up to the medical examiner's office to take over the case.

Putting her on the stretcher, they brought her to the ambulance and soon were off to the hospital. There, she would be officially pronounced DOA and the family would be notified by hospital officials.

Back at the house, the neighbor had gone into Emma's house through the back door and searched for Paul's phone number and the house keys. She found keys but still hadn't found his number. She looked for Emma's cell phone but couldn't find it. Then she realized it might be out in the yard where Emma fell. Not knowing if Emma had it with her outside, she checked anyway and found it near where the body had been. Looking on it, she found a number which could have been his and dialed it.

When the connection was made, it was him and she was the one who gave him the bad news about Emma. Not her death, but what she had discovered and about her being taken to the hospital. She also told him she had the keys to the house and would give them to him when he arrived at the house. After recovering from the initial shock, he thanked her and stated he was on his way back.

***

At their building in San Luis Obispo, Maria and Calvin worked in their respective labs, researching the possibilities of the spread and where the colony might go next. They needed to find other nests quickly. Time was not on their side in this situation because of the close proximity of the residential areas.

Maria was tempted to call a hospital to see if anyone had been stung by something unknown, but she was hesitant. The last thing she wanted was to start a panic. They had enough problems with this pandemic going on. This was no time for another epidemic, albeit a different type. Yet she really wanted to know. But she would have to be quite discreet about it. Maybe she would speak to someone at the hospital in person with whom she could be confident about not spreading their discussion with anyone else. Picking up her purse, she headed down to San Diego Memorial to find out what she could.

When she arrived, after checking her mask, she identified herself and asked to meet with the lab supervisor. She wasn't sure if he or she was the right person to speak to about this, but she had to start somewhere. The hospital volunteer at the reception desk contacted the lab and let them know about their official visitor and her request. A minute later she hung up.

"You can take the elevator to the fourth floor. The elevators are right around the corner there," she pointed out. "Ask to speak with Sondra."

After thanking her, Maria followed the instructions. When she arrived at the lab, she asked for Sondra and was soon met by a tall, slim, middle-aged woman with short, coiffed-up brown hair and large, rimmed glasses above a white mask. She looked more like a professor than a lab worker.

"Hi, Maria? I'm Sondra, the supervisor here. I understand you are here in a professional capacity?" They shook hands.

"Yes, I am. I am an entomologist working for the state Wildlife Department, entomology section. I'm also affiliated with USD."

Sondra's eyebrows raised. "Entomology? Really? And a professor! University of San Diego?"

Maria smiled and nodded, having expected a surprised reaction. "I know what you're thinking. If you can keep this confidential, at least for now, I will explain the reason why I'm visiting your hospital lab."

"Ok. Obviously it must be important enough to speak to a supervisor and too important to discuss with a regular lab worker. Come on to my office."

She turned and Maria followed her to a small, neatly cluttered office with a computer and, unfamiliar to Maria, lab gadgets. She sat at her desk and motioned for Maria to have a seat beside it.

The entomologist began to explain a little of what she was doing and what she and her colleagues were searching for. She mentioned the hornets which suddenly appeared in the area, which again raised Sondra's eyebrows.

Sondra quickly interjected herself. "And you are wondering if anyone here in this hospital may have been stung?"

"Well, that would be a start, yes. What I'm getting at is, if anyone has been stung by anything recently, like within the past three or four days, would it be possible to determine what the venom is in that person?"

"You should know that I can't divulge confidential info on any particular patients because of HIPPA laws, without their official consent. However, I can speak on some things without referring to anyone in particular.

"To start off, if we knew the culprit, Doctor, we would already know the venom. We know what's in bee venom and wasps as well. Most hornets we know about also, although rarely have I heard about this hospital getting any patients with those stings. But that doesn't mean none have come in, mind you. And you say these are hornets?"

"Right. But these have never appeared here before and they are not native to the US. These are Japanese Giant Hornets, about two to three times the size of our own." She forged into her purse and pulled out a picture of one and showed it to Sondra.

The woman covered her mouth as her eyes widened a bit. "Oh my heavens! Good lord, that is nasty looking."

Maria continued her spiel. "Unfortunately, their behavior and their threat to animals and people are as bad as they look. In this particular case, you CAN judge a book by its cover and be right."

"How in the world did they get over here?" It was clear the woman was flabbergasted.

"Long story, Sondra. I can't explain it now. However, they are in the area and if they have stung anyone, their venom will be in their blood. But it will be unique from bees and other stinging insects. It's something that should be tested for in stinging cases with unknown sources. In those cases, the presence of acetylcholine must be specifically tested for in the patient's blood."

"Acetylcholine? Are you serious? That's a neurotransmitter!"

Maria nodded in agreement. "Yep. But it turns out our brains aren't the only places this is found. These giant hornets from Japan have high levels of it in their venom. And you know what that chemical can do outside of neuro-transmitting."

Indeed she did. Although she wasn't a chemist or doctor, as a laboratory supervisor she knew her biochemicals quite well. This chemical was an absolute necessity as part of brain and nerve functioning throughout the body. Without it, humans would never be able to function properly. This chemical was meant for humans to move and react as they do.

But outside its transmission purposes, it stimulates pain receptors throughout the nervous system. In other words, it increases pain levels exponentially, which in turn increases suffering. Unbeknownst to either scientist, this is what happened to Billy and Emma. Neither case had yet been broadcast on the news.

The two women looked at each with full realization of the new dangers to the community.

"I don't think we have any patients in this hospital with unknown sting cases. Let me check." Sondra started typing on her laptop, searching the screen for appropriate cases, if there were any. While she did that, Maria glanced around, taking in the layout of the laboratory from what she could see through the window of the office. It looked like a typical lab in a hospital, so nothing really stood out.

"So. We have no admissions with this problem. I'm going to check the ED, see if they've had any new cases in."

She typed, then shook her head. "Doesn't look like there's anyone in the ER."

"What about Children's?"

"Ok, let me get into their site. We have the same software so that should be no problem."

Again she typed. This time she got a hit.

"Yes," she said. "There's an eleven-year-old boy in the ICU. Oh my gosh! Let's see…he came to the ED there a couple of days ago." Then she went on to explain the circumstances and everything except the name and any references to his identity because of the HIPPA laws.

Maria hid her excitement but then realized that there was a problem.

"Oh my. I really need to talk to his parents. How can I do that if I don't know the name? What they tell me and the information I have could have an impact on his case or treatment. I need to be able to get past that law without anyone breaking it."

"Hmm. You're right. Hold on."

She typed some more and wrote down a name and other information. She then gave Maria the piece of paper she'd written on and gestured her to wait while she picked up the phone.

Maria looked at her talking to someone on the other end. Yes, she was trying to get a hold of the boy's doctor or nurse. She explained the situation and the request being made. The nurse came on the line and Sondra explained the request, who Maria was and her reason for being there, and that if the parents were in the boy's room, would they agree to speak with her if she came over?

"Hold on a moment. I think the mother is in the room. Let me check with her."

"OK, I'll hold."

While Sondra held the phone to her ear she said softly, "I'm about to find out."

A minute later she got the ok. Maria got up and thanked the lab supervisor for her help. She quickly looked at the piece of paper with the boy's doctor's name and number on it, stuck it in her piece and left the office. She was anxious to find out what she could. If the boy was stung by the Vespa M., it could be a bad sign of things to come. She could only hope not.

6

In Riverside it was a warm sunny day. The baseball game was going on in one of the park's two ball fields. The nine youths manning the in and outfields were spread out and ready for the batter. It was top of the fifth inning. Jonny Westerfield was at bat. He was his team's power hitter who had scored more home runs than anybody else there. It was First Congregational in the top of the inning.

The game was just for practice and fun, though. They were youth teams from two churches: the First Congregational and the Holy Trinity Lutheran Church. Once a year the two teams got together for a fun game. Everyone knew each other. After the game, congregation members from the churches gathered together for the post-game cookout. Despite the different denominations, everyone got along well and there were never any issues regarding their differences in the ways they worshipped. After all, they all worshipped the same God.

The pitch was thrown. "Ball one," said the umpire.

The first baseman smirked. "Ok, let's strike him out Tom," he said under his breath.

The second pitch came. The batter didn't swing. "Strike one!" yelled the umpire.

The first baseman gave Tom the thumbs up. "C'mon now. Only two more to go."

The tension in the air was felt by everyone. Even though it was just a fun game, still the onlookers felt it. It was a game and it was only human to feel that way when you have a favorite you hope to win.

In the bleachers, onlookers were sweating but enjoying the game anyway. Two teenage boys were rooting for their younger brother who was playing in the league. He was now the left fielder for the home team. The score was one to zero, home.

The teen brother named Brad stood up and reached into his pocket for money. He looked down and asked his other brother Stan if he wanted a coke from the vendor.

"Sure," replied Stan. He reached into his pocket for his allowance money. "Hey, bro, while you're there, get me a small popcorn with the coke." After giving Brad his money, Brad left to get their stuff from the vendor.

In the meantime, the pitcher was winding up for the next pitch. There was one out so far. Just two more to go before Holy Trinity would be up to bat. The throw was made. "Strike two!" yelled the umpire.

The home crowd cheered, with some father fan yelling out, "Let's go, guys. One more strike. Let her rip!" he yelled to the pitcher.

The batter for First Congregational, the visiting team, felt the drop of sweat come down from his brow. It was eighty-seven degrees but he was completely tuned out to that. He could be *dripping* with sweat. But when he concentrated on something, wild horses couldn't pull him away from it. Right now, his concentration was complete and absolute. He readied for the pitch and was determined to get this one.

His eyes looked at the pitcher as he saw the windup. It looked like this one would be a faster pitch. He was right. It came at him full force and was right where he wanted it to be. He swung and made the connection. The smack could be heard by everyone there. The ball went so high the onlookers couldn't see it. Over the infielders in a second and then the ball flew over the outfielders. They all ran as fast as they could toward the outermost fence with their mitts ready. The ball continued and went over that fence.

It went high into a tree that was just a few feet away on the other side.

It slammed into the huge nest that no one knew was there. No one in the area had expected a home run, let alone a grand slam. There was something else no one would have ever expected. The swarm of hundreds of giant hornets exploded out of the hive in a fit of ferocious anger. They followed the invisible airwave vibrations that the ball had left as it traveled toward them. They flew directly back toward the players and the onlookers. These were not just angry from the disturbance of their home; they were murderously enraged.

Sometimes it takes at least a few seconds, sometimes more, for the brain to process what the eyes are seeing. Vision is usually interpreted almost immediately by the brain. Sometimes seeing can lead to difficulty believing.

The swarm looked like a black cloud. There were so many of what comprised it that the numbers seemed to appear in the thousands. It was moving as a dark cloud of low buzzing. The players quickly saw them coming, and then the onlookers. Immediate shock and seconds of delayed brain processing were revealed by everyone's faces. Over the fence they came. The outfielders were the first to react and run back toward the stands, yelling, "Get out. Everyone get out!"

They were the first to be struck. Each of the three outfielders were stung repeatedly as they desperately attempted to wave them off with their arms. It was about as futile as trying to stop a cannonball with bare hands.

The infielders were running toward their parents who met them quickly, but they too were soon covered with giant hornets and nearly everyone was getting stung. It was clearly a mass attack, indefensible. A woman had called 9-1-1 just before getting into her car. To her horror, she watched everyone getting attacked. Someone ran to her car, begging her to open up as they knocked on the back window while being assaulted from behind. She had locked the doors without thought. She wanted to let the person in but realized if she did, the insects would follow her right in and they would all be in trouble.

They reminded her of the killer bees movie she had seen a few years ago. In fact, these acted just like them. Only these were more terrifying because they were at least two to three times larger than the bees. What the hell kind of wasps or hornets were these? Were they some kind of mutation or new undiscovered species?

Soon the fire department arrived and then the police. Two officers who had gotten out of their cars were running around in a panic all over the area trying to find shelter or to get back into their cars. They, too, were constantly flailing their arms trying to fight their attackers off. Some people collapsed to the ground, soon covered by the giant insects. Of those people, unfortunately, a large percentage of them would soon die because of the multiple injections of the toxic venom. Hornets continued to fill the entire area in furious continuing flight patterns above panicking people.

All first responder ambulance personnel, as well as police and firefighters, realized they were caught in an extremely precarious situation. Without special suits, they were equally fair game to the insects. Only the firefighters had the special fire suits that had some semblance of temporary protection. They were the ones who went in, wearing them and oxygen masks to cover their faces. They did their best to hose down as much of the area as possible, hoping to at least chase the hornets away, if not kill them.

A number of people had made it into their cars, but not without getting stung at least once. By now local police and county sheriff's cars were all over the place. But knowing what was outside made it difficult for them to leave their cars. Their first gut reaction was to go anyway and try to save people. However, they had a real dilemma.

What good were they if they got stung to death themselves?

There were a number of people on the ground. One of the officers focused on one of them and decided he had to go and rescue that person, regardless of the hornets. He quickly looked around. It looked like the swarm had been chased away by the fire hoses. The ground was wet and some of the few stragglers still struggling back to their cars were soaked.

He got out and ran to the man who was struggling to breathe. The officer looked over his shoulder and saw the ambulances in the area and waved his arm over for one of the EMTs to come over and get this man. Other responders left their vehicles.

Looking back down at the man who grimaced in pain, the cop knew this man was in no condition to answer questions, except for his name.

"Mike," he managed to softly say out loud to the officer.

"Hi, Mike. I'm Randy. Listen, I'm getting you help now. The EMTs are on their way. Are you allergic to anything like bee stings?"

Mike continued to grimace and groan, finally squeaking out, "bees".

The EMTs arrived with their equipment and a stretcher. Officer Randy passed that information on which made them work even faster. The victim could die at any time and they had to quickly pump some epinephrine into him before he did. Having given him that injection, they quickly put him on the stretcher and within three minutes he was on his way to the hospital. The ED would soon be inundated with sting victims.

***

By this time, the second queen born three months earlier, had now well-established a nest and plenty of workers to serve her needs. The nest was expanding. As more eggs hatched, more drones and workers increased the population. Many scouts had gone out in search of beehives and found one.

Consequently, the workers followed the pheromone scents of the scouts back to the hive where they destroyed the entire bee population and took the body parts back to feed their young. They were now taking over the area. Other insects were also on their menu and there were plenty of those around. For now.

***

It was now late August, a little more than a month since the hornets first arrived on the shores of California. Unknown at that time was the fact that there had been *two* queens which were transported and had escaped from their confinement on reaching the US. This would prove to be significant later on. At the time because of this, the spread and infestation into surrounding areas was virtually guaranteed. Good for the insects, bad for honeybees, people, and animals.

Although not everyone decided to go to the Riverside Hospital ED, those that went believed they were in serious medical trouble. When the doors opened and a crowd of people walked quickly at the same time to the check-in desk, all the registrars could hear were the rantings of people in pain and distress and talking about terrible stings. They had no clue what they were talking about but decided more reinforcements were needed asap. Something was going on.

At the same time, ambulance EMTs were bringing in Mike from the ballpark who'd been found on the ground by the police officer, Randy. He was shaking, almost like semi-seizures, and had vomited while on the stretcher.

Staff quickly brought him to one of the ED rooms where they immediately hooked him up to monitors and got his vital signs right away. A doctor came in to perform an assessment and quickly realized the seriousness of the situation and got him started on IV solutions for hydration. He ordered an IV medication to control and stop the vomiting, and bloodwork to be taken stat. For now, the man was in good hands.

Whether he would live or die depended on their proper diagnosis and treatment. They were told he was stung, but by what no one knew for sure. Huge flying insects is what was reported. A precautionary dose of epinephrine was administered.

It wasn't long before they found out. With rumors of giant wasps or hornets floating around the ED and those words being said out loud by incoming patients, the ED staff realized the situation could be far more serious than they immediately thought.

7

"Thank you for meeting with me, Mrs. Jansen."

The two women shook hands outside Billy's room on floor five of the Children's Hospital.

"That's ok. Dr. Hernandez, you said?" asked Sandy.

Maria nodded. "I just have a few questions for you. Your answers could help me determine if we can help your son in some way."

They had to move to make way for a hospital housekeeper moving her cart. "Whoops, sorry," said Maria.

The cart lady smiled, saying, "That's ok. No problem."

"There's a family room a couple of doors down on the right. Let's go in there," suggested Sandy. Maria readily agreed and a minute later they sat down in there with the room all to themselves for the moment.

Sandy brushed her dark blond hair back. "Now I think I'm ready."

Maria started in calmly with her questions, wanting to know what happened just before, during, and just after she discovered Billy on the ground outside. Sandy then explained the entire story up to the point where her son was transported by ambulance to the hospital.

"So you have no idea what stung him?" Maria asked.

"No. No idea at all. I looked around but didn't see anything."

"Any hives of any kind that you noticed in or around your yard?"

"You mean like bees?"

"Mmm, bees, wasps or hornets. Any of those?"

Sandy thought for a minute. "We used to have a beehive in one of our trees in the back. I haven't noticed if it's still there or not. I don't go out in the back except to monitor the pool. I don't go in very much. Once in a while. Billy loves to go in. He goes in almost every day during the summer, sometimes with his friend next door."

"Are you sure it was a beehive?"

"Pretty sure. I mean, it looked like one to me. Funny thing is, I didn't see anything flying in or out of it."

"Ok." Maria wrote something down. "Were you there for more than a minute?"

"Oh sure," exclaimed Sandy. "I stood there for, hmm, I'd say several minutes at least. I wanted to know if anybody was home up there."

Maria was already formulating a plausible theory in her mind. She believed her for one important reason. The Vespa M. did not usually make hives like that in trees. They were primarily nesters, finding holes in subterranean areas such as under rotten tree trunks lying on the ground, or in any other holes in the ground where they could create a few combs for the queen to lay her eggs. On occasion they would nest in or up a tree.

"When you checked your son, did you see any bee stingers stuck to any part of his skin?"

Sandy remembered that she didn't. She had initially thought that odd because she had first believed bees were involved.

"No, didn't see any. I was surprised because I know they lose their stingers and die after they sting. And I thought bees had done this to my boy."

Maria wrote down, *"No stingers or bees found on Billy J. No bees seen in area. Beehive in yard tree appeared deserted."*

"What are you thinking, Doctor?" Sandy asked curiously.

Maria sighed. "Well, I have a better idea of what we're dealing with. There's no hard evidence, yet, as far as whodunit. I can only theorize the best case and the worst-case scenarios. First, the best case.

"It's possible that this is a one-time thing. An unknown stinging insect got your son and he's had some kind of anaphylactic reaction to it for which he's now being treated. By the way, I am *so sorry* for failing to ask at the beginning. I really am. How is your son? Is he stabilizing, I pray?"

"Oh, he seems to be stabilizing. He's awake and talking some now. The doctor says he is improving. With another day or two, he'll gain his strength back and will almost be ready to come home, thank God. Thank you so much for asking."

"You're so welcome. And I am very happy to hear that. I'd like to go in and see him for a minute after we're done here. Would that be ok with you? We won't be much longer here. Almost done."

Sandy smiled. "Of course. Billy might be thrilled to meet a new scientist friend. He won't know what an entomologist is. I'll just say you're…"

"The bug lady!" they said at the same time. Both women laughed at that.

"Ooo, I don't know how you do it," Sandy said. "Studying bugs gives me the creepy crawlies." Sandy shook and made a face.

Maria smiled. "It's funny how people can differ so much in their likes and dislikes. Both my parents hated bugs and killed them whenever they could. My sister also. Yet me? I didn't do that. Just the opposite. I'd collect them in jars and just look at them in fascination, wondering all kinds of things about them. Not one of them scared me. Not even spiders, which my sister was deathly afraid of. If I had a jar in our bedroom with bugs or spiders in it, she would not go in the room while it was in there."

Sandy nodded. "Wow, that is something. The only time I get scared is when one lands on me. Anyway, didn't mean to get you off the beaten track here. Now my curiosity is getting the best of me. Tell me what's the worst-case scenario."

Maria told her what she believed the culprit was.

"There's no hard evidence yet and so far no one has actually seen them. What I do know is that it wasn't a bee that stung your son. You said he's not allergic to bees or any other insect venom. What this was, there are now two possibilities. One, he may now be allergic to venom and this was a wake-up call to that. Two, it's an insect of unknown origin."

When she had been at the main hospital earlier, before she had left she had asked Sondra to see if she could get Billy's blood tested for the acetylcholine. Sondra told her once the doctor's order was obtained, she would be able to do that.

"I'm waiting for a certain blood test result on your son. If that result turns out positive, then I will know which particular insect stung him. It could be the Asian or Japanese Giant Hornet."

Maria almost blurted out the other known name for it: the murder hornet. She caught herself in time. The last thing she needed was to cause panic in this poor mother. The alternate name was applied because of all the people it had killed back in Japan, without provocation. They were as aggressive, if not more so, than the African killer bees. But they were worse because of their ability to sting as many times as they wanted. One hornet stinging a person, having this ability, could cause a lot of damage in the victim as well as death.

Sandy went pale. "What?" she exclaimed. "Giant hornet? Are you serious?"

Maria nodded. "I'm afraid so, IF this is what it is. I won't know until the blood test comes back. Nothing will be sure until then."

Sandy looked at her in shock. "But...but how are they properly treating him if they don't know? And why wasn't this test given initially?"

Those were very good questions, and Maria answered them as factually as she could while avoiding too much negativity. She said just enough to satisfy the need to know while leaving out the worst-case scenario. She didn't want to jump the gun on that because she'd yet to receive confirmation of the test results. If she needed to and when the time came, she would let Sandy know. But for the moment, Billy seemed to be medically stable and his prognosis was good. Why cause needless worry at this point?

"Do you have any more questions for me while we're here?"

Sandy looked down and sighed, then brought her eyes back up to the scientist's. "How come he seems to be better now without them knowing the test results? How could he have been properly treated?"

She hadn't told the woman about the acetylcholine. Rather than confuse her, she explained that his pain level was likely increased by whatever venom was injected into him; that it would have gradually subsided with the pain meds, and that the epinephrine that had been given to him at the beginning had not worked. That and the fact that he hadn't been given any since then suggested to her that maybe he was not allergic to bee venom but could be to that of the hornet. It was best to find out for sure from the doctor since she wasn't a medical person.

After her explanation, Sandy seemed to accept that but understandably remained nervous about the whole situation. Maria then decided that now was a good time to see Billy before she left the hospital. Sandy agreed, stood up and had her follow her to her son's room.

After a few minutes, she assured Sandy that she would ask to have someone let her know regarding the blood test results for the venom component. If the giant hornet was involved, it meant that not just Billy, but the entire community might very well be in jeopardy. They needed to find that nest and any others that were in the area before someone else was attacked.

She hadn't yet heard the news about Emma Compton or the young ballplayers and their families. On her way out, she decided to contact the San Diego County Department of Health and bring them into the loop. This could turn out to be not just a county health crisis, but a statewide one as well.

8

The Children's Hospital ED was suddenly inundated with multiple patients coming in screaming. The staff had never seen anything like it before. It was a nightmare in the middle of the afternoon. Despite many parents having been stung trying to protect their kids, they also were suffering the same pain. The attack had been swift and unrelenting. The attack was from what seemed like thousands of them sweeping across the playing field in a merciless onslaught which confronted anything and everyone.

Most of those who ended up covered by the aggressive insects collapsed and quickly died. Those who were allergic to insect venom of any kind died the quickest. Others were able to gather up their kids and get into their cars. However, even those parents were suffering pain and agony. Parents who drove to the hospital endured the symptoms of the venom coursing through their bodies. Just the fact that it was happening to their children kept them just able enough to get to the hospital. Hospital staff quickly realized that the parents of the children were suffering the same symptoms.

When police received the report of the ballfield attack, they had already known about the attack and death of Emma Compton two days before. The communications on the police radios alerted the media who, in barely any time at all, showed up at the Children's Hospital. The hospital and police had to quickly send out their public information officers to release the information they could to the public.

When it came out on the local news, everyone dropped what they were doing to watch and listen in horror at the events that had unfolded. No one could have imagined that something like this could happen in their community. Why? Why here and why these people?

Maria was one of those that had just learned about the Emma Compton case and ballpark event. There was no question in her mind now. She no longer needed to find out the special blood test results on Billy Jansen. The attack that occurred, especially on the ballfield, would not have occurred from bees or even regular hornets or wasps. This was worse than African killer bees and there could be only one insect that would be worse and more deadly. These were killers that needed no provocation.

She didn't hesitate to contact the powers-that-be for her department up in Sacramento. Without question, the state needed to become involved. They could let the governor know. Only he would have the authority to notify local and county officials to declare a state of emergency in the affected areas in and around San Diego. Until the nests could be found and eradicated—she was sure there were multiple nests—all residents were at risk whenever they were outside anywhere in the county. The health crisis had begun.

But *they had to find those nests*. All of them. That would require multiple numbers of scientific teams and a large assemblage of assistive personnel. Her headquarters office could, with the proper authorization, send wildlife and game personnel along with more state and local entomologists, down to their area.

She stayed on the phone for a while until they connected her to the one person who could help her the most. Miranda Bingham had the most experience and was now the Director of the Entomology branch of the Department of Wildlife and Game in California. Maria had worked with her once a few years back before she became director. Out in the field, Bingham had discovered the eggs of a rarely seen beetle that only lived in certain rural areas. She knew almost right away what the species was, whereas Maria hadn't ever seen those before and therefore had no clue.

"Well hello there, Maria. Long time no see or hear. How are you?"

"I'm fine, Miranda. It's good to hear you again. I hope you're well. Too bad we have to talk under these horrible circumstances."

"Yes, I know. I heard the news and to say that's disturbing would be an understatement." Miranda was a very pleasant, cheerful sounding person, even when she talked business. To anyone who didn't know her, it was quite easy to underestimate her. But because Maria knew her, she didn't want to beat around the bush.

Maria then explained in detail everything she had found out so far, from the Billy Jansen case to the latest on the ballplayers.

She let Miranda know that she had two small teams looking for nests in the area but they had yet to search hundreds of acres of more wilderness areas. It was overwhelming for them and a most daunting task as well.

"And you say you found only a deserted beehive and not the hornet nest—rather not any hornet nests yet?"

"I'm afraid that's correct. I suspect the hornets killed off the bees."

"But you didn't actually see the hive yourself?"

"No, I didn't. I just spoke to Sandy Jansen and her son for the first time today. He's in the hospital as being the first known victim stung. His mother was there and we had a little chat, after which I went to see her son who seems to be improving, thank God."

"Hmm," she grunted. "So, these are the only cases so far?"

"So far," Maria replied.

"Well, this is what I would do if I were you. Sounds like you're going to have your work cut out for you. You will likely need a lot more people than you have now to help out with this because this situation has the potential to spread like a raging wildfire."

Maria nodded. "I agree. Go ahead."

"I would suggest that you first go see it yourself and look around for any signs of bees or bee parts. Make a record of what you find. Have your teams continue to search areas they haven't already. In the meantime, talk with some of the neighbors around the Jansen residence. Find out anything you can regarding hornet sightings, whether regular vespas or others. Include sightings of bees. That's important. We need to know if any bees at all are around that area."

"I will certainly do that."

"Already there's been one death down there that we know of. That's one too many. Tragic, to say the least. But from what you told me about the attacks on the ball players and their families, that calls for a state of emergency. When there's one mass attack without provocation, there is guaranteed to be more. Especially in a highly populated area. Where they came from we will have to find out. Did they originate from those containers or from the north of us?

"So… I am going to contact the Wildlife Department commissioner and have the governor notified of all this. The request will be to have a local and potential state health crisis declared as well as a local state of emergency. I want you to keep me updated regularly at least every two to three days."

"Ok."

"Here's my numbers." Bingham then gave her private extension and cell phone for calling or texting.

"One more thing, Maria."

"Sure."

"What about the media? The public should be made aware of this."

"Already thought of that. I will have our PIO take care of that and it will be on the news as soon as we can get it on there."

After Maria had thanked her and promised to keep her updated, she thought about how much had to be done on her part as well as the state's. Now that Miranda had given her the green light to go full out in her investigations and search for the mystery nests, she picked up the phone again to contact Sandy. She had to tell her that she was now convinced her son was the victim of a giant hornet attack. Plus, she now had to take some serious precautions for her own safety.

***

Up in the foothills of Escondido, just east of San Diego, the team searched the area based on a report from local hikers. It was the strangest report they'd ever heard and the most chilling. Because it wasn't what they saw. It was what they *heard*. The sound itself was loud enough to be heard from even a discreet distance. They knew, in general, what could make those kinds of sounds. But it was too frightful for them to get any closer and visualize where they were coming from. They believed it might be African honeybees, aka killer bees. A huge nest and swarm of them.

The searchers, wearing their full bee netting and outfits were prepared for that. They were neither from Maria's group nor from the state. A rumor from someone had reached one of the hikers who then told their group that it was thought there were killer bees in the area because a couple of people had been stung over in San Diego. Whatever story was started, it apparently got distorted as it spread to more and more people. For whatever reason, it may have been misunderstood in the very beginning and now the searchers were hunting for a possible killer bee nest. Apparently, they hadn't yet heard the news on television.

The woods weren't very thick in the area, but they still had to watch their footing. There was an occasional boulder along the way and a few clumps of rocks. Because of this uncertain hilly terrain, their progress was slow.

The air was warm and dry. Two of the five searchers from the private lab of Sandicki Labs Incorporated were carrying backpacks containing certain items they might need to repel and contain the bees within a certain area. At least that is what the items were supposed to do. They kept their face masks off until if or when they arrived at the target area.

"Hey, Tom, any idea if we are nearing the target yet?" asked one of the searchers toward the back.

Tom was the leader. He turned around. "Not yet, but I think we are getting closer, according to what those hikers said."

The hilly terrain would certainly be tiring to most people, even if in good physical shape, after climbing or walking on it for a while. Trying to dodge boulders and rocks while looking for a nest or hive in the trees and being on the lookout for those killer bees at the same time was a challenge that none of them preferred to repeat.

After about another twenty minutes, Tom stopped suddenly and put up his hand for the others to stop. He heard no birds chirping or any other sounds but the deep buzzing in the distance.

"Hear something?" asked someone from behind him.

"Shh! Wait a minute," said Tom in a whispery voice.

They waited, listening. "Hear that?" he said.

"Yea. What the hell...? Does that sound like bees to you?" asked someone from behind him.

"I'm not sure," replied Tom. "Might be a large swarm. But I don't know. Doesn't sound quite right."

He dug into his front pouch he was carrying and pulled out a small pair of binoculars to see what he could see in the distance. He didn't want to lead his team into something or to confront something they weren't prepared for. Surprises out here were not welcome for what they were doing.

The buzzing sounds were constant. Not sure of which direction they were coming from or how far away they were, he now knew they were heading right where they wanted to go.

Tom had been an entomologist with a specialty in bees for seventeen years. He knew bees like the back of his hand. Europeans and Africans sounded alike and each of those bee types were exact duplicates in appearance to the naked eye. The only difference between the two was the aggressiveness level.

After about five minutes, he turned to the team.

"I think I know which direction it's coming from. Let's be careful and we'll walk slowly. You know what to look for, so from this point on we need to put our face masks on. Make sure they are tight against your face. Everyone let me know when you're ready."

Speaking to the second man from the last, he made a final note before proceeding into the danger zone. He looked up at the tree he was standing next to. Its lowermost branch, about ten feet off the ground, was broken and bent.

"Note this tree," he told the team. He pointed up to that branch. "That's the mark of it. Consider this the entrance to the danger zone. Don't take your mask or gloves off while in this zone. Harry, take whatever items you need out of the bag now."

Harry dug into his bag and removed one of the three cylinders he had. Those cylinders contained a chemical gas under pressure which produce smoke when it hits the air. It was harmless to bees but they don't like it and it would chase them away temporarily.

Each member of the team was heavily suited, masked and gloved. Even their feet were covered so completely that there was no space between the bottom of the pants and the shoes. No insects could get in. They were, in effect, suit-quarantined to the max.

"Ok, Harry, you all set?"

"Yep. Ready to rock and roll."

"'K. Let's walk slowly."

Proceeding slowly and with caution, the buzzing seemed to increase in volume and intensity with each step they took.

None of them saw or knew that they were being watched. There was no one else around.

Tom and the rest of the team scanned the area, visually searching up into the trees and below them. Sometimes bees took advantage of hollowed out areas in tree trunks when they had the opportunity. Hives were not always used. Sometimes bees used the closest thing they could to a hive. Usually they preferred to be above the ground.

As they slowly made their way through the trees and occasional thick shrubbery, they seemed to be the only ones making sounds besides what was making the buzzing. No birds were seen or heard and no squirrels were seen at any time since they entered the woods.

When the team reached what seemed to be the peak of the buzzing intensity, Tom put up his hand. He looked up for the hive he expected to find. But he saw nothing. Where was it? The buzzing seemed to come from all around them.

While he and a couple of others looked around and up in the trees at the trunks, others were looking down. They knew they were at ground zero for the source of the buzzing, and large flying insects started flying around them.

Tom looked down and he suddenly froze. Inside his large, windowed head covering, his jaw dropped. It took only a few seconds for his brain to process what his eyes had just discovered.

"Back off. Back off now. Slowly!" he said firmly.

"Tom, what the hell; back off for what?" asked one of the others as they started to comply. They'd never heard alarm in Tom's voice before.

As they backed away slowly, reality began to sink in.

"These are not bees, guys." Tom's worst fears became reality.

By this time, the entrance to the ground nest quickly filled with hornets ready to exit. Tom noticed it in stunned silence. These looked like flying predators of the worst kind. More like a close *encounter* of the worst kind. Again, he told everyone to back away and keep going. When they got far enough away, he yelled to turn and run back the way they came. He knew that for the moment they were in trouble. They were expecting bees because of reports of the killers being in the area. Instead, they were now vulnerable and exposed as if they weren't wearing anything.

The bee suits were ineffective against the vespas. Their stingers were long enough to easily penetrate them and into the wearer's flesh.

One took flight and landed on one of the team members and he soon yelled in pain. Many of the others followed.

The men continued to run toward the wood's entrance as the swarm quickly overtook them. Each of them was quickly covered with giant hornets which repeatedly stung them, forcing agonizing cries of pain from each. Despite that, they continued to run until finally they reached the open area where they could see their vehicles.

One of the men collapsed and then another as the toxic venom quickly pumped through their bodies. They continued to struggle and fight their way back. Despite his tormentors stinging him, Harry managed to open one of the chemical cannisters he was still carrying and sprayed all around them to try and get the attackers away. The chemical was meant for bees *and* hornets. Because these were giant hornets, which could be loosely compared to American hornets on strong steroids, the chemical had some effect but not enough to make much difference. It wasn't strong enough and there wasn't enough to spray more than the required amount for regular hornets. Some of the insects flew away but many others continued their attacks.

One of the victims turned out to be allergic to the venom. While the other victims continued to fight their way out of the forest, the one allergic team member thrashed around on the ground in his struggle to breathe. As Tom, the last member to leave the area, reached his colleague, he saw the man turn blue under the mask and his eyes bulge.

"Mac, stay with me, stay with me!" he yelled to his fallen comrade as he picked him up and positioned him over his shoulder and then started running. He ignored the murderous insects stinging *him* as well, not feeling the pain for the moment. All he could think about was getting his friend and colleague back to the van and to the hospital.

"You're gonna be alright, buddy. Stay with me, pal," he said to the now unconscious man.

At the clearing, those exiting the woods were now free of their attackers. All were in pain but alive and able to walk around. One of them called 9-1-1 and reported their location and situation. Ambulances were now on their way. They were unaware that the media and police would not be far behind them.

Once Tom caught up with them with Mac over his shoulder, the others had removed their masked hoods and suits. Tom put Mac down on the ground and the others immediately gathered around.

Tom removed Mac's hood and mask, only to reveal what appeared to be a facial rictus of death. His face was purplish, and his lips extremely swollen as well as his eyes and throat.

"Holy shit, Tom. Is that Mac?" one of the men asked. Mac's face was so bloated they almost didn't recognize him.

Instead of answering, Tom checked for a carotid pulse. Then he put his face down near his mouth and nose to check for breathing. He felt neither.

"He's not breathing and there's no pulse. I'm starting CPR."

"I called already," someone said. "They're on their way."

Tom began CPR as the men around him tried to process what had just happened and what had happened to Mac. It seemed like hours rather than minutes before the first of the ambulances arrived, followed by two police cars.

The scientists were gathered at the edge of the grass near the parking lot and were quickly spotted by the first responders. After a brief assessment and seeing Tom giving CPR, the EMTs took over. They ripped his shirt apart to clear his chest area and started using their portable defib kit on the patient. While another EMT radioed in to the trauma center at the nearest hospital, the EMTs attempting to revive Mac made another two attempts at resuscitation. There continued to be a lack of any vital signs in Mac. They looked up and shook their heads at the EMT on the radio.

Then a paramedic came up to assess the situation. Orders came over the radio. He was to inject a dose of adrenaline into the heart to try and get it started. It was a last-ditch effort to revive the stricken man and was a one-shot deal. They were in the field and couldn't perform everything that might be done in a hospital setting.

The paramedic pulled the medication out of his kit along with the appropriate large bore needle. Working as fast as he could, he pulled the medication from its container into the syringe.

"Alright, give me room here," he said.

With the needle in one hand, he quickly checked for the exact spot he needed. He swabbed it with an antiseptic in the other hand and inserted the lengthy needle all the way until he was sure he was in the heart.

Then the paramedic dug into his kit and pulled out a tube and airbag.

"Someone hold his head. I'm going to try and vent tube him."

He got above Mac's head and tilted his chin up, looking for the airway and opening to the trachea. His heart sank when he saw that the swelling was so great down his throat that it didn't look good for insertion of the endotracheal tube. He had to try anyway as best as he could without causing any injury.

Carefully he took the tube and very slowly attempted to insert it. But he was quickly met with resistance. Re-tilting the chin and head, he painstakingly made a second effort. It was no use. The man's airway was closed off by the swelling. He had literally suffocated from the swelling.

The paramedic thought about doing an emergency tracheotomy. But first he had to recheck the heart.

"Got a heartbeat yet?" he asked the EMT.

"No."

With no available airway right now, their only chance of saving the man was to get his heart restarted. "Rick, call trauma again. I'm going to try and defib again."

While Rick got on the phone and updated the situation to the hospital trauma team, the paramedic cleared the area and applied the defib once again. The man's chest quickly lifted up and back down. The machine still detected no heartbeat. The joules were less than the maximum for the machine.

Rick got off the phone. "Doctor says try one more dose of adrenaline, half of the original. Defib one more time. Increase the joules to three hundred and advise the results." Joules was the amount of electric charge in a defibrillator. In a portable one called an AED, three hundred and sixty was the maximum.

"Alright, let's defib again. Maybe we can get it working this time."

He turned the knob on the machine to the ordered charge, made sure the area was clear and pressed the button. After it was fully charged up, it made its final warning and then sent the electric charges into the man's heart.

After removing the pads, the EMT checked for vital signs. All breathing had stopped. The paramedic was ready to do the emergency trach, but it was a no-go. If the heart had started or even if it had some movement, he was ready to instantly perform it. Once on the right spot, it would only take less than a minute or even seconds to perform. But without even the slightest response from the heart, it would be useless. The EMT contacted the hospital. It had been almost seven minutes since the man went down with cardiac arrest. Six minutes was the point when brain damage would begin from lack of oxygen.

On orders from the hospital physician, they had to call it and transport the body to the hospital for further analysis.

Tom and the other men were devastated. They couldn't believe it. What the hell? How could a sting destroy a person like that? If it *was* a sting. Mac was strong and healthy as far as they knew. He'd never even called in sick. For them, there would be no going back into those woods. Not today. He told everyone that was it for the day.

Tom's next plan was to contact Mac's family right away. That would be the worst thing he'd ever done in his life. Although a couple of the other men were stung, only Mac had suffered the way he did and died. It hadn't been known before this that he was allergic to bee and hornet venom. But it seemed to make him more aware and skittish of all biting and stinging insects. It would always remind him of what happened to his colleague and friend.

Other ambulances came and took the other victims to the ED. One fatality was one too many in Tom's mind.

9

Two days later at San Diego Children's Hospital, Doctor Jurgensen was the hospitalist on shift, sitting at one of the physician computers on the medical/surgical floor. The screen he was looking at displayed the latest lab results on one of his patients, Billy Jansen. Much of the bloodwork showed some results that were concerning: low red blood cell count, an alarming increase in white blood cell numbers, and an increase in urea and creatinine: byproducts of cellular metabolism that must be filtered out from the blood by the kidneys and expelled in urine. The fact that there was an increase of these in Billy's blood would concern any doctor. In addition, combined with the decrease in red blood cell count, these increased numbers indicated that something serious was going on that must be addressed as soon as possible.

What that something was could be from many things. As in police detective work, doctors were all too frequently medical detectives. They had to rule out all the least probable before they could get to the most probable. That could take time and time was not on Billy's side. Many of the same symptoms could be caused by a number of different diseases and illnesses.

For now, Billy was stable but still required to be on oxygen. He was half lucid and partly aware of what was going on, but not fully. Even so, that was promising. The doctors had to find out about the sting and determine for sure what kind of toxin was in the boy's blood and affecting his organs.

The doctor continued to scroll down until he got to the toxicology section of the lab report. That's when he stopped scrolling. "Oh my Lord," he muttered under his breath.

He went to the orders screen and typed in new orders for Billy.

Toxicology revealed that the boy was suffering from the venom of a deadly hornet, specifically that of the *Vespa Mandarinia Japonica.* He'd heard of it before. From what he knew, the only way the Japanese Giant Hornet could get to the states was by ship. He had heard that some were suspected of having entered the US and had hoped what he heard was nothing but rumors. Now he knew the information was true. What's worse, they were apparently now in their part of California. This was a very long ways from Washington state. He somehow doubted they migrated all the way down here. Regardless, he didn't have time to dwell on this.

After his orders were typed in and flagged to be read and followed through asap, he stood up and went to another one of his patients. He would check in on Billy later and ensure that the treatment was in progress. He heard a little about the sudden huge influx of patients here who had been attacked by large insects. But before he could find out more, he'd been called to a new case. Word was spreading rapidly throughout the hospital and he would find out soon enough.

State Entomology Lab

Maria had returned the day before to try and determine whether the insects had spread north from the San Diego area. There had been nothing more she could do down there. After finding out that Billy was still stable in the hospital and that he was being treated for his severe allergic reaction, she returned to continue her investigation. In addition to this area, she had to find out if areas north of LA were also finding unwanted invaders.

"Hey, welcome back." Calvin Kablinsky had a habit of coming in quickly enough to nearly startle her almost every time. Once again, she almost jumped. But it was just his coming in. It was his talking all of a sudden at just the right moment when he entered.

"Good grief, Cal," she exclaimed with a hand on her chest. "You are exceptionally adept at scaring the hell out of me!" She had been bending over at a paper on the counter when he'd made her straighten up as if she'd been struck by lightning.

"Oh, I'm sorry, Maria. Didn't mean to do that. Guess old habits die hard. Are you ok?"

She brushed back her hair. "Yea, I'm fine," she replied. "Just try not to do that again. Give me *some* clue that you are nearby." Her smile told him she had, once again, forgiven him.

Both scientists had been colleagues for a number of years because they worked well together. Although both were experts and worked with all kinds of stinging and biting insects and arachnoids along with the less harmful, it was Maria who worked with the bee and hornet families, including European and African honeybees, yellow jackets, and a number of subspecies of wasps. Calvin took on the mostly ground dwelling biters and stingers, including various species of centipedes, millipedes, numerous varieties of dangerous stinging ants, and many others which were not well known to the general public. Most people would consider the subjects of his studies and expertise the very antithesis of pleasurable work.

"So did you find out anything down there?" he asked. Curiosity wasn't his only motivation for asking. Often they worked together to resolve a difficult problem or major issue. They were not merely individual scientists, but a team as well.

She told him about the boy in the hospital and information about other attacks in the area, including at the ballfield. That day had certainly not been good for either the players nor the hospital staff. But especially for the players and their parents.

Calvin was mildly surprised at the ballfield attack. That did not sound like typical behavior, even for those monstrous things. Although they could attack unprovoked, the field was nowhere near where they nested. The motivation for their attacks was no less a mystery than how they first got up to Washington state in the first place. Because there'd been so many casualties, the news went global.

"Tell you what," Calvin said, "I will stop my current project for a bit and help you on this."

"Cal, you don't have to do that. That will bring you off focus on what you've been trying to accomplish."

He frowned at her. "Oh hogwash," he replied. "Trying to determine how long it takes for a South American millipede larva to develop and hatch during their winter down there? Convince me that discovering *that* is more urgent that what's happening here and I will continue that."

Maria could only smile. There was nothing there to convince him.

"Ok."

"Good. Now what would you like me to do? This is your case."

"Um, ok. Do me a favor and check as much as you can for any reports of these things, either by sight or by recent attacks on people or animals that are suspected by these vespas."

"North of here?"

"Right. And I'll take care of all points south, down to the Mexican border."

For the rest of the day, the two scientists worked on their computers and their phones. Neither realized what was occurring in certain other areas.

Stockton, California

It had been only two weeks since the chemical leakage spilled from a small chemical plant into the nearby forest pond just outside the city. A brook adjacent to the plant just outside the perimeter gates bordered a wooded area which led slightly downhill to a pond. Neither the pond nor the leakage was huge. If there had been any fish in the pond, the chemical would have killed them. But no one fished there anyway. As close to the city limits as it was, it was still hidden in the forest and rarely did anyone venture out there. Most people didn't even know it was there.

Stockton is a northern city between Sacramento and Modesto lying along the San Joaquin River. As with most cities in California, it has its tourist attractions, including a park with nature trails, a nature center and a fish-stocked lake. Nearby surrounding areas also cater to tourists with additional attractions as well.

Its population is over three hundred thousand and always growing. As with all cities, it has its bad points along with the good. Most residents deal with both, but life continues to move forward as usual. Most of the people there either weren't aware of this remote pond hidden in the small forest or knew about it but had no interest in going there. Besides, there were numerous other ponds and lakes that could hold secrets or mysteries that no one yet knew about.

The area was always dead quiet except for the chirping of crickets in the early morning or at night. No birds drank from the water, otherwise they would soon find themselves grounded forever. The chemical had no smell that could be detected, except by the most acute noses. The water tended to overflow its shallow banks during heavy rains. It normally affected only the grass near the banks which left it brown and dead. The only thing near the water was an odd hole in the ground, small and inconspicuous. The nearest trees were just a few feet away and displayed no effects from the contaminated water.

***

From within the darkness, it looked out. The army was behind it. They had just recently hatched but their growth did not stop. The genetic norms had somehow been bypassed. As a result, the hole expanded to three times its original size as it struggled to make its way out, making it easier for the others which followed.

The black and white panorama which it saw through its black eyes was pixelated. But it could see and identify what was out there. It was hungry, but for what it didn't know.

Slowly it crawled out until all of its four inches stood outside. Others behind it followed. As it beat its large wings, others followed suit. No person could see that there were dozens in numbers when all had exited the entrance to the nest. As the army looked around, its hunger to attack intensified. Each of them beat their wings as if planes preparing for takeoff.

Genetically, they were programmed to find and destroy all nests of the enemy, kill and feed on the enemy and bring parts of the bodies back to their own offspring. But there was something about these that had an additional terrifying feature which defied other genetic norms.

In an area on another side of the pond, others came out of their nests in huge numbers. For them as well, there was a new genetic norm that took over what they had once been. Somehow they could sense the other colony on the other side. Perhaps they could smell the pheromones. But they knew. The others were not the enemy. It was the entire world all around them that was the enemy, save for their own kind. The one thing that was common between their old and new genetic norms was that they never tolerated the enemy. Rivalry was not required for them to destroy and kill. The world was not ready for them. But they were ready for *it*.

There would be many more to follow them. Inside both nests, the queens were laying more eggs. They would need food. The hunt was about to begin. Dusk was settling over the landscape. The armies lifted up into the air, each with its own schedule but equal intentions and determination. The extraordinarily loud, low buzzing of the armies was too distant from the city to be heard by anyone. That would change as some flew toward the distant lights, while others flew through the forest to search for their normal prey. Their intent: bring back all the bee parts to their nest to feed the hungry larvae. The intent of the others would soon become clear to their victims. They left total silence in their wake. For the first time, no chirping of crickets broke it.

***

Two weeks later, Calvin had discovered that the hornets, now being dubbed by some as "murder hornets" because of the human fatalities they caused and unprovoked aggressive attacks, were migrating south from the state of Washington and were now deep into Oregon territory. What made things worse was that they seemed to now be well-established in California as well. Their migration now threatened the very existence of the honeybee population up and down the entire West Coast.

Humans were also on their list of victims albeit for a different reason. The scientists knew that humans were a threat to the hornet's existence, which could be a reason why they so fervently attacked people at every opportunity. What they *didn't* know was how they had the intelligence to hunt for people when people weren't even around their area. What made them want to intentionally hunt for humans instead of tending to what they normally did in nature?

To Calvin and Maria, these particular hornets, if not their species in general, displayed behavior that mimicked a higher level of intelligence. Their primary case example was the attacks that occurred on the ballfield the week previously. That event hit the news faster than the fastest speedball coming from the pitcher. There were no known areas around that playing field that could possibly hide a vespa nest. It was a large open area which had residences and some businesses outside of the park in the distance. Trees there were sparse and small in size.

After conferring with Maria, Calvin came to his first conclusion regarding how they got here in their state.

"Stands to reason, Cal, that our culprits definitely got here via an outside source. For whatever reason or however it happened, one or more queens escaped. This is bad."

Calvin looked at her with a frown and eyes that agreed. "Yea, no kidding. First we have the Golden State Killer who is finally captured after decades of looking. Now we have the Golden State hornets who are out to kill more people. Only these are even worse. They don't discriminate."

Maria looked at him with a sheepish grin. Her colleague sometimes tried to be funny. But she knew that this was a joke that could not be disputed.

"Find anything out in your research so far?" she asked him.

"Well, we know that they first appeared in Washington. We also know that there was no way they flew all the way across the Pacific from thousands of miles away just to establish residence here. So once again we can blame it on the human species. They could've been transported."

Maria nodded. This was another example of human error and negligence that caused the US infestation of dangerous indigenous wildlife and insects. Who knew how far back the introduction of Burmese pythons into Florida and other southern states went? Or how long ago people started to keep other even more dangerous exotic animals that were never meant to be pets or kept in private captivity? In 1957, the African killer honeybee escaped their quarantine in Brazil to eventually invade the southernmost states in the US after migrating all the way through Central America and Mexico.

"Well, so far we haven't gotten any new reports," Maria said. "But we need to do battle because what's happening and what has already happened is not acceptable."

Calvin nodded. "I agree. Despite my love of insects, this is a species I have no use for. They may be useful to the environment in their own natural habitat, but I don't believe that could ever apply here. We have enough of a decrease in the population of European bees here without having these things make them go extinct."

"And they seem to be deliberately going after people, for God's sake!" she exclaimed loudly, almost yelling, startling Calvin in his chair.

Her outburst seemed to suggest these things and events troubled her more than she let on. Rarely did Maria get passionate about something. The more she thought about it, the angrier and more determined she became.

"Now, now dear lady, don't get your thinking machine in a tizzy. Yes, that is a problem of course. We have to figure out why. But first theanswer must be known as to where all their nests are. We find them, we know all the locations of the queens. We find them and for them it's apocalypse now."

She looked at her colleague. Oh, if only it were that simple.

"Nice plan," she replied. "There's only one problem with it."

Calvin looked at her. "Oh, and what's that? We certainly have the resources to destroy all the nests. That includes lots of teams. All we have to do is locate those nests."

Maria looked down. The one problem was a major one. Without *its* resolution, the plan could never be completely successful. Cal continued to look at her, while trying in his mind to guess what it was.

She lifted her head and met his eyes with her own. "We don't know how many queens there are. There could be more queens than there are nests right now."

Calvin looked at her. He was surprised at himself for not thinking of that himself. She had a point. It was a considerably bigger problem than first realized. His frown grew along with his concern.

"Yes, um… there is that problem too," he conceded.

"Sorry I scared you," she said apologetically.

Both scientists knew they had a lot of work ahead of them and wasted no time getting back to it. When it came to the safety of people, time was not on their side.

10

Maria once again had checked in with Children's Medical down in San Diego but was told no new sting cases had yet come in. Billy Jansen, after nearly a week there, was ready to go home. His full recovery had been a relief to her. She was happy for him and his family. Although she was married but didn't have any children of her own-at least not yet- still the motherly instincts in her would kick in whenever a child was hurt or ill. It was troubling to her to see a child injured or ill enough to have to go into the hospital. It was bad enough for an adult, let alone a child.

She picked up the phone to make some calls she had planned for a few days. There were other issues that needed to be addressed besides the current one.

Meanwhile, from *his* lab, Calvin was doing his own research, managing to schedule some time each day to help Maria if she needed any for any particular issue. Today was fairly quiet. He checked the various local state offices for any reports of invasive breakouts but so far no new ones were reported. That didn't mean none were discovered.

It was nearly 11:30am. He'd been working here since 7:00am and he needed to stretch his legs and grab a coffee. First things first, though. He had to see a man about a horse. His bladder was nearly bursting. A minute later he was out the door. He didn't hear the phone suddenly ring back in the lab as he entered the men's room.

***

The Evening Before

The buzzing was loud but unheard. They were on a mission but they didn't regard it as that. Something drove them to seek out and attack. While the other split-off group was in the process of doing what it was meant to do, this one had a different purpose. It was about as unnatural as it could be.

They were hungry, but not for food. They saw the trees and grass below them pass quickly underneath as they headed for the lights which were getting closer. In an open area behind a house, they saw a creature moving around on the ground. It didn't matter that they didn't know what it was. Their flight path tilted downward heading right toward it. Because it was getting closer to dusk, the animal never saw them coming.

It started running around the gated back yard, barking and trying to hide while things flew out of the darkened sky. It yelped helplessly as large unknown things covered it and stung it repeatedly. Its yelps and squeals were heard by the residents who ran out the back door. Trying to process in their minds what they were seeing that seemed to be killing their dog, in the darkened yard they saw only something wriggling under a coat of what looked like gigantic wasps or hornets.

"Oh my God!" the woman yelled.

Even the dog's face was covered with the things. The yelping had stopped, but not the terror.

"Mom, what is it?   What's happened to Benji?" yelled a child's voice from behind her. Benji was their lab who had been let out for a bathroom break before returning back in.

The woman immediately took her son inside and slammed the door shut. When she turned on the backyard light, the things immediately lifted up from the dog's body and flew toward the light, hitting and smashing the cover and bulb to pieces, leaving the back porch in darkness. Only the light from the kitchen allowed her to see around the immediate area outside.

The woman was in shock. Warning her child not to go outside, she had a brief absence of rational thought and didn't know what to do.

When the shock finally wore off, she knew she needed to report this to *some*body. Lacking the knowledge of who exactly to call, she could only call 9-1-1. Unfortunately, her husband was out of town on a business trip. Who else could she call but the police?

While she waited for the police to arrive, she looked out the window of her back door. The dog lay still. Tears flowed uncontrollably out of her eyes as she realized Benji was no longer with them. His body lay still and lifeless out there. Only five minutes previously, she had let him out as they normally did around this time each evening. One minute he was there, the next minute gone. It was almost surreal.

The violent slam against the door window startled her so intensely that she almost fell back onto the floor. The horror of what she saw made her wish it was only a nightmare or horror movie. She could see the large bulbous black eyes. It had yellow and black stripes on the thorax and the largest weapon she'd ever seen.

Even in her terrified state of mind, her brain was able to take in more of what it looked like before it flew off. It had appeared to be about four inches long and was either a mutated giant yellow jacket or hornet, with huge mandibles that looked like they could do some damage, and the largest stinger she had ever seen. That looked to be about half to one inch long and more dangerous looking than a hypodermic needle.

"Mommy, what is that thing?" Her little girl had been standing behind her in equal horror, teary eyed and more scared than she'd ever been before about anything.

"I don't know, honey," she replied. "Looks like a big hornet."

Her seven-year-old started crying. "Did they kill Benji?"

The woman cautiously went back to the door to look outside the door window. The dog's body still lay there. Unmoving. There seemed to be no more of the things around it. The thing that slammed against her window had flown off. But from what she saw of just one of them, she realized there was no way the dog could have survived what she had witnessed. If they could do this to animals, then it was a foregone conclusion that people were equally vulnerable.

"It looks like they did, honey," she replied in a weepy voice, turning around and hugging little Sally to her. "I'm so sorry, Sally."

As her daughter cried against her in her arms, she did as well. Benji had been just as much a part of the family as them. As they stood together for a few moments, Sally's mom, Susan, regrouped her thoughts and remembered she had called for the police.

She gently moved her daughter from her and looked down to her face. "Listen, baby, someone is coming to help us with this. Why don't you go in your room and find something to do?" She wiped the tears from Sally's face.

"Ok. Mommy, why did this happen? Why did they kill Benji?"

Susan hugged her daughter again. "I don't know. I wish I did." She could only stare ahead, secretly wondering if this was the beginning of something that should never be.

"Go," she told the girl. "I'll be in shortly."

After the girl left the kitchen area, the front doorbell rang. It must be the police from when she called earlier.

She opened the door to two Stockton police officers. She invited them in, introduced herself and explained what she had witnessed and that she didn't know who else to call but needed to report it to them at least.

The officers were obliging and asked to see the area in the back yard if it was clear of the insects. This was not a crime and not something they ordinarily investigated. Since they had been dispatched, they needed to check it out anyway. They knew the appropriate people to call for various situations.

They told her to stay in the house in case any of the things came back. Because they had heard stories before of giant bugs of some sorts being in other areas of the state, they weren't entirely sure if those had anything to do with this.

Walking around to the side of the house with their flashlights, they saw the dog's body in the middle of the yard and knew immediately that it was dead. There was no movement or any sign of respirations.

The male officer looked down at it and then squatted down to examine the dog's face. His jaw dropped with already widened eyes.

"Uh, Brenda, take a look at this."

The female officer came over after looking around the immediate area. "Oh my gosh," she said, not too shockingly as she saw some swelling on the dog's body. She knew dogs because she bred them for some years before joining the ranks of the city's finest. This swelling she had never seen before, not even in sick or injured dogs. She hadn't yet seen the face.

She walked closer to her partner and looked down. There was some swelling to its face. But it was the eyes that shocked both of them. Her jaw dropped as well. This poor dog had to have suffered the most painful, agonizing death that anything, man or animal, could possibly endure. Her hand went to cover her mouth as she tried to shut off thoughts of that. But it was nearly impossible.

It looked like the animal's eyeballs had been punctured and literally ripped apart. They were flattened and bloodied, with pieces of eye tissue sticking out. This certainly did not look like the work of a predatory mammal. The officers did not see any bullet or normal stab wounds.

There were no bite wounds that they could see, no bloody wounds of any kind, other than what had been done to the eyes.

"Birds, maybe?" asked the male officer, Ron. He knew his partner had experience with dogs.

Brenda didn't reply, still staring at the dog's face and eyes.

"What do you think, Brenda?" he asked again. "Birds?"

"Uh, no. No, I don't think so. Besides, the description Mrs. Tompkins gave us was not of any bird. Birds wouldn't have done that to the dog's eyes. Usually they peck them out. These were ripped and torn apart in their sockets."

Ron stood up. This was as disturbing as any murder scene. The question was, what now? He looked at the distraught woman who was trying to maintain her composure.

"Mrs. Tompkins, I know this is hard and I am truly sorry about your loss. I can arrange to have the body removed if you like." He noticed her nodding and starting to cry.

"Yes please," she squeaked out.

"Would you like to have a necropsy performed?"

"What?" she asked, wiping her eyes. "Necropsy, what's that?"

"It's what they call an autopsy on animals. Basically, it's done for the same reasons as on a person. In this case, it might show what killed the dog. If it was those things you mentioned, it might be a good idea to know that."

Susan nodded. That made sense. Even though she was sure those things killed their pet and family member, she wanted to know and have everyone else know as well.

"Ok then."

"Dispatch, five twenty-seven," the officer said on his shoulder mike.

And thus began the process of removal of the body, examination, and confirmation of the cause of its death. For Susan and her family, it would be the end of their investigation but just the beginning of a much larger one, a nightmare that would soon involve the entire state of California.

***

Back in the lab, Calvin returned to his desk to continue his research. He saw a blinking light on his office phone and checked the caller ID. It had come in just a few minutes before as he headed to the rest room. He saw that it was from a Dr. Rosenthal. *Now who the heck is that?* he thought.

He picked up the phone and dialed in to his voicemail. Dr. Rosenthal turned out to be a veterinarian in the Stockton area. As he listened to the message, his eyes narrowed and mouth turned downward in a frown. He normally didn't do this unless something compelling concerned him. This message did.

He pressed the hang-up button after listening to it all and called the doctor back. After they connected, he listened to the report over the phone. The news was disturbing and was already more than twenty-four hours old. Dr. Rosenthal was the doctor who had done the necropsy on Benji, the three-year old Labrador retriever. No word had spread to the community as yet as far as the doctor knew. But from what he determined, Cal's office needed to know.

The puncture wounds observed in the dog's eyes were apparently done by something biologically long and sharp, not unlike a scorpion's stinger.

He said that it was too soon for the toxicology report to come back. So no conclusive report would be made until then. This was a preliminary report to the state to give it a heads up. But it wasn't just based on the eyes.

All over the body, including the snout, there were hundreds of puncture wounds as if the animal was stung by thousands of whatever they were. The swelling on the face was enormous. He knew those weren't made by bees because there were no stingers found anywhere. Bees leave stingers behind when they sting and then they die. Hornets or wasps don't. There was no question the dog had suffered immensely. This is what had the vet worried. And for good reason. People.

After several minutes on the phone and getting contact information for the Tomkins family, Calvin rubbed his face and sat staring for a minute or so to process this information. This situation was beginning to seem more serious than first thought. He picked up the phone to call the area hospitals and clinics. The question was, were there any human victims after the ball park incident?

Meanwhile in her lab, Maria was busy on her computer looking up reports from southern areas of the state regarding more incoming sting victims. She was alarmed to see that three more people from the ballfield had died of their sting attacks. This was from that event a week ago. Despite efforts of medical personnel, they couldn't save the victims. According to the medical experts, several possible conclusions as to why they couldn't save them were arrived at.

One, too much time had passed between the attacks and treatments. Many of the medical personnel were not so sure that this was the reason because they had gotten there fairly quickly, considering the number of ambulances that were needed. First responders would have acted as quickly as they could, started treatment right away as they were transporting, and got them to the hospital within minutes.

The second possibility was the hypersensitivity of the victims to the venom: being so sensitive to the venom that treatment would be ineffective if not done immediately. That, too, was in question. But it

couldn't be ruled out. Not yet.

The third thought was given to the issue of amounts and potency of the venom itself. Everyone by now knew of the invaders being the newly named "murder hornets". Their larger size would, of course, suggest larger stingers. They could be like hypodermic needles. They, by themselves, would cause a little pain if penetrating one's skin. That's all. Combine them with venom, and it would bring the pain up to a whole new level. It was the venom, not the stingers, that caused all the problems in victims. The latter were scary enough. It was the former that everyone had to worry about, whether allergic or not.

From most stinging and biting insects, when envenomation is a possibility or certainty, those victims who are allergic would be given either IV epinephrine, Benadryl or other antiallergy drug to counter the allergic reaction; or they might be given an antivenom, depending on what the envenomator was and if antivenom was available. In this case, Maria wasn't sure what the culprit or culprits were. She suspected what had attacked the dog because she had learned what the MO was. Familiarity breeds more familiarity. She could always find out from the Children's Hospital in their treatment of Billy Jansen. Was there a link between what happened to Billy and the dog?

As she researched in her computer, she almost jumped in her chair at the sudden ringing of the phone. She picked up and listened as Calvin reported what he had just been told. The news was not good and she realized now that her worst fears were coming true.

"First of all, Cal, we have to remain calm. Before we alert the powers that be in the affected areas, we need to establish a current territorial perimeter so far of these things. In this state. We know they are already north of California."

"I got that and concur," he replied.

"Find out if they have reached areas around Sacramento, west to east and north to south of the city. Select suburb towns to call, hospitals, etc., wherever you can find out about any serious sting cases. Anything at all."

"Ok."

"I'll cover all areas surrounding San Diego in all directions and the southern half of the state. We need to find out as quickly as possible. These things are on the move and they are becoming a serious threat. Not just to our local bee population."

11

At their home in Modesto, the Sondheim family was packing the car in preparation for their imminent departure to Yosemite. It would be about a two hour drive from their home and they planned on staying for a week. Despite the fact that they lived most of their lives in or around Modesto, they had yet to discover the natural wonders and beauty of this world famous park that was only about a hundred miles away.

Ronald Sondheim was a construction engineer who worked more than forty hours a week. Sometimes up to fifty depending on the work project. He'd been working with the company for almost fifteen years. Although some may have thought of him as a bit of a workaholic, he wasn't truly one of those, although he did take his work very seriously and loved his job. Still, his family would always come first in his life. He was dedicated to his Jewish faith and that dedication would always take a front seat in all their lives. They would all need some kind of break.

So he decided to take the family on a little vacation seeing as he had plenty of time on the books. He chose to take one week at a time now, and maybe in another three months take another week. Rather than take what he accumulated all at once like others did in his company, he preferred to split it up.

Now in his mid-forties, he'd been married to his high school sweetheart, Marilyn, for nearly as long as he'd worked for the company. She was a part-time paralegal who enjoyed splitting up the week hours for working at home rather than at the office. Though she was five years younger than he was, she was almost a younger replica of himself yet with enough differences to make their marital relationship interesting.

Even so, they were as compatible as a married couple could be. Having their two children turned out to be visible proof of that and for each of them was quite a blessing.

Little Bobby, age thirteen, was no different than any other boy his age to those who didn't know him. To those who did, he was better than that. He was loving and caring, seemingly an inherent trait he got from his parents. His younger sister of two years, Suzie, sometimes was a little rambunctious but managed to maintain good behavior most of the time. She seemed to appreciate the protectiveness of her brother.

As Ron loaded the back of the SUV, Marilyn brought out a bag of goodies from the house. So far in the car they had luggage filled with clothes and most other things, including toiletries that most people brought on overnight trips. The kids were bringing out a few of their toys.

"Not too many of those, guys," Ron advised them. "We are almost full out here. Just bring a couple each, ok?" He had just enough room for those toys they had in their hands.

Bobby brought to him his plastic baseball bat and ball.

Ron smiled down at him with a reserved look. "You sure you want to bring those, buddy?" he asked him. "I don't know if we'll have the chance to use them.

"Just in case," he said. "Would've brought my regular bat and ball but then these are lighter. And better in case we don't use them."

Ron laughed, getting a kick from that seemingly illogical logic that his son came up with.

"Ok. Just put them right there," he said, pointing to a spot near where the back door would close. Bobby put them there and said he had to make a final bathroom stop.

He ran into the house and then Suzie came to Ronald with a couple of her entertainment things in a bag. He knew she loved her cell phone and its games she loved to play and that it would be in the bag. He didn't know what the other item was but didn't care. As long as it was in the bag and the bag could fit in the back area of the vehicle. After putting it in the last available spot, he closed the door and they were set to go.

"Got everything, sweetheart?" asked Marilyn from the house.

"Yep," replied Ron. "Double check to make sure you have everything you want to take. No more room in the back for anything else. I'll go check all the windows and doors."

After making sure the house was locked up tight on the inside, he set the timer lights to go on and off at the appropriate times. He believed in having some security while they were gone. So far there were no burglaries, and he wanted to keep it that way. After everyone made their final pit stops in the restroom and they had their travel drinks, they left the house.

The back door was always locked so they didn't have to worry about that.

In five minutes they were on their way to an adventure they would neither forget nor want to remember.

***

Unknown to Calvin and Maria as yet, 9-1-1 calls were being made in Burbank and Pasadena, both just north of Los Angeles. These were atypical calls. Not from gunshots, traffic accidents, homicides, or a cat trapped in a tree. But from stings, allegedly from giant insects. The callers sounded terrified as they unsuccessfully tried to be as clear as possible about what they had witnessed; seeing the victims who were in serious and dire need of medical help. As a result, some emergency rooms were being inundated with patients having been stung by sources unknown.

***

A few miles north-northeast of San Diego in the area of Escondido, a couple of hikers were making their way through the surrounding hills.

Sally and George Takaris were a young couple, both in their twenties, who occasionally enjoyed outings, either cycling or hiking. Today was a bright sunny day with mild temperatures. They had decided to walk instead of ride because they wanted to enjoy taking their time enjoying nature.

It was late morning. Already they had been on the trail for an hour but were far from tired. Through some of the trees they could see distant homes in the valley below. It was a beautiful scene which they had seen before, as this trail was quite familiar to them.

"George, can we stop for a minute?" asked Sally. "Need a swig. My throat is dry."

"Ok," he said happily. "Might do the same, now that you mention a dry throat."

After both downed some water from their travel mugs, they looked around briefly and then up the trail they planned to follow. In the distance, they could see another trail which forked off to the right, a bit further from the hill's edge. It appeared to go deeper into the wooded area and was not a path they had taken before. Not that it was forbidden or anything like that. They just had no inclination in the past of going that way. Plus, they didn't know where it led.

They weren't quite hungry yet, so the lunch they had in their backpacks could wait a bit longer.

"Hey, want to check that other trail out?" George asked his wife. Despite their unfamiliarity with it, he felt adventurous today.

She looked at it with an uncertain expression. "Hmm. I don't know, honey. We don't know where it leads to. What if we get lost?"

George looked at it as if it could give him the answer.

"Well, it's got to lead somewhere," he shrugged. "Besides, if it gets to the point where we don't know if we're getting anywhere, we can always turn around and head back to our regular path."

She reluctantly agreed. That's what they would do if they suspected they were getting too far from civilization. After putting their closed mugs back in their packs, they headed toward the new trail. At the fork, they took one more glance at the regular path, then proceeded forward.

It was a little past noon when they decided to stop and have a bite to eat. There were no benches or anywhere else to sit on this path, so they accepted having to eat standing up. It wasn't the first time they'd had to do this.

A few minutes later, they were off again. This path wasn't very different from their normal one. The only real difference was that it led deeper into the wilderness area. Every turn led them to a straighter part of the trail before it turned again.

"Ouch, damn!" Sally tried to contain her yell as she lifted up her right foot.

"What's the matter, sweetheart?" asked George, concern in his voice. He turned toward her.

"Oh I just got a rock or something inside my shoe. Hit the wrong spot. I'll be alright. Damn, I hate when that happens."

She flipped her slip-on shoe over and the little pebble fell out.

"Yea, I hate that also. Shit happens. You gonna be ok to continue?"

Sally sighed. "Yea, I'll be fine. How long have we been traveling on this trail?"

George looked at his watch. "I think about half an hour."

"Maybe we should give this another twenty minutes or so. If we don't see anything by then, we can turn around."

Sally's suggestion was reasonable and he agreed. Who knows? This trail could go on for miles. The longer they traveled on it, the longer they would have to hike the way back. Best, he thought, to set the time limit. Twenty minutes and no more, he decided.

Just before they set off again, George spotted something curious on the ground to the left side of the trail. He was just going to take a quick look and then they'd be on their way. But the nature of it caused him to pause and look at it longer.

That didn't escape Sally's observation. "What? What are you looking at, George?"

He bent directly over it and knew what it was. "Looks like a piece of a honeycomb," he replied. She looked down at it but didn't think much of it.

"A honeycomb piece? Ok. So what? These are the woods, you know and bees probably have hives all over the place here."

Sally had always been the skeptic in the family. So it was not surprising that she would find this discovery a little drab. Certainly, it was nothing to get excited about. Really!

George stood up but continued to look at it and then the immediate area surrounding it. Then he saw another piece where weeds and grass met the dirt of the trail. Further on into the bush, he saw other pieces around. They were not small. Some were as large as a dinner plate while others were saucer-sized. Scattered around those were smaller pieces of various sizes.

"George, what are you doing? C'mon. We have to get going."

He stood straight up but couldn't help having the feeling that something was a little off here. He was no entomologist. It was just a gut feeling and George was not good at ignoring gut feelings.

'Uh, Sally. I don't know. Something's not right."

He started looking around and thought he saw something else ahead of him.

"Not right?" she asked. "What do you mean?" She was more curious now than annoyed. Knowing George, she knew he had to play this out until he was satisfied. She had tried countless times to distract him and get him focusing on other things. Nearly all her attempts ended in failure. So much for trying.

At a tree just a few feet ahead, he saw more remnants of a beehive and the hole in the trunk he suspected where it had once been. There were a couple of chunks inside of it along with what looked like a few dead bees. Scanning the area of and around the hole, his eyes drifted downward toward the base of the tree and stopped. They widened in surprise. "Holy cow! Oh my lord!"

Sally's jaw dropped. She had never heard her husband utter those words before.

"What? George, what do you see?"

"C'mere, hon. Take a look at this."

He moved aside as she came up beside him. She looked at the hole in the tree trunk, seeing only the hive chunks.

"No," said George. "Look at the ground below it."

As her head tilted downward, her look of surprise cloned his. "What the hell?"

They'd never seen anything like it before. It was a huge pile of dead bees. Neither knew what to say. It was obvious to them that something had killed them and destroyed their hive. The first thought that came to their minds was that people had come along and done this. Why not? Humans did everything else bad, much of the time for no apparent reason. Why not something like this even though it made no sense?

Suddenly, Sally sensed something but it wasn't good. Her eyes had sensed a slight movement in the trunk hole. Despite the darkness of the hole, she had detected something round, about one eighth the size of the hole and blacker than its surrounding darkness sticking out from the side. Then something stuck out from the hole. Although it was very small compared to everything around it, it still seemed abnormally large. Yet she didn't know why. All she knew was that it hadn't been there a second ago. The fact that she didn't know what it was made the hairs on the back of her neck stand up and she backed away.

"George, we gotta get out of here." The alarm in her voice was disturbing. Sally never spooked easily. This was something he had to pay attention to.

"Honey, what is it? What's the matter? They're dead! They're not going to hurt you," he told her as reassuringly as he could.

She grabbed his right arm and pulled him back without turning. He saw the terror in her eyes and knew for sure something was wrong.

He looked at her face with that grimace of terror, quickly starting to feel the same without knowing why.

"Let's get back to the trail," he said. "Now."

On the trail, they stopped and Sally took some deep breaths as George gently held on to her. They stood there quietly for a few minutes. Color returned to Sally's face. George patiently held her and waited for her to tell him what she had seen.

On calming down, she explained to him what she had seen. Not sure if it had been an apparition, a bad omen or if had been real, she described it in detail. The part of it which she'd seen.

As he listened, he was trying to process the information. His eyes went from staring into her as she talked to looking down after she finished as if he was trying to think hard of what it could be. There was no question in his mind that it was spooky as hell. If it weren't for that big pile of dead bees, maybe it wouldn't have been so unnerving. Then his eyes stopped suddenly. A thought had hit him but it was a terrible one.

His eyes returned to hers. If what he thought was true, they did indeed need to get out of there. Out of the woods as soon as possible. He didn't believe the strong danger he was sensing was a product of his or anyone else's imagination.

"Let's go. I think our hike is over for today."

She followed him quickly, not wanting to argue. Right now, home never seemed more welcoming.

They passed the fork and returned back down the trail from which they had first come. He told her he would explain what he believed after they got home. Soon they were back in their car.

They didn't know that had they gone any further and just a little ways past that tree, they would have come across a dead hiker. The face of the person was so bloated and swollen, identity of the gender would only be possible at an autopsy. The body had been downwind from George and Sally. They wouldn't have sensed or smelled it.

***

By this time, the news of the hornet invasion in California had gone national and then international. It was on all the local and nationwide networks. California didn't yet know that the US President was now interested and concerned. To him and his staff, they had to keep tabs on the situation there in case the governor decided to declare it a disaster zone. President Thompson knew Joe Capulette for many years. He was not only a friend but a party colleague whom he had supported in his run for governor three years ago. Joe would not declare the state a disaster zone unless it was truly that. So far there was no word but he decided to give Joe a call anyway. Besides, if the problem spread that fast, it could spread east. That made it a potential problem for public health nationwide.

San Luis Obispo

Maria took the call. It was from an urgent care clinic in Escondido which surprised her. They never got calls from such a medical place. Could this be a report of another victim?

After identifying herself, she listened to the caller who was a physician's assistant or PA named Brian Johnson. He told her that they were having a routine day no different than any other. A patient was brought in with a possible sting. It was a twenty-eight-year-old woman accompanied by her husband, Eric. She'd been stung viciously on her left arm multiple times and it was now twice its normal width and quite reddened. Her pain was so great and agonizing that she could barely talk. Her state of mind was near delirium and she was clearly ready to pass out.

Eric had helped her into the exam room where Brian quickly examined her and realized she was in serious jeopardy. After taking her vital signs and seeing her blood pressure drop dangerously low with her respirations shallow and her apical pulse racing dangerously high, he knew she was near going into shock. Picking up the phone, he called 9-1-1 and asked for an ambulance stat. Time was of the essence.

He then explained to Eric what was happening. He notified the other staff at the clinic of the ambulance being on the way. In the meantime, he checked to see if he could find where exactly on her arm she'd been stung. Brian could see Eric was trying desperately to hold it together and commended the man for keeping it that way. He knew how hard that was, especially seeing a close loved one possibly dying in front of his eyes.

When asked, Eric explained to Brian how he had found her.

"I was in the backyard of our home when I suddenly saw her scream and swatting at something. Something big was attacking her in the air. I mean it was huge and it was definitely not a bee. Looked more like a wasp or hornet but I never saw one that big before. It was swirling around her as if it was trying to find a spot to land. I found a flat tool and started swatting at her, trying not to hit her.

"I missed. Then the thing landed on her arm and her screams became really loud and bloodcurdling. That's when I knew it had stung her. But she continually screamed. I think the son-of-a-bitch kept on stinging her. Oh man! So as it did, I took advantage of that moment and gently hit against the back of it until I crushed it. But it took a bit of force, more like a very forceful pat."

He then took a wadded up handkerchief and showed it to the PA. He opened it up and there it was. It was at least three inches long. Yellow and black stripes. Crushed. The PA looked at it in shock, seeing the largest stinger he'd ever seen on an insect. He realized the woman now was in serious trouble.

"Ok. Wrap it back up. Bring this with you to the ER. You can't go in the ambulance because they will need to work on her on the way. Give it to the medical personnel there. I will call them and make sure that it gets to the proper persons for analysis."

"Is she going to be alright?" Brian could tell the man was worried and scared for his wife and for good reason. The venom was coursing through her body and could shut down her vital organs if this was not dealt with properly soon enough. He didn't want to give him false hope; but neither did he want to paint a picture of doom for him.

"She has a chance. Let's see that she gets there asap." He patted Eric's shoulder and noticed the tears of fear and dread in his eyes.

Just then the ambulance personnel came in and Brian quickly gave them his report, letting them know that Eric would be going there with the dead culprit to hand over.

After taking her vital signs and realizing the desperation of the situation, they quickly got her into the ambulance, called it in as a life-threatening trauma and were soon off. Brian got on the phone and made his report to the ER personnel. He prayed silently that she would make it and that he would not see any more patients suffering as she was. At least not today.

12

Forty miles southeast of L. A.

If there had been any hikers or other adventurers in the area, they would have noticed the unusual silence. The experienced would have immediately noticed the change in the air. It seemed like a dead area. Even the novice hiker/adventurer would have sensed that something was not right.

There were no sounds of birds chirping and no rustling of leaves from the frequent squirrel movements. Even the air was eerily still, with not even the slightest breeze. It was as if the world had come to a stop, pausing to see if life as normal would catch up.

The area of the forest was remote. Few hikers had come this way in the past and none recently. There was actually nothing to see except forest anyway. Trails around here were far and few between.

The nest was hidden from easy view, although it didn't matter. Nothing was around anyway. But it was huge. The low buzzing was loud enough to be heard a hundred feet away. It was one of many. Perhaps hundreds. If a person had seen the nest, it might give the impression of being either a fox den or that of a ground squirrel. Only the buzzing sounds from invisible inhabitants gave it away as not being either.

Much of the buzzing involved intercommunications between its inhabitants. Those communications could have been related to anything. All too often there were calls to go on the hunt, to do battle, or to invade. This was what they did and had always done. For some reason, they had become larger and more savage. Everything was their enemy and they were the same to everything. They were ready. But it wasn't time.

Their scouts hadn't returned yet. They would and when they did, they would communicate to the others any finds of more beehives in the area as well as other nests in the area. Any and all hives would be located and destroyed and all their inhabitants killed. Anything that got in their way would be attacked and killed, including other species related to but not their own. They would be relentless and merciless.

Their time would come soon. Somehow they would work together with others of their kind from other nest sites in the area. Although just one of them could prove fatal to a victim, hundreds or even thousands of them would prove unstoppable and catastrophic. It was not their goal to destroy all life. Just to destroy and kill. It was not in them to sense their limitations if they had any. Whatever had made them more aggressive and savage was forever beyond their ability to know.

They would not know about any other nests in the area until the scouts returned. The queen did not have to know. Her only role was to lay eggs, which she was doing. But she would defend herself and her young if she had to.

There was, within them, excitement to leave the nest and get out there to do what they instinctively believed was their destiny. Because there could be other nests in the area, their new increased intelligence would make some kind of primitive coordination with others possible. Somehow, the hunt would result in coordinated attacks without thought to any future or consequences. Because they couldn't think. Not in the same way as people.

Around their nest, no human would see the dead squirrel and bird, both which had wandered a little too close and paid the ultimate price.

***

San Luis Obispo lab

The specimen had been received a couple of hours earlier. The container had been marked "Urgent". It was not a designation often used for shipped specimens. As the assistant to Maria and Calvin, Norm's job was to first assess whether a specimen required further analysis by the experts. He was trained to look for certain information. But if he found the maximum amount of details he was allowed to assess and saw that increased expertise was needed, he would notify Maria who would then take custody of the specimen.

Opening up the dark plastic container after removing it from the plastic hazard bag, he looked at the crushed giant hornet. Although the label tagged to the bag indicated what it was, it was the sight of it that had real impact on the researcher. He'd never seen anything like it before. Although insects did not scare him, otherwise he would never have worked here, this one gave him the chills. It was a monster, almost as if it was from a horror movie. For such an insect, even three inches was gargantuan. But he knew there were likely other types of insects of equal length; just not the flying, stinging kind.

He knew that this specimen had to be passed on to the scientists. Before he sent it to Maria, he examined it very carefully with forceps and tweezers in gloved hands, starting with the head. It was fascinating to him because he'd never seen anything like this before.

Its two large black eyes were compound eyes. He noted what looked like three small, round, eye-like dark areas on the top of the head. He realized these could be smaller eyes, but he wasn't sure. Its antennae were at least a half inch long and bent downward. The mandibles were thick and proportionally sized. To him, this indicated these were exceptionally powerful and could do some serious damage to its natural prey.

Its thorax was brown and below that was its brown and yellow-banded abdomen. The wings were dark and appeared longer than its body length. They had to be strong and powerful enough to lift its large body.

But it was the stinger that made him realize the serious danger of this insect. He already knew it had some serious venom that this stinger injected, and that this species was invasive to this country and not the normal species of wasp or hornet. He measured it at precisely three and a half inches long, longer than any other species of flying stinging insect. He didn't want to think about the pain this could cause or the suffering from the injected venom.

He didn't know what the gender was, but figured it was a male because the queens are always female and stay in the nest. It didn't matter anyway. This would need to be passed on to his boss and he called her to let her know he was sending it. He was smart enough to know his cut-off point for his assessment.

Minutes later in another part of the building, Maria received the specimen and opened it up to take a look. Being quite familiar with this species of hornet, she immediately noticed something different about this one. It was larger and considerably more so than its Japanese cousins. She measured it. Three-and-a-half inches. The norm for this species was two inches. Did she have some kind of mutant here? Or was it an example of what was over here? Right now, there seemed to be more questions than answers and she needed to find those answers before more people were harmed.

She knew it wasn't the queen. The only time she flew was to establish a new nest for her to lay eggs.

The phone rang and Maria picked it up. It was Cal.

"Maria, I just got a call from a vet down in San Diego. He's the one who did the autopsy on that dog that was stung to death. He just got the toxicology results in from the lab."

"Oh yes. What'd he find out?"

"The dog was, in fact, stung to death by the Vespa Mandarina. They found mastoparan and mandaratoxin in its blood, enough to kill at least ten or more grown men. It never had a chance. They are very deadly toxins. They also found acetylcholine in its blood and tissues, which increases the pain level if in the body. It's supposed to be found only in the brain."

That immediately rang a bell in Maria's mind. "Yes, I found out about that last one from the lab at the hospital in San Diego. That really surprised me. But they never mentioned about those other two you just mentioned. Mastoparan and that other."

Those were deadly chemicals that ate through human tissue or, in this case the dog's, destroying red blood cells, and causing kidney failure which almost always resulted in death if not immediately treated. Cal was right. Benji the dog was likely already dead before the last sting was inflicted.

"That's because the test has to be specific for those chemicals or toxins. Otherwise they will not show up in any standard lab test. He tested for all three because apparently he had become familiar with the symptoms and what was going on with these hornets. He probed and researched for some of the components of their venom. So the tissues were tested for all three. Not to mention the fact that the dog was not the first animal casualty from those things he examined. He was, in my opinion, brilliant."

Well, well. So the venom was far more dangerous than she had believed. It was very bad news. Their enemy was quite formidable.

"Ok, looks like they've got a serious threat down there. Maybe here too. Did you find out anything regarding the northern part of the state?"

Cal looked down at his notes.

"I've been getting calls from various sections in and around Sacramento and parts east. There have been occasional reports of people noticing increased black swarms of something in the air above them. I mean these reports stated that these were swarms of something so huge that they looked like black clouds. Some people believed they were locusts."

"Were these swarms more around Sacramento or sporadic in various areas?" she asked with some increasing anxiety.

"From what I gather, Maria, most were spotted in various areas, mostly around where people live."

Maria just stared into the air. Her jaw dropped just a little. But that was all it took for her to exhibit alarming surprise. She was mostly a non-alarmist.

"Cal, those were not locusts."

"Yeah. I know. This would not be the season for them anyway."

"If they are these Vespa mandarina, we are in serious trouble."

"Yea, no kidding. I'd say we need to get the word out fast to every-one at the top." Cal hesitated for a moment, then asked, "What do you suggest?"

Maria thought briefly. "What bothers me is that they don't usually act aggressively unless they are bothered by intruders into their territory. These are behaving far from their normal behavior. And what also bothers me is that they are considerably larger than the norm of their own species. I wonder if there is a link between their unusual size and their behavior."

Cal shook his head. "You got me, Maria. But we need to find more of these things. Was this one hornet a fluke or are they all this size?"

She looked down at the dead hornet. "Good question, Cal. Good question. Whatever the answer is, we have to find out fast. What did you find out about the northern area hospitals and clinics?"

He looked down at his notes. After clearing his throat, with his finger he ran down a short list he had made, naming some of the smaller clinics east and just north of the city. He told her about two patients brought into the Sacramento General's ED with severe stings, resulting in incredible swelling and pain around the sting sites, with more redness and swelling extending further out from the sites themselves. There were multiple sting sites.

Other reports he mentioned were from two clinics reporting two sting victims, one at each of them. So far there were no catastrophic numbers. Hopefully, it would never get to that. But there was no guarantee. She herself had found out in her investigations that there were a number of victims further south after the Jansen boy and the dog. In fact, the number was considerably higher than in the north. As to why, she couldn't figure it out as yet. It didn't make sense, especially after the initial intrusion into this country began in the extreme northwest of the US Washington State.

One thing she was sure of though: the number of victims was increasing from three weeks ago. The problem was also spreading. She felt tension in her stomach and a feeling of foreboding. Was this a dark omen, a precursor of things to come? Was this becoming what could be catastrophic to the state of California: an invasion? It was time to update the director. She would be responsible for passing this new information on to the governor.

***

Outside of Stockton, CA.

It wasn't long before word got out everywhere that not only certain areas but the entire state had a serious problem. This was equivalent to a microbiological epidemic of a very nasty bug. This problem might not be so readily dealt with. Once the governor was notified, all health agencies, fish and game agencies, and statewide scientific agencies were notified of this emerging crisis. As more victims reported being attacked everywhere, additional reports were coming in of more nest sightings being discovered in more areas.

Living in a middle-class closely knit neighborhood on the outskirts of Stockton, Tommy and Jack Bindell were close-knit brothers who sometimes enjoyed exploring around when they got bored or had nothing else to do. Today, they took advantage of the bright sunny day to see if they could find anything of interest in the small woodsy area beyond their back yard in Garden Acres, a small town east of Stockton.

Because they were teenagers, both being just two years apart, they were allowed a certain amount of time by their parents to explore, as long as they didn't venture too far from home. The conditions for them being allowed to do this included letting their parents know their location and where they would be going and what they would be doing. Most importantly, they would need to return home by the set curfew time. In other words, before dark. Their dad, Robert, made sure at least one of them was wearing a working watch. The boys agreed to it all.

The ground was sort of rocky and a little hilly but that didn't seem to bother them. They'd been to this spot before. The only wildlife around here were squirrels and birds. There were no bears or cougars in this area. At least not that *they* knew of.

The younger brother, Jack, sometimes got a little too frisky and almost tripped a couple of times. The last thing they needed out here was for him to fall and break an ankle. That, Tommy thought, would be the un-coolest thing that could happen.

It was truly amazing to their parents that both seemed to like nature and being outdoors. Usually between siblings there were differences. Even between twins. And there were between Tommy and Jack. But for both of them to enjoy nature equally was not very common between two brothers. But that certainly was nothing to complain about.

Whenever they came to a hill to go up, Tommy was always curious to see what was on the other side. That meant climbing up it. He liked climbing more than Jack. That was one of the differences. Jack knew that his older brother was determined to climb this hill as he was with most. He didn't want to be left behind, so he followed him up it. Besides, it was part of exploring, right?

At the top, the boys stopped to look down at the small valley not far below. The descent wasn't steep, less than a thirty degree angle. So they ventured forth to check out the small pond below. They had never been to this part of the woods before and hadn't even known about that.

Making their way down, they reached the bottom and stood at the pond's edge. Jack picked up a stone and threw it in the water.

"Gee, I wonder if there's any fish in there," said Jack.

Tommy shrugged and also threw in a pebble he'd picked up. "Beats me," he said. Each of them kept picking up pebbles and throwing them in, watching the ripples break the calm smoothness of the water where the stones landed.

"Maybe we can come back and fish here sometime," Jack continued.

"Heck, we have the poles and gear."

Tommy looked around the area. He didn't really pay attention to the stillness and silence of the air. Except for the lack of bird sounds. He did notice that and wondered to himself if there was anything to it.

Jack started walking along the water's edge, looking down at the barely perceptible movement of the water as it gently hit the dirt bank. Something he saw caught his curiosity and he kept looking at it. As he kept walking, he kept seeing it along the edge but had no clue as to what it was. In fact, he wasn't sure if it was anything but decided to bring it up.

"Hey, Tommy."

"Yea?"

"What's this red stuff along the pond bank?"

"What red stuff?"

"C'mere and see for yourself."

Tommy came down and looked at it, perking up his curiosity.

"Hmm, what the heck is that?" he asked, more to himself than his younger brother.

They both kept looking at it.

Because the pond was not very big, Tommy suggested they each walk in opposite directions around it to find out if this red went all the way around.

"Think it's blood?" Jack asked.

Tommy shrugged again. "Don't know. Maybe. But from what, I have no idea. It's weird, though. Let's walk. You go that way," he said pointing toward his left, "and I'll go this way. Let's see what we see."

Slowly they made their ways around the pond, getting ever so closer to meeting up at the right side of it. Still trying to figure out what the stuff was, they concentrated on what they were looking at, failing to see the black, fast-moving cloud high above the open area that surrounded the pond. It was steadily growing bigger. Not a normal movement of a real cloud.

Jack looked up at Tommy who was still walking slowly toward him. Then Tommy looked up and back to Jack. There was something in the air they sensed.

"Hey, um, Tommy. You hear that?"

"Uh, yea. Sounds like a buzzing. Chainsaw maybe?" Tommy listened more. "No. Don't think so," he answered himself. "Sounds too low and continuous."

As the buzzing became louder, the direction it was coming from became more apparent. Both boys looked up. It took more than a few seconds for their brains to comprehend what they were seeing. It was something that could be from someone's worst nightmare. Or from a Wes Craven horror movie. They knew what they were seeing was very bad; yet they didn't know *what* they were seeing. What they did know was that they had to get out of there right now.

"Jack, c'mon," Tommy yelled as loud as he could over the continuously increasing buzzing. "We gotta get out of here. Run!"

Jack didn't have to be told twice. He started running back in the direction they had come from. Up the hill. Tommy was close behind him. They stumbled and kept trying to keep from tripping as they climbed as fast as they could. Behind them, the buzzing continued to increase in volume with the nearing of the black cloud.

Panic started to set in to both boys, starting with the younger one. The buzzing became louder. Its lowness of pitch made it more terrifying to them. They were afraid to look back, so they kept running. At this point they weren't sure any longer if they were still going in the right direction. Tommy sensed that if they stopped now, the cloud of whatever it was would be on them.

Their running slowed down. They were almost out of breath. Finally, they had to stop before they collapsed. They were still in the woods with no familiar landmarks yet in sight. Bending over, they tried to catch their breaths. When they looked up, something from the cloud engulfed them. Their eyesight went completely black and the last thing they heard and felt were thunderous buzzing sounds in their ears and multiple stabs of agonizing, searing pain all over them. Until they heard, felt, and saw no more.

13

As Maria sat in her home one evening just outside of L.A., she listened to the local news as always. That evening it was reporting something familiar to her and it immediately caught her attention. People needed to know about this because what was being reported could affect people or industries everywhere, and not just in California.

"There is a growing concern among state and local officials for the decreasing population of honeybees. Although reports of this have been made over the past several years throughout the country, it seems to have worsened significantly in the state of California. Reports of a new invasive species of insect called the "murder hornet" is considered a possible cause for this bee population decrease. The bees are considered a prime source of food for these dangerous insects which originated in Asia and Japan. Although they were initially spotted in the United States in the state of Washington, they've now been seen and reported here in California. What's even more disturbing is that attacks on people and pets have been reported in various areas of the state, from northeast of Sacramento all the way down to the San Diego area. Already numerous fatalities have been reported. Lisa Harrington has the story from Los Angeles."

Then the screen changed to the field reporter in L.A. Maria turned the volume down. She didn't need to hear what she already knew. So the news was now officially out. Now that the public knew, would it change anything? Would people now take extra precautions? How do you stop something from attacking and killing people and animals when you can't see it until it's too late?

She decided to take steps as soon as she got back to her office in the morning. Despite the fact that there was no sure way to stop these things, something had to be done to protect the public. This could now be considered a public health crisis and the state DPH would have to be brought into this.

The ways to attack the problem and get it under control wouldn't happen overnight. Cooperation would have to be obtained from all the hospitals and most of the major walk-in and urgent care clinics in the state. A statewide alert would have to be made to all healthcare facilities, among a number of other things. But she would worry about starting it in the morning. In the meantime, she sat and heard the rest of the news but listened to very little of it. Her mind was going a mile a minute. For her, morning couldn't come fast enough.

***

That same day on a trail in Escondido, a hiker detected a stench that she would never forget, equating it in her mind with the smell of death. At first, thinking it was a dead animal, she rounded the bend then suddenly came across a bloated body in the middle of the trail. The sight of the disfigured, purplish face shocked her to her limits. She couldn't tell if it was male or female. Quickly picking her cell phone out of her pocket, she called 9-1-1 and gave her location as best as she could. She reluctantly agreed to wait until they arrived, but not near the body. The fork on the trail a few hundred feet back was close enough for her.

***

Yosemite National Park

The Sondheim family was settling in a rented cabin just outside the park in the late afternoon. There was a restaurant nearby, a few other nearby cabins, and a large souvenir shop. Although Ron and Marilyn were excited to be there, they were able to contain their excitement, unlike the kids who just couldn't wait for anything to begin.

They had just finished putting their clothes in the bureaus and toiletries into the bathroom. They had the kids do the same as they attended to their own.

They were staying in one of the log cabins with two bedrooms: a master and a smaller one for the kids. It was comfortable, simple and very cozy. There were simple accommodations for cooking if they had brought their own food. It was almost like getting a room in a hotel, only better. The one bathroom had a shower but no bathtub. That was fine with them. The cabin also had a living room area and provided a TV. There was even a fireplace. The logwood walls made them feel like they were truly in the wilderness and closer to nature. That's what made it better than a hotel.

"Hey, Dad, can we go to the gift shop?" asked Bobby, while little Suzie was looking at one of thegames she had brought along.

Ron looked at his watch. It was a little after 5:00pm.

"Kind of late for that now, bud," he replied. "It'll be open again in the morning. We can check it out then before we go into the park. But the restaurant is open now. I think we should go have something to eat, don't you?"

After they all readily agreed, the family headed over to the restaurant. Although it was still light out, they could've gone into the park. The entrance was right there near their cabin. But it was late and touring the park would, more than likely, be an all-day affair. In fact, people had reported that it would take a lot more than one day to see all of it because there was so much to see. The plan was to settle in and relax for the evening and they could start the next morning early. But first they would enjoy their first evening meal on vacation.

In the morning after they'd all had a good night's sleep, they left the cabin at 7:30. Breakfast was first on the agenda. A quick walk brought them to the restaurant. An hour later, they finished their meal. After Ron paid, they left and walked over to the gift shop to check it out as he had promised. He checked the hours of operation on the sign and saw it was open until 8:00pm.

"Get only two items, kids," Ron told them. "We'll be here for a week so you can get more later."

After picking out an item each, Ron paid for them and they headed out, with Marilyn following behind the kids. He was surprised they didn't pick out everything in the store. Maybe they hadn't seen everything and picked out the first things they liked. It was probably that and wanting to get into the park, he thought.

After they were all in the car, they headed toward the entrance gate where they paid the fee and then went in. There were signs with names of destinations pointing straight ahead, and to the right and left. He wasn't sure which one to take. In the back seat, the kids looked out the windows trying to figure out what they were seeing. They had never seen such heavy thick wilderness before. To them it was mysterious and intriguing and they weren't sure what to make of it.

Between Ron and Marilyn, they chose to take the right road. After all, what difference did it make where they went first?

They would see most of it, if not all, during the length of their stay here. Along the way, they saw some beautiful scenery, which included open valleys and mountains in the distance. They knew El Capitan was in the park but weren't sure exactly where it was. They likely missed seeing it listed on the signs back there. Unfortunately, Ron had forgotten to take the park map with him. He'd left it back in the room.

"Did you bring the map?" asked Marilyn. Ron smiled. They must be bonded. Her timing always seemed to be right on cue.

"No. Left it in the room. We'll kind of feel our way around here for now. Tomorrow we'll have the map and plan right where we want to go."

"Ok," she nodded, accepting that.

Having driven at least a couple of miles, they were now deep in the wilderness country. There had been signs both in the cabin and just outside the front entrance warning visitors of the wildlife. Strong encouragement had been posted to stay in the vehicle if large wildlife such as bears were spotted nearby. For hikers, signs advised to stick to the posted trails and not to wander off of them. There was the occasional emergency phone on a pole that a hiker or other tourist could use if in trouble for any reason.

Ron noticed these things but didn't think too much of it. They weren't hiking and he had no intention of getting out of the car, unless they spotted a spectacular scene he wanted to take a picture of.

As they proceeded down the road further, spotting more scenic views of mountains and rolling hills, valleys, and a river below them, he noticed a sideroad on their right which was heading downward.

"Hey, let's go take a look at the river down there. Want to see it?" he asked no one in particular.

Not surprisingly, the kids yelled out "yeah!" at the same time.

Marilyn looked at the road he was turning onto, then turned her head to him. "Ron, there's no sign here or posting. How do you know it's going down to the river?"

"Has to," he replied. "It's going down, right? Can't be going anywhere else."

She couldn't argue that, but still couldn't help wondering. Going into the unknown made her nervous. She hoped he was right.

For several minutes they drove slowly down the road, which seemed to narrow the further down they got. The forest was thickening. Ron was thinking they must be getting close to the water by now. The kids kept looking out the window. Marilyn kept looking forward and out her side window. No one said anything for those minutes.

Finally, "Daddy, are we getting close to the water?" It was Suzie.

Ron looked to his right. "I think so, honey. Think I might be hearing water."

Despite what he thought he was hearing, there was no visible indication of the river as yet. Above them, the thick forest trees on both sides of the road umbrellaed the road which darkened the area.

Marilyn looked at Ron, now concerned. She was starting to get a bad feeling about this, and decided she'd better say something. They had actually been driving down this road for about half an hour and there were no indications they were getting close to the river below. There were no emergency phones along the roadside because there were no light poles.

"Honey, I think we better turn around. We should have gotten to the river by now if this was where it was heading."

He didn't say anything. Marilyn knew he was frustrated, as they all were. Where the hell was this road leading to if not there?

"Ok," he sighed in resignation. "First spot we come to that I can turn around, I will."

The road had narrowed so much that they couldn't do even a U-turn here. And as he drove further looking for an appropriate spot to turn, the road became even narrower and less paved. The forest here looked thicker than behind them. They seemed to be in the middle of a jungle. What made it even more ominous was that there was not one sign, not even the smallest, that stood along either side of the road. Ron's heart sank as he realized he'd made a huge mistake turning onto an unknown road with no sign to indicate where it was heading. He stopped the car.

"Dad, are we lost?" asked Bobby. He didn't sound scared, but his voice betrayed his worried concern.

Marilyn answered almost immediately, not wanting the kids to be scared, especially at this beginning stage of their visit here. They were here to have fun, not to be frightened.

"No, honey, we're not lost," she said looking back at him. "We're on the same road. Just trying to find a place to turn so we can head back the way we came. Then we can get back on the main road and continue into the park."

"How we gonna turn around? The road looks awful skinny."

Leave it to Bobby to put it like that. Marilyn looked at Ron, wondering herself. Ron looked at her with a sheepish grin. No one else could do it but him. He put the car in reverse gear and turned to begin the long, slow, treacherous trek back.

"Ok, here we go, everybody. Be patient, we'll get there." He said that more for himself than for the others, who remained silent.

As they slowly made their way in reverse, it was obvious to him that going forward on this road gave absolutely no indication of the difficulty of going backward. Not surprising. There were a lot of things, he thought, that people took for granted. This was one of them. He was, at the same time, looking for a spot he could back the car onto so he could do the much-needed U-turn.

As they came to the first bend to the right as one looked behind, he almost clipped a sapling. Ever so slowly the road became slightly wider, but still was nearly imperceptible. A straightway for about fifty yards, then a sharp bend to the right. As he tried to compensate for an overturn, his right foot inadvertently pressed a little too much on the gas pedal and they accelerated backward quickly.

Ron realized he had directed the car toward the edge of the road. A split second before he hit the brake, there was a thump below them, as if they'd run over something. Then the back of the car slammed into a tree and one of the rear tires sank deeply into something. The kids screamed and Marilyn yelled out a loud, "Whoa. Ron!"

"Oh my god, is everyone ok?" Ron was frantic and apologized to everyone. "Bobby, Suzie, are you ok?"

Although they were a little shook up, they said they were fine. Marilyn was straightening her hair as a nervous gesture, afraid to say what she was really feeling in front of the kids. She had to be strong for them.

"My foot must have pressed too hard on the accelerator as I was going back. Sorry everyone. That definitely won't happen again. I better check the back end." He opened the door.

"Yea, I think you better," Marilyn agreed. She hated to think what it looked like back there. It would not have occurred to her that a smashed back end would be the least of their worries.

From what he saw, the right taillight was gone and about a foot of that side fender was bent in but not terribly. It would cost them but wouldn't break the bank. Their car insurance would take care of it. Still, it was not something he would ever be proud of. Damn! Even so, they would be ok as long as the car was running and they could get out of there. But now he would have to go even slower, which would take them considerably longer.

There was a new problem he realized when he looked down. The thump they had all heard and felt in the car apparently was the rear right tire going into a hole in the ground near the tree. The hole looked fairly large and the tire had sunk almost halfway into it. Not a good situation. '*Shit*', he mumbled to himself.

He quickly walked back and got in. He told Marilyn of their predicament and what he was going to do. They had their cell phones and could call Triple A if they needed to. But first he would try to get them out of this.

He pressed on the gas. The engine was revving up and the car moved slightly forward in its attempt to get out of the hole. It wasn't quite making it and he repeatedly gunned the engine, trying to get enough momentum to get out of that hole. Several times he almost made it, but the hole seemed to tighten its grip on the tire and the car kept rolling back into it. It was frustratingly discouraging for Ron, to say the least, but he kept trying anyway. Marilyn had to remind him about the gas consumption. She would call Triple A on her phone. When he finally stopped, he looked at her, dejected in his failure to get them out of the situation he had caused. He nodded. "Ok; you better," was all he could say.

The eerie silence around them was broken by sounds of low, thick buzzing. The sounds slowly increased in volume and were continuous rather than intermittent.

"You hear that?" said Ron.

Marilyn nodded. "Yea. Don't tell me we hit a beehive." The sounds grew louder quickly. "Good lord, Ron," she exclaimed. "Are you kidding me? We hit a darn beehive in the middle of nowhere here?"

Ron looked around. How could this be possible? The kids looked around out the windows in the back. They asked if they were in trouble.

"No, we'll be fine, kids. As long as we stay in the car, we'll be ok." Ron knew it was his job to make sure that they all would be. Marilyn had just got off the phone, angry and even more frustrated than before.

"What's the matter, hon?" Ron asked.

She turned to him quickly. "No signal. No freaking signal. Can you believe it? Try your phone, please."

Ron removed his phone from his pocket and checked the screen icons. He had no signal either and informed Marilyn. They looked at each other with expressions of *now what are we gonna do?*

Suddenly, something large and dark hit their windshield. It hit the glass so hard it made them all snap back in shock. But whatever it was flew off and they couldn't tell for sure what it was. What they knew was that it was large. A bird was the first thing that came to their minds.

The buzzing was now very loud even through the car's enclosed space and closed up windows. It sounded like it was coming from everywhere. In the back, the children started crying with good reason. With Ron and Marilyn also frightened, they knew they were in trouble in more ways than one but still they didn't know from what. Whatever those things were, they knew they were the targets of something or some things. It was terrifying for all of them.

The buzzing grew louder and louder. Much of it was coming through the car roof. It hardly sounded muffled. Ron and Marilyn realized that if it sounded this loud *inside* the car, being outside right now would be tantamount to suicide. If the sounds didn't kill you, whatever was making them would. It was then that one of the sound makers made its first appearance to them.

***

Garden Acres, CA.

That evening, the Bindell parents were frantically making calls to the homes of all the friends of the boys they could think of to find out if they'd seen them. Tommy and Jack had been gone for at least six hours and hadn't returned. Curfew for them from their hike was two hours ago. It was now 6:00pm. There was still no sign of them.

Once they realized no one had seen them, their father went out in the car looking for them at all their usual hangouts. The mother called the

police and reported them missing, describing them and their ages. Although both were in their teens, they were never delinquent in anything. Even from school. Despite their perfectly normal teenage quirks, they were pretty much reliable, the mom told them. The thought of them running away was out of the question. Besides, Jack who was the younger boy, was diabetic and he wouldn't ever run away knowing he had to have his medication.

Fortunately for them, the police would not make them wait the usual forty-eight hours as with older teens or adults. They made it an official missing person's report and began by putting out an APB on them. The mother told them where they said they would be going, which was fortunate for all parties concerned.

Many teens who go out on little escapades either tell their parents where they will supposedly be but in secret go somewhere else; or they go where they said they would but get "distracted" on the way back home. Another more sinister reason is what parents dread most of all: abduction. For now, it was much too soon to determine which it was.

It wouldn't be dark until about 9:00pm. At least too dark to make an accurate search possible. And that was only an hour away from now. Police worked quickly to set up a search team and get them out in the area where the mother reported they would be. They sent an officer to their home to interview and obtain any pictures of the boys.

"Mrs. Bindell, has this ever happened before?" asked the officer.

"No, never!" Those two words shouted out her worry.

He took notes and then the pictures she offered him of what they looked like. Her description of where exactly they would have hiked, a location they had visited several times before, was extremely helpful to the searchers and quickly gave them a valuable starting point.

"May I take these with me?" he asked. "We will return them when they are found."

"Oh of course. Please." She was noticeably shaking.

"Don't worry, ma'am. We'll find them. They probably took a wrong turn and maybe got a little disoriented. Your description of the area very likely will speed up the process of finding them."

He thanked her as he rose to leave. "Please be assured we will do everything we can to find and safely return them back home."

Although he didn't want to give her any false hopes, he also didn't want to paint her a morbid picture either. Right now, anything could've happened to them. It was not the time to bring up any negative possibilities because there were too many of them. But still, he had a gut feeling. All too often, gut feelings in cops were not good signs.

Ruth's husband arrived back home after looking for them in the area with the car but not finding them to their dismay. The fact that the police were at their home made the situation more serious than what he had thought. The fact that they still hadn't gotten home worsened it even more.

He had decided to then go on a foot search himself and he knew where to go. Because he himself had brought them to that same area where the police were told to search. It was a year earlier and they had decided to take a nice Saturday afternoon stroll together.

"Bob, watch the time. It's starting to get darker. Bring a flashlight just in case but don't try searching when it's dark." Ruth didn't want to have to worry about him as well.

After reassuring her he'd be back by or before dark, he grabbed a flashlight and headed off while he still had a little time left. She watched him from the window of the back door and soon he was swallowed up by the forest.

Although it was suppertime, food was the last thing on her mind. Inside, she was going crazy just waiting around, waiting to hear something from somebody. But she had to do something to keep her wits about her. So she decided to prepare some kind of meal for when her husband and the boys returned. Because of the lateness of the hour, she believed he wouldn't be gone that long.

***

He'd been out for about thirty minutes but there was no sign of the boys. As it was getting darker, navigating became more difficult and things were harder to see. There was no doubt he would have to turn around soon. Although he was following the same game trail he had initially brought them on that day a year ago, underbrush had started covering parts of it so he had to look carefully to make sure he was still following it.

About fifty yards further ahead he thought he saw the clearing that he remembered had a pond at the bottom down a slight incline. That would be his final search area, not only because it was getting a little too dark to proceed further, but also because he and the boys hadn't gone further on past that. If he was going to find them, this would where it should be.

He called out to them.

"Tom! Jack! Hey guys, this is Dad. Can you hear me?"

He didn't care if it sounded a little corny. If they were out here and could hear his voice they would answer. Only silence was his reply. He repeated it all the way to the pond. But there was still no answer. That fact made the silence around him even more ominous. He felt the hairs stand up on the back of his neck because now there was the feeling of dread. If something had happened to them, he feared it wouldn't be good.

He looked around the pond and was determined not to leave it until he covered every area around it. After quickly circling the perimeter while keeping his flashlight working ahead of him, he decided it would now be pointless to search any more tonight. It was getting too dark to see anything. Reluctantly he headed back up but made sure he was lighting the way ahead of him. The air was cooler than when he'd set out and he felt the annoying high buzzing of mosquitoes, despite the coolness. It was still slightly humid which probably explained their presence.

Back on the game path, he walked a little quicker as he neared the forest edge. Somehow the light from the flashlight lit up something dark off to his right. It was well off the path but close enough for him to determine that it was not something that grew here. That stopped him in his tracks. What the heck was it?

He brushed aside some saplings and decided to check it out. It looked like a red and white striped object. As he neared it, he stopped and widened his eyes. Getting closer to it he recognized Tommy's shirt. He was too shocked for words. He squatted down and cried out to his older son who lay face down on the ground. Turning him over, he saw a face he didn't recognize yet knew it was him. It was bluish purple and so swollen even around the eyes that it seemed he was in a horror movie.

But he knew it was him. It could only be him. After checking for a pulse and not finding one, he looked for breathing but there were no respirations. Initially he knew Tommy was dead. His were the desperate actions of a father that wanted to refuse to believe his boy was dead. Now where was Jack?

He depended on the flashlight almost completely. Shining it everywhere in the dark and slowly panning the area with it, he thought he saw the lighter shirt of Jack just about fifteen feet away, partly hidden in the underbrush. He went over to it and discovered the body of his younger son. He was laying faceup and his face was also unrecognizable.

It, too, was purplish, swollen and with eyes swollen shut. There was no breathing or a pulse on him either.

He knew he couldn't just pick them up, especially in the dark. Fortunately, he always carried his cell phone. After removing it from his pocket, he called 9-1-1. Then after reporting the situation and where he was located, they asked that he remain on that spot with the flashlight and keep his cell phone line open. When they asked about their condition, he told the dispatcher that he believed they were dead because of their physical condition and the lack of breathing and pulses.

By this time, he was in tears and could barely control his voice.

"Don't hang up, and don't move the bodies, sir" they advised him. "Police officers and medical personnel have now been dispatched and will be there very shortly."

They again reminded him not to hang up so police could home in on his phone's signal. He complied and waited there, teary-eyed and in shock while his brain was still trying to process what he'd discovered. It was little comfort to know that now no search party would be needed.

After the first responders arrived, he'd have to call Ruth immediately. The news would devastate her just as much. Life had now forever changed for them. Children were not supposed to die before their parents, and both of them were now gone. It wasn't fair. It just wasn't fair.

14

Yosemite National Park

As if the continuous buzzing wasn't bad enough, now they were visually confronted. They were they the largest insects they'd ever seen. Their appearance reflected their deadly aggressiveness. In fact, in Ron's mind, it seemed they *wanted* to attack his family and wouldn't give up until they did.

"Ron, what are these things?" Marilyn screamed at him.

He was just as much in shock as she was and no less scared. "I, uh, I...I don't know. Giant, uh, bees maybe? Mutations or something?"

Soon, one then more climbed down the windshield and the other windows as well, blocking the light. The low heavy buzzing was continuous, just adding to their frightening situation. One look at one of them and Marilyn blocked her mouth trying to stifle a scream. But the kids in the back saw it and they filled the car with their screams. How could you tell your terrified children that everything would be ok when you were just as frightened and didn't know what to do?

When one of the insects turned and faced them, it was almost surreal. Ron felt they were in the middle of a horror movie that turned into reality. The large black eyes were looking at them. Its large mandibles opened and shut slightly and its long stinger looked deadly as the pointed end lay against the windshield. They were all literally staring death in the face. For the moment, Ron believed they were safe. It was clear these weren't bees. There was no way they could get in through the vents because of their size.

His mind was racing to try and figure out their identity. Then it came to him. He remembered reading an article in the newspaper about it. But these were supposed to be in the state of Washington, not California. What the heck?

But these could not be anything else. There were no other insects this big. In fact, these looked *bigger* than the ones reported.

"These are the Japanese Giant Hornets!" he told her.

Marilyn's eyes widened at him. "What? Are you serious? They are supposed to be…"

"Yeah, I know," he interrupted her. "In Washington. Obviously, they migrated down to here. Oh, good lord, I wonder if anyone else knows about this."

She turned her head to face the hornet-covered windshield, hard pressed to keep from thinking gloom and doom. In the back, the kids remained too scared to maintain their crying. Their silence and the looks on their faces said it all. She turned her face to them and reassured them as best she could that they would come out of this ok. They were safe as long as they stayed in the car.

All the windows were now covered by these things. No doubt so was the car's roof.

Despite the lack of signal strength on their phones, Ron didn't know what else they could do other than try to keep calling out on them. He continued to try, thinking maybe an atmospheric fluke would allow at least one signal to get through. Meanwhile, the buzzing was now increasing.

"Ron, what are we gonna do?" Her voice was now quiet and subdued but understandably with tension. Marilyn looked at her husband with hope that he might come up with some plausible plan. If they were to survive, they had to do something. Right now, exiting the car would be tantamount to suicide.

He looked at her and knew he had to think of something. He was their supporter. Their strength. Their protector. There was no way he was going to let anything happen to his family.

"Alright, listen everyone," he said unsurely. "Listen. I have a plan. "Kids, listen, I need your attention please. We will be alright as long as we stay in the car. Whatever you do, don't open the doors or windows." Although he probably didn't have to tell them that, he had to remind them of their situation. His plan, if it worked, would allow them to follow through on it. But not yet.

Marilyn knew she had to stay strong along with Ron for the kids' sake. They were the rock that the children needed to support them. Without that rock, they would sink.

Having their attention, he decided to say some things to them which might give them some hope, as well as to himself. He didn't know if they would be the correct things to say or if they would be factually correct. But he had to try.

He turned sideways in his seat so he could look at them all.

"Look. Here's my idea. First, when it's dark or these things have left, I am going to try and get the car out of this hole that has a grip on the tire. Maybe if I try enough the tire might catch enough traction to get us out of there."

Marilyn started to say something but Ron put up his hand. He knew what she was thinking. She closed her mouth.

"But I won't try for more than a minute. Chances are if we don't get out of it after that time, we probably won't without outside assistance. So, a thought occurred to me. Something we may have to try later on."

Marilyn's brows furrowed. "What do you mean, Ron? What do you have in mind? You have some way to chase these things away? I mean, *look* at them!"

He looked at them and it brought to mind something he had read in the paper not long ago. In the newspaper, they were called "murder hornets." By the looks of them, the pseudonym seemed quite appropriate.

He let out a breath and looked at the hornet-covered windshield.

"Later on? Why later?" Her voice started rising from the anxiety of it all. Realizing that, she quickly lowered it so she wouldn't scare the kids. She realized also that the question was stupid but resulted understandably from her fright.

"Marilyn, do you really have to ask that? Look at the windows, for Pete's sake."

Now for the information he hoped he was right about. Even if he was, the plan would still be on the dangerous and very risky side.

"From what I understand, most flying insects, other than mosquitoes and gnats, go into hiding at night. I think they all do, when it's really cool. I think we are going to have to leave this car and walk back on foot soon after sundown. I think when it's dark or cool enough, these things might leave us alone. For some reason, they don't fly at night. At least not that I know of."

"Daddy, are we gonna take a hike?" Suzie, despite her age, wasn't happy about the prospects of a long walk. She was smart enough to know they were in trouble.

Ron turned around and looked at the both of them. "Yes sweetie, we'll be leaving the car later to try and walk far enough for us to use our phones. So we can call for help."

"But why aren't the phones working here?" asked Bobby.

Ron then explained about strong and weak areas for phone signals. When he told him that this area was not picking up any probably because the mountains might be blocking some of them from reaching their

phones, he seemed to understand and settled back in the seat. For now, the answer seemed to appease them. But the tension remained.

"So, are we going to have to walk all the way back to where we turned on to this road?" asked Marilyn.

Ron shook his head. "I don't know. I hope not."

"How far do you think we came?"

"Maybe a mile. Or two. I doubt more than that." But he wasn't sure. In fact, it was likely more than that. He did his best to minimize the seriousness of their predicament.

"We have to walk at the very least as far as the first signal we can pick up with either of our phones. Or I have another thought. You can all wait in the car and I'll go for help. At least you'd be safe."

"Oh no you don't," Marilyn quickly responded. "You're not leaving us here! No way. How would we know if you made it or not? There's no way we would know with our phones not working. And even if you found a signal with *your* phone, mine doesn't work here."

She's right, he thought. *So much for that idea. In the trash you go.*

For several minutes they sat in silence as they contemplated the only option they could come up with for seeking help and, possibly, surviving at all.

"I don't want to walk out there at all," Marilyn said softly, followed by a sigh. "But looks like we don't have much choice. Still better than being left alone out here."

Damn these devilish creatures. Why couldn't they have stayed where they came from! Her hatred for them now knew no bounds.

The thought of walking in the dark through an even darker forest on an unknown road leading to god-knows-where was not something that any of them looked forward to. But their options were limited. They couldn't stay here forever. As far as Ron was concerned, no one might come down this road anytime soon. If at all. The only silver lining then was, despite all of this, they would be walking toward a "safety zone." Back toward the entrance where there was help.

Marilyn was constantly thinking. Leave it to her to think of another problem. But it was a potential problem that should never be ignored, especially in an environment like this.

However, the last thing she wanted to do was scare the kids. This was scary enough to adults: *bears!* She wrote the word down on a piece of paper and showed it to her husband. He hadn't thought of that and his jaw dropped slightly. His eyes rose to meet hers. Damn. She was right!

Still, the possibility could not make them stay here because *here* was a certain death trap. At least out there, despite the dangers, they had a fighting chance.

He told her so without mentioning bears. She hemmed and hawed about it. Not because she wouldn't do it. It scared her.

"What would you rather do, stay here where we are sitting ducks for these things or for whatever else comes along?" he persisted. "Or would you rather take a chance and get help? I think we will be perfectly fine. Just have to stick together and keep our wits about us. We can do it. I know we can. At least with these things in hiding we have the freedom to move around. And the farther we get from this trap, the closer we will get to help."

He thought of wolves too, but damned if he was going to mention them also. They had enough to worry about without bringing out all the dangerous possibilities Mother Nature could throw at them. He needed the kids to cooperate, not panic.

Marilyn looked down deep in thought. She almost wished they hadn't come out here. If they had stayed home, they wouldn't be in this predicament. But then, how were they to know something like this would happen?

"Ok," she nodded in agreement, then looked at him. "Ok. You're right. We can't stay here. Even if these things weren't here, we'd probably have to do the same thing."

He breathed a mild sigh of relief. "Yea, we would. Except that we wouldn't have to wait for dark. Ok. That's the plan."

He looked around. All the windows were still covered with the giant hornets. Only slight slivers coming through between some of the packed bodies revealed the daylight. But he couldn't for the life of him figure out why these things were after them. Until the thought occurred to him. And he realized it was actually their fault for the insects attacking them. They had driven into their home. The hole. It had to be.

He didn't initially know that these hornets had *ground* nests, not hives like bees or other regular species of wasps. If that was the case, they all needed to steer clear of the hole the car was trapped in.

He didn't want to talk about it right now. There were too many things going on. The plan to save themselves later was one of them and it was at the very top of the list.

"Why don't we relax and hunker down until it's time, everyone?" advised Ron.

It would be a number of hours before dark. All they could do now was relax as best as they could until the time came. Because of the long wait, that time couldn't come fast enough.

***

Stockton

From Garden Grove, the bodies of the two Bindell boys were transferred to the medical examiner's office in Stockton for autopsy because the deaths were unnatural. Although people suspected what killed them, no one knew for sure. Authorities as well as their parents had to find out for sure.

The purplish bloating of their faces and the quick start of decomposition suggested their deaths were agonizing and quite traumatic. They had suffered as no one should. Even the forensic pathologist who was doing the autopsies was taken aback by the number of stings and trauma to the bodies. Toxicology had to be done as soon as possible because he believed it would provide the clue to what killed them.

It would take a few days for the report to come back. After blood and tissue samples were taken, he performed the external and then the internal autopsy. The former revealed the incredibly large amount of sting marks on their bodies, bruising, and extraordinary swelling. Each of the boys had been stung multiple times. Hundreds of times all over. The internal autopsy would reveal any damage caused to the internal organs by whatever venom had coursed through them. Although the boys had been fully clothed, the stingers of the unknown sources had gone completely through the clothing and penetrated their skin and tissues. They had virtually no protection from whatever attacked them.

Three days later the toxicology report came back. The results were basically the same as with other victims who had died: large amounts of acetylcholine and other neurotoxins found in each of the bodies. More than enough to do the job. The boys never stood a chance. The coroner's office then contacted the local police who then notified Robert and Ruth Bindell. They were both shocked and devastated by the news and the identification of their killers.

Word quickly spread to the news media. Soon it was all over the news throughout the state. This added to other news of people in different regions of the state being attacked, many having to be hospitalized. Although many survived when treated quickly, others weren't so lucky. It was now the government's consensus that California was now under siege by the now-dubbed "killer hornets."

***

San Luis Obispo

Maria and Cal were now keeping track on a large map of where all the attacks were taking place throughout the state. Maria immediately contacted the closest field offices of their department to each of the affected areas in California and suggested deploying search and destroy teams to find and eradicate all hornet nests within their region. She emphasized the extreme importance of finding all of them. When they truly believed they had accomplished that and could find no evidence of any others in their area, they were to report back to the home office after their destruction.

They knew that it would be almost impossible to know for certain that every single nest was destroyed. Destroying the nest was one thing. Destroying all the insects was quite another. All it took was for the queen to escape and the problem would begin all over again. But they had to have the best effective game plan and this was the best they could do for now. As the situation developed further, so would the plan.

Maria was on the phone. Someone from the San Joaquin County Medical Examiner's Office had called her with news that was not good.

"Both of them?" she asked the ME's pathologist who'd made the call.

"Yes, I'm afraid so,' he said. "They were found by their father who decided not to wait for the police search party. He'd gone briefly looking out in the community with his car, then returned home and found out they'd been in the woods rather than the community. He immediately went out to look for them. It's unfortunate he found them the way he did. They were already decomposing at a quicker than normal rate even in these outside conditions because of the trauma caused by the venom and pain."

"Oh my god!" she said. "That's awful. So, I assume it was the hornets?"

"Yep, it was. As with many other unfortunate victims, they were quickly attacked in overwhelming numbers. It wouldn't have mattered if they were allergic enough. There were enough stings on both of them to kill two elephants and then some. The venom had taken over the bodies and systematically destroyed their organ systems. They stood no chance, even if they had been adults."

She didn't regard them as just tragic statistics, because she was human and regarded each and every case as significant and noteworthy.

"What were their names and ages?"

The doctor looked down at his notes. "Thomas and Jack Bindell, ages seventeen and fifteen, respectively. Lived in Garden Acres.

"Well I appreciate your call, Doctor. If any other cases come in would you please let us know? We are keeping track of all reported cases so it'll help us better to do something about it."

He agreed readily to do that.

After the call, Maria sat there for a few moments to process the new information. It was mindboggling in a terrifying way what was occurring. As she was getting ready to get back on the phone again, it rang. It was Calvin from his lab office.

"Hey, just got a call from San Diego Memorial. A twenty-eight-year-old woman was brought in several hours ago with a sting on her left arm. She is non-allergic to bee venom, yet her entire arm was swollen to twice its normal size and she was having breathing difficulties."

"And it wasn't a bee," she said. She knew where this was going, remembering the previous call about her and the crushed specimen which she had received. Another victim by the same culprits. There seemed to be no end to their deadly rampage.

Before the ER nurse could respond, Maria told her about the last call and the specimen they had assessed and confirmed the species. "Is she going to be alright?"

The nurse said her prognosis was good. She'd been lucky and had been brought for treatment right away. Had there been a delay it might have turned out differently.

Maria got on the phone's building-wide intercom and paged all department field and support personnel to report to the main conference room at 1:30pm. They now had a terrible statewide crisis on their hands and any unnecessary delay in fighting back might cost more innocent people their lives.

To obtain her blessing on Maria's first official aggressive move, she needed to contact the director, Miranda Bingham. Her plan required her approval. Considering the ongoing situation in its increasing seriousness, she had no doubts she would get it. Soon enough, she did.

15

Yosemite National Park

It was a little past dusk when the family noted most of the insects were gone from the car windows. The chirping of the crickets was heard through the closed windows which was a good sign, and the scene appeared serene. Not one car or other vehicle had come by during the hours they'd been there, so Ron knew this was not a road that would be taken by anyone except park personnel. Yet he wondered why no park staff had driven by. Perhaps the reason was at the end of this road: wherever that was. It had seemed endless. But they probably would never know what lay ahead.

Marilyn was dozing. When he looked in the back, so were the kids. He was not able to doze. It was approaching leave time from the car. Despite his determination to do this, he couldn't kid himself. He was quite nervous about it. After all, walking in the dark in the middle of a national forest when no one was around and where there were dangerous predators that could be lurking within every shadow, not to mention killer hornets being around, was just not anyone's favorite activity.

Before getting out, he started the car and tried several times to get it out of the hole. As before, the tire just spun and moved forward a little. But that was it. He would see just how deep it was when he was outside. The sound of the car's engine revving and its movement woke them up.

"What's going on, sweetheart?" Marilyn asked him.

"The things are gone," he replied. "Tried getting the car out but no luck. We need to get ready to leave the car. I'm going to get something out of the trunk before we go. Make sure the kids are up and ready."

He got out and after a quick search, took the crowbar out of the trunk. It wasn't much but it was all they had that could be used. Even against a bear or wolf, it was better than nothing.

Marilyn looked around and realized how very dark it was now. It was a frightening dark. She might be a horror movie buff, but reality was very different from Hollywood. If the moon was out, there was no indication of it. For all they knew, the clouds were covering it or the entire sky. But she forgot about the tree canopy overhead. That made the area dark even in daylight and wouldn't show the moon if it was out.

"Are you sure you want to do this?" she asked, when he returned to the opened driver's door.

"Well I'm sure I *don't* want to do this. Decision made. We have no options. The sooner we start out, the sooner we will get help. We won't get any of that sitting here."

The night was not cold but cool enough to keep any stinging or flying biters away. Marilyn looked at him with an expression that conveyed what she was feeling. *What have we gotten ourselves into here?*

He found some spring water bottles and handed one to each of them and one for himself. "Bring these with you in case you get thirsty. Might need them."

"Are we leaving the car, Daddy?" asked both of the kids at the same time. He turned sideways again for the final time.

"Yes, we are getting ready to. Keep your jackets on."

'Honey, can you get the small flashlight out of the glove compartment?"

Luckily, he kept one in there just in case. Even though it wasn't powerful, it was some kind of light. He'd have to conserve its use to preserve the life length of the battery. The next-to-last thing he wanted was to end up with dead batteries before they reached the gate to the park. He knew right now that the whole park was closed. No one knew they were even there. That was the last thing he wanted to think about. What a lousy time to have no bear spray or Mace.

She gave him the flashlight and then he briefed everyone before they exited. They were to stay close together at all times. They could talk and even make noises. They didn't have to be quiet. Marilyn looked at him like he'd fallen off his rocker.

"What?" she asked in wonder.

"Yea, why is that, Dad?" asked Bobby.

Ron, then realizing his near-mistake said, "No one is around and you won't wake up anyone so it's ok."

In Marilyn's ear he whispered, *"Bears need to know ahead of time humans are around so they won't attack."* He'd learned that from TV documentaries about animals. He wasn't absolutely positive about the "won't attack" part. But he knew the chances were at least greater that they *wouldn't* attack than if they startled the creatures. *But what if they ran into one anyway?* The thought was too terrifying to even say it out loud. That would surely cause a panic. He didn't know if he was doing the right thing by not saying anything. He didn't even know if he was doing the right thing by having them all walk out there. All he could do was check the cell phones for the first indication of a signal. He had to think positive. They were more likely *not* to run into one. He chose to believe that. Hell, it just might be true.

"Ok. Everyone ready?"

They all nodded. "Alright. Let's go."

They knew the hornets were gone. Ron came back in unscathed, so he was right. They hid at night. Somewhere other than the nest their vehicle had destroyed.

For them it was difficult to believe that anywhere could be this dark. After a few minutes outside, their eyes adjusted to the foreboding darkness and they could make out the road in front of them. The forest on either side of them appeared pitch black and threatening. The only sounds coming from it was the chirping of the crickets. If it weren't for the hornets, walking in the dark would never be an option.

Every so often, Ron turned on the flashlight to help them maintain their bearings and location on the road. They stuck together, not so much because Ron told them to, but more for feelings of some sort of safety. They had no idea how long they would have to walk. All they knew was that they had to get away from the danger area of the car.

"Honey, any idea of how long it took for us to drive down this road from where we first took it?" Ron had an idea why Marilyn asked this.

"Oh, I'd say about fifteen or twenty minutes. Maybe twenty-five tops. We weren't going that fast. Walking back to the starting point, it might take us maybe forty-five minutes to an hour. Depends on if we keep walking or have to stop for pee breaks."

So far no one complained about having to go. But they also didn't want to admit being too scared to think about peeing let alone actually go.

"Daddy, Mommy it's scary out here," said Suzie as she sobbed.

Bobby didn't want to admit his fright so he didn't say anything. But his parents knew. Although the background silence was deafening, the chirping seemed to reassure them that they were alive and ok.

Unfortunately, there was no assurance of their safety anywhere along the way. Even though Ron and Marilyn knew there was no such thing as the boogeyman, at least in their minds, the kids had heard of such a thing and

were afraid to ask if he was out there in the woods. The forest or woods anywhere can be exceptionally creepy for anyone, especially at night.

"We'll be fine, sweetie," Marilyn replied to her daughter. "Just keep walking and watch your step, ok?"

Ron was almost tempted to have a little sing-along as they were walking to try and keep their spirits up and also keep them from thinking scary thoughts. He talked himself out of it. This was not the time, he decided. Besides, he didn't feel like singing and was sure the others wouldn't want to either.

He guessed that they might have been walking for about twenty minutes or so when he thought he heard something off to the right in the darkness of the forest. It was a rustling sound and then more of those sounds.

During daylight hours, he wouldn't be overly concerned about that. But at night, those same sounds sounded louder and had a way of sending chills up and down one's spine and causing hairs to stand up on end. Those sounds could have been from anything because there was a lot of wildlife out here. Animals, ranging from squirrels and mice to bobcats and you name it, were out here.

Looking at that darkness when the sounds are occurring, it would take all your emotional strength to resist succumbing to the terror within you and running away as fast as you could.

If he had been alone, that's probably what he would have done. Not a good idea, though, when you have a family to protect. And that's what he had to do now. He had to be strong for them if he was to succeed in getting them out of here alive.

"Any idea what time it is, honey?" asked Marilyn.

Ron thought for a minute. He couldn't see his watch in the dark. The numbers no longer glowed.

"I don't know. Sunset, I believe, was about forty or forty-five minutes ago. That would make it now, I say, about nine or nine-thirty. My best guess."

They kept walking side by side with each making sure the kids were following close behind. They were still there remaining quiet. Under normal circumstances they would be quite the opposite.

After about another fifteen minutes, Bobby complained that he felt a pebble in his shoe. So they stopped. Ron took his flashlight and held it down toward his son's foot while Bobby took his shoe off and let the small stone fall out. Soon they were off again.

"You alright, Suzie-Q?" Ron sometimes called his little girl that as a nickname of affection.

"Yea, I'm ok. Are we gonna get there soon?"

"Shouldn't be too much longer now, hon." Then he pulled out his cell, letting Marilyn know he was going to try to call out now. He said to keep walking.

There was a faint signal but not strong enough to connect with anyone. He hung up and told them he would try again further up. By this time, they were all frustrated at their continued inability to get help. But Ron was determined that they would see this through until they did get some help.

As they continued to walk in the dark, Ron thought he saw a faint glow of light far ahead in the distance. He wasn't sure and didn't want to say anything as yet, not wanting to get his family's hopes up. His eyes continued to stare at them. They didn't go away so he then knew they were actually there. Could they be finally reaching the beginning of this road? He told Marilyn that.

"I'm going to try the phone again," he told her. When he dialed, the signal strength was just enough to connect with a 9-1-1 operator.

"9-1-1. What is the—" then static "—ture of your—" static again "—gency and loca—" static again. *Damn it,* he said to himself.

"Hello, 9-1-1? Can you hear me?" he yelled into the phone.

"I can barely…" then more static and silence. The timing numbers on the call were still working. He was still connected but without an audible signal.

He realized what the rest of that sentence was. Hanging up to save juice, he let his wife know they still didn't have enough signal strength and encouraged everyone to keep walking. He'd try again when they got closer to the lights.

Up ahead they heard some loud rustling. The family immediately stopped in their tracks. Walking in the dark in the middle of nowhere was bad enough. Now, they were hearing loud sounds that could be threatening. They could hardly see in front of their faces. Those sounds were accompanied by soft grunting. They heard, first two higher ones, followed by a deeper one.

While Ron's heart sank, all the hairs on him stood up immediately at the same time. Whatever their sources were, the sounds were not made by wolves. Wolves howl. These didn't. And there weren't any bark-like sounds either. Small wildlife doesn't make these kinds of sounds, at least none he had ever heard of. It didn't take a rocket scientist to figure out the possibility here. He now believed they were in mortal danger.

He had considered that running into bears was possible but not too likely. They were, of course, known by everyone to be in some national parks, mostly Yellowstone and other famous ones. But here in Yosemite it didn't seem as likely. Maybe he was wrong in his assumption. But this was neither a good time nor place to have the wrong assumption.

"Did you hear that also?" Marilyn asked him.

Ron stared ahead. "Uh huh." He spoke quietly. "Good thing I brought the crowbar."

There was more rustling, this time even louder. It was at least fifty yards ahead to the right. With their eyes adjusted to somewhat ambient light on the road, Ron was the first to see the large black spot on the road with two smaller ones near it. From what he could tell, they seemed to be about seventy-five to a hundred yards ahead of them. He strongly suspected what they were but couldn't tell if they were looking at them or even sensed them right now. The surrounding darkness with the blacker figures hid their features. They were moving slowly on the road.

He turned to his family and spoke quickly and quietly. There was no way he could now keep from scaring the kids but they had to act as quietly as they could and just as quickly. He whispered as loudly as he dared.

"Ok, listen. Listen to me. We have to all get to the ground slowly. Don't ask questions. No time. Get to the ground and roll yourselves up into as tight a ball as you can with your head close to the ground. Be as quiet as you can. Do not, I repeat, do not move quickly. Put your arms over the back of your head and neck and keep them there until I tell you it's ok."

Bobby whispered while trying to stifle his sobbing. "Daddy, I just peed in my pants." Ron and Marilyn could also hear little Suzie crying, but softly. Bless her little heart for trying to hold it, thought Marilyn. He looked out into the road. The black figures were moving diagonally but in *their* direction. *Oh shit!*

"Ok, down now. Don't talk."

Seconds later, they were all on the ground in the positions Ron had told them. He was thinking he never should have brought them here. First it was the wrong turn they made, then the car got locked into a hole which happened to be a killer hornet nest. Now this. Their lives were in serious jeopardy, with their only weapon a crowbar. How much worse could it get?

He was thinking brown bears. And a mother with two cubs. That meant a much worse confrontation than with a lone bear. A mother will defend her cubs even if she only *thinks* they are threatened. There doesn't have to be an actual threat. She wouldn't be able to distinguish a real threat from a perceived one. His learning from TV had paid off. To some degree. He knew that playing dead when confronting bears often worked and the bear or bears would eventually leave the potential victims unharmed if they believed they were dead.

But what he didn't realize was that there was never a guarantee. In addition, playing dead does not work with black bears. Only brown bears or grizzlies. If you're lucky. With the blacks, you have to use a different defense. To his knowledge anyway.

What made their situation worse was that there was no way to tell which kind of bears were up ahead. The darkness hid their true colors. In effect, they were truly blind to an appropriate defense.

They all lay in balled up positions on the road with their arms in protective positions. In the distance they could hear the breathing of the creatures and an occasional grunt. At one moment there was a loud snort. Ron guessed it was mama. He was afraid to look in case she spotted his movement.

But Ron didn't realize how lucky they were. They were downwind from the creatures. And because they didn't move while the creatures stood still, they weren't heard. He waited a couple of minutes and hoped that they would cross the road and disappear back into the forest. He looked up slowly, just enough for him to determine if they were still there or not. They weren't.

After whispering to them to stay still for another couple of minutes, the family waited until Ron felt it was safe enough to get up and continue on their way.

A few minutes later they were once again on the move, getting ever closer to that front gate. Walking in the darkness on an unlit road in the middle of a huge forest, in Ron's mind, was no less than hair raising. Every little noise they heard along the way came from within the forest darkness and would be enough to set even the bravest soul on edge. Sounds from unseen sources seemed to permeate all around them. Despite occasional whimpering from the kids who stayed close behind, Ron knew he had to get them back safely. The only way to do that was for them to keep pressing ahead. They had to get out of this area.

"Are we almost there, Daddy?" It was Bobby.

"We're getting close, son. Shouldn't be too much longer," replied Ron.

"I'm getting tired," said Suzie. "We've been walking for a long time."

"Keep walking, honey, we're getting close," said Marilyn. She wasn't sure if that was true or not, but she didn't want to make things more difficult by admitting to that.

Several minutes later, Ron thought he saw lights up ahead. As they continued to walk and he continued to see them, he told the family and they started to walk faster. Soon they had indeed arrived at the fork where they had turned off to the right. Although they had reached an area of safety, they were not quite out of the woods yet. They had to make a call to someone. Because the park was now closed, Ron didn't know if he'd be able reach anyone for help getting their car.

Fortunately, their hotel was close enough to the park entrance where they could walk to it in a short amount of time. Not realizing they had been walking out there for at least an hour, they saw the lateness of the hour on the lobby clock. The front desk receptionist was still there and told Ron that he wouldn't be able to call for service to get his car until the morning. Ron thanked her and it wasn't long before they were in their beds and fell asleep more quickly than usual. For now, they were once again safe.

San Luis Obispo

Once Maria got the all-clear from Director Bingham, plans were set to send out specially equipped teams throughout the state to destroy all hornet nests. It would be a daunting task which would take a lot of time and effort. Yet it had to be done because of the danger to all lives and the communities.

There were no special chemicals necessary to destroy this kind of hornet. In fact, surprisingly, regular flying insect killers could be used. But they had to use a lot more of it because of their size and extreme aggressiveness. Unusually large amounts of it would have to be obtained or its potency increased significantly.

From all the reports she had heard on TV and received, these insects were, for certain, overly aggressive. Much more than they should have been, even for this species. From the various attacks and accounts from witnesses, Maria was not one to scare easily. She was an entomologist and a top-rated one at that. Sometimes what she believed came to match the facts, which was not always good. The hairs stood up on the back of her neck when she knew this was one of those times.

These swarms of giant hornets were predatory to *humans* as well as honeybees. That was not typical of any insect species that she knew of. Not even in Japan. There, they attacked only when provoked or threatened. In her twenty years of research and studies, she had never seen or heard of anything like this. But, time was not on their side. She had to figure it out. That would not be easy.

Something had caused or triggered the increased aggressiveness in them. She was thinking that maybe they came in contact with something unnatural or that something found *them*. Whichever the case, she put that further up her priority list of things to do.

At her lab desk, the phone rang. Maria answered and was told by the front desk receptionist that she had a priority call from the governor's office. Although she had talked with them before, this was the first time the office had called *her*. That could mean only one thing. She hoped she would at least have some answers that she knew the governor himself would want to know.

While she was told to standby for the governor, she waited a little nervously. When she had called his office previously, she had not spoken to him but to one of his assistants. This time she was about to speak with the man himself.

Finally, a loud click, then a female voice.

"Dr. Hernandez, here's Governor Capulette."

Governor Joseph P. Capulette was a first term governor who did his best to always try to stay on top of everything, especially when the government and the people might or would be affected. He had always been the typical politician but with a remarkable ability to convince anyone of almost anything. Some thought he was so good at talking that he could convince people that the sun rose in the west instead of the east.

But he was a fair, no-nonsense governor who listened to people and paid attention to constituents or higher up state employees with news that could be critical to the state. He was about to find out some of that news right now.

"Dr. Hernandez, how are you? I hope I'm not disturbing you at a critical time." For a middle aged man, Maria thought he sounded much younger.

She sat down and smoothed her hair back.

"No, governor, this is a good time for me. I'm fine, sir, thank you. And I hope you are as well."

"As well as can be expected. I'm kept pretty busy all the time as you can expect. Can be tiring, I have to say. But if you are a director, you can understand that. As a governor, multiply *your* busiest day by ten and you will know. Anyway, I don't want to take up much of your time."

"That's alright, governor. Take whatever time you need. What can I do for you?"

"Well, first off, Director Bingham referred me to you because you're the primary scientist involved in this issue and you're highly recommended anyway. I had already spoken with Miranda which is why I'm now talking to you. I'm calling about my concern, not to mention everyone else's, about this hornet thing. Can you fill me in a bit about the how, why, and what's to be done about this? First of all, how did it get into our state?"

Maria explained to him about what had happened at the docks in Los Angeles several weeks ago. She mentioned about the insects already being in the state of Washington. It was still uncertain if any of them had migrated south. What they were surer of was that at least one or two queens, possibly more, had escaped from the LA docks, but no one seemed to know how that happened or when.

She explained to him about their over-aggressiveness and information comparing these to their cousins of the same species back in Japan. She wasn't certain as to why these were different, but what she told the governor just then is what she had kept to herself for a while until she found out more. Being predatory to humans as these seemed to be was not typical or common. She considered the possibility of something causing them to mutate into something else. Something worse. But she asked the governor to be cautious about passing that information on until she was able to validate that theory. Every day she was learning something more about them. But she didn't want to start a panic.

"So, if I'm mistaken," he started to ask, "it sounds like our fair state is under siege by these insects. A lot of people have died, so far, from these things. What will it take to stop their spread and eradicate them in a timely manner?"

Maria started to explain to him what was needed and what the plan was. What needed to be done would require a significant number of people for the search, find, and eradication process. Numerous teams would need to be distributed throughout the entire state from north to south to cover all of the most likely areas of infestation. Special head-to-toe suits would be necessary for all active personnel involved, with materials thick enough to withstand the penetration of, possibly, half-inch stingers. The logistics would be enormous, not to mention the cost.

But the governor knew this might be a possibility. What had to be done was not a matter for debate with anyone. The citizens of his state were in peril. The gloves came off, in a manner of speaking, when it came to saving innocent lives. The state had to respond quickly to minimize the possibility of any more deaths.

"Ok, you've got my blessing and support, Maria," he told her. "Do whatever you need to do to get rid of these things. You have a seemingly impossible amount of territory to cover. I will authorize as many people as you need for all counties to cover for everything they will need. I will inform Director Bingham and give her my full support and official authorization to provide you with all the people, equipment, and materials you will need."

Maria was surprised at how much the governor was going all out against this thing and she breathed a sigh of relief. He was practically giving her carte blanche to take care of this crisis and assuring her that her boss was completely supportive of her as well. She would have no trouble getting what she needed.

The task she faced was daunting, with millions of lives counting on her. There were tens of thousands of square miles of territory to be searched. It would almost certainly be one of the greatest scientific hunts in the history of the US. The responsibility for getting it done weighed heavily on her. Unfortunately, more lives would likely be lost before the eradication process was completed because it would take time. For now, the planning and implementation process would have to start immediately. She called Calvin over in his office and then a meeting of all her staff. Time was not on their side.

16

Visalia, CA: One month after the invasion began
At this time, it was still unknown to anyone, including the
scientists, that there had been more than just a couple of queens
that had escaped from the original cargo. Someone had actually
covered up the truth. The effects of that coverup and the
numbers of hornets that had actually escaped were now being
felt by the general human population. It was no different here at
Kingfield's Beekeeping Farm. Not yet.

Charlie Kingfield had been a beekeeper, or apiarist, for
twenty years. He loved the work and the results it produced. He
knew that many people regarded it as easy pickings; that one
could just go in with gloves on and take the honey with no
problem.

The fact was: most people had the wrong impression.
Beekeeping is not easy work, despite what most people believe.
For one thing, it can be dangerous without proper protection.
Especially if you're allergic to bee venom. You have to be able
to control them and prevent them from escaping to areas outside
the confines of the apiary, or man-made beehive area. You have
to know what types of bees you have, among other things.

Charlie had two types of honeybees: *Apis*, or regular type
European honeybees, and *Melipona*s, or stingless bees. Although
he had no allergies to bee venom, he always wore the
appropriate headgear and suits. Whenever he checked the square
wooden columns of beehives, he always carried a smoker with
him. He used the smoke that came out of it to keep them calm
and under control. Without it, he'd be quickly covered in them.

Although he could go out without the special suit, except for
the headgear, he chose not to do that. In the event the smoker ran
out of the contained smoke, he didn't want to lose control of the
bees around the hive and have them sting his bare arms. Some
beekeepers wore only headgear, but Charlie didn't want to be
foolhardy.

His apiary was located in the far end of his huge backyard.
His house was a raised ranch in a neighborhood of widely
spaced-apart suburban homes. His wife of thirty years stayed in
the house most of the time. He loved Melba nearly more than

life itself and he knew she felt the same. Their grownup two children had left the homestead several years ago, were married and now had lives of their own in different parts of the state.

He and Melba had moved to Visalia, a town in the middle of the state north-northeast of Los Angeles, from Bakersfield. After Charlie retired from his truck driving, he chose to continue his beekeeping activities which, during his driving years, he had done as a part-time hobby-like activity. It was now full-time for him. The honey his bees produced, as well as other products, provided him with a comfortable additional income to his retirement and social security. Besides, he loved the work anyway and didn't plan on stopping anytime soon. This was a much better area for doing this than Bakersfield was. Where they lived, the homes were clustered too close together. There, he had to severely limit and more tightly contain his apiary.

"Hey Charlie, supper's almost ready. You about done out there?" Melba had to almost yell for him to hear her, especially when he had that headgear on.

Charlie checked his watch. "Oh my gosh, that time already?" he mumbled to himself. It read 4:55 pm. *Crap. Time sure flies when you're having fun,* he said to himself.

"Ok, hon. Be right there." He knew he could safely leave the bees to tend to themselves. They neither would escape nor have any reason to. It wouldn't be too long before dusk anyway. At that time, they pretty much settled in to the hives, where the queens would keep them quietly and calmly busy. If one could imagine that.

From the corner of the yard, the scout saw everything with its huge eyes. Although it didn't see things like humans did, it could certainly detect the large funny-looking creature that exuded mist. It didn't know what it was, but it did notice what it was taking care of. It felt their vibrations in the air and sensed their pheromones. It saw them flying around and heard their buzzing. It knew what they were. Here was a jackpot and it was *here* that it would lead troops to. Undetected by anyone or anything, it left the tree branch and headed back to the nest.

***

Breakfast the next morning was scrambled eggs, bacon and toast. And of course, coffee. It was 9:00am and Charlie wanted to get started outside. He didn't have to be at the hives all day but needed to check the honey shelves. Any that were full he scraped the honey off into a special container. But only after he smoked the bees first. This routine he did every three or four days per shelf. He had to keep track of which shelf to check on particular days.

Already the sun had been up for a couple of hours. Another sunny August day. "How's the sausage? Done ok?" asked Ellie. For some reason, she always asked him that. She had always made it the same way as she did everything else. After a while, he just accepted her redundant question and said as always, "It's just fine, honey."

The older couple, for the most part, led a quiet life. Their marriage was one filled with ups and downs as in most marriages, but with pervasive success at keeping it unified and loving. Even with occasional problems that kept coming up, they always worked well together to solve them.

Their two boys, Tom and Steven, were now successful men in their own right. Tom was the younger one who after college became a financial analysist and was doing well in his career. His marriage of three years was a happy one so far and resulted in the birth of their first child-a daughter whom they named Tara.

Steven was still single, four years older than his brother, but had a girlfriend who he seemed to care a great deal about. He was training to be a plumber. Although not college trained, his technical training would eventually land him a very good, high paying job in a profession that was more blue-collar, yet still professional.

Both Charlie and Melba were sad to see them leave the nest, but yet happy at the same time that they were ready to take on the world themselves and become successful. It made them feel they raised them right and they felt good about that.

Now with a new post-retirement career, Charlie could enjoy work at home and still make some money. He believed he could not have it better and was grateful for the way his life had turned out.

Giving his mouth a final swipe with the napkin, he got up and brought his plate to the sink, finishing off his cup of coffee at the same time.

"Good breakfast as always, sweetheart," he told his wife. "Better get out there and check on our friends."

"Ok. Be careful out there."

That was another habit of Melba's, always telling him to be careful out there. As if he didn't know it. But that was alright with him. It just told him she cared.

"Sure will. If there's enough, I'll replenish our near empty jar of honey."

Whenever they got low on their household jar of honey, he would just refill it, as long as it didn't dig too much into the profits. He had to be careful about that. It was too easy to go down that road. If it became a habit, then control of his business would be lost or damaged. He wanted to maintain the required stability to keep it going.

After donning his suit, he went outside and walked toward the apiary area. The hives were on their stands in a closed-gate area at the far end of the huge yard, almost a hundred yards from the house. He needn't worry about any of them escaping because the bees were always too busy doing what bees normally do. Even though they would leave the hives to collect pollen, their hives were their homes and where they made the honey. So their return was always guaranteed.

Charlie kept looking at the area as he walked toward it. For some reason, he sensed something was a little off but couldn't put his finger on it. The hives, even from seventy-five yards away looked a bit ghostly. He didn't hear any buzzing as yet and was still a little too far to see any of them. It was just a strange sense that he had.

Without realizing it, he picked up his pace. Within the headgear, he wasn't aware that his breathing had increased a bit. It was getting awfully warm inside of it. He stopped briefly to take it off to give himself a bit of a break. He would need to put it back on when he got to the bee gate, as he called it. Sweat ran down his face from his brow and he did his best to wipe some of it off with his suited arm.

With headgear in arm, he continued his approach to the gate, his eyes and ears focused on the hives. The three stands slowly became visually larger and revealed nothing to him, neither visually nor audibly. At the gate he stood absolutely still, stared at them and listened. He felt the hairs on the back of his neck stand up. Something was wrong.

Putting his headgear back on, he opened the gate slowly in case he was misinterpreting what he was seeing or not seeing. All three stands of the hives were ghostly and silent. He stared at them, seeing no sign of the bees. What the hell?

As he stepped to the first stand, he felt the sounds of crunching under his docker shoes. He had never heard that before. Not here. He looked down and saw the pile of dead bees. His jaw dropped. *Oh my Lord!*

He stepped back and looked down at the bee corpses. Hundreds of them. His eyes scanned to the right and immediately homed in on the other two piles of bee corpses. For some reason he looked up and around the area, as if he would see the cause of all this. He saw nothing.

Walking quickly to the first hive, he opened up the shelves starting at the top. There were four shelves of honeycombs in each shelf of the three stands. There was no need for him to grab the smoker which he kept on the table beside the hives. He saw hundreds more bee corpses on the shelves, some shelves with more, others with less. He knew he had far more bees than these. In his mind, many might have escaped from whatever killed their hive mates.

He had no clue what that was and didn't know if those missing were still alive. Whatever had happened, it had destroyed his business.

After carefully examining the entire area, he removed his headgear. There was not one bee in the entire area. For now, there would be no more honey in the near future. Before animals got to whatever honey was there, he would need to remove it. Even without looking he knew there wouldn't be enough to sell, so he would keep it for themselves. But his investigation would not end until he found out what killed his business as well as his bees.

After removing his suit, he went to the nearby shed and pulled out clean-up tools, unaware of the danger and tragedy that was about to befall him.

He returned with a special vacuum. The shed had been wired with a working outlet that he had plugged the vacuum into. Keeping the gloves on, he also carried a shovel in the other hand.

Back at the hives, he turned on the vacuum and started sucking up the dead bodies. Then he noticed something. Bending over, he looked closely at some of the bodies and saw something strange that he had overlooked before. Most of the bee bodies were missing their heads!

Carefully picking one body up, he was stunned to find that the head had been removed with surgical-like precision. How could this be? What on planet earth could do such a thing in this way to bees? And the next question was, why? After looking again at other bodies, it appeared the same was done to them as well.

Charlie didn't know what to do at this point. For now, cleaning up the bee bodies seemed pointless. What he had to do was collect the honey that was left, then worry about the clean-up later. He had discovered something strange and ominous. Although he was a bee expert, he was *not* when it came to things that killed bees. Especially this way. One thing he was sure of: It was no disease that killed his workers.

***

The leader was slightly bigger than the rest. It was roughly three and three quarter inches long. Like most of the rest of the animal world, size did matter. Only the queen ranked above it. The hundreds of its followers waited patiently for it to make its move. Once it did, all would be close behind.

It was on a tree branch and the others were perched on nearby ones. As its large black multifaceted eyes focused on the upright creature a few yards ahead, it was waiting for the right moment. Earlier they had done what they were meant to do and killed off all the honeybees. Their young were now feeding voraciously on the bees that had been returned to the large nest deeper into the woods.

The upright creature bent over, then stood up straight again. He wasn't moving away. But it wouldn't have mattered anyway. Without warning, the leader took off, followed quickly by all those behind him.

The buzzing was loud and the creature ahead moved suddenly in response.

The swarm nearly filled the sky with blackness. It caught Charlie off-guard and left him with very little response time. He never saw them coming. In seconds they quickly descended and covered his unprotected face and body. Unfortunately for

Charlie, no one could hear his blood-curdling screams because he had forgotten to turn off the vacuum machine. His face was pierced hundreds of times with highly potent venom, their large stingers piercing his skin and flesh nearly to the bone. His heart rate quickly accelerated along with his breathing.

Once the venom reached his bloodstream, it coursed through his body rapidly and began its catastrophic damage to his organ systems, starting at the cellular level. Underneath the giant hornet covering on his face and the rest of his body, the tissues swelled almost instantly and his skin was turning a deep, purplish red. As his mouth opened to scream, hornets entered it and starting viciously stinging the inside of it as well as his tongue. One went down his throat causing him to violently choke. Charlie could no longer scream or make any sounds.

Even his eyes were stung and were now bulging out. His breathing soon ceased as Charlie collapsed to the ground. His heart stopped and a few seconds later he was physically, then clinically brain dead. Just one or two stings might have killed him. He received hundreds. The only cure to his painful, agonizing suffering was death. The only sound heard was that of the vacuum machine.

***

San Luis Obispo, the next day

After talking to Calvin and delegating him to the most urgent tasks he needed to take care of regarding the entire northern half of the state, Maria continued with her phone calls to all the various regional substation offices and labs within the boundaries of southern California. She basically had to do the same thing Cal had to do plus some.

With the green light given by the governor, she was able to obtain all the lab and scientific personnel she needed to combat the crisis within the entire state.

"John," she told someone on the phone, "teams of ten are assigned to search and destroy. Use the daylight hours to your advantage. I am going to fax you a map showing reported areas of infestation and where attacks have been and are still happening."

John Welford was the entomologist assigned to the Escondido substation, in an area where he and his family lived.

He, as well as the other stations, were each assigned a team of ten people, most which were experts in either entomology or a related field. All had experience in some form of pest control and knew how to search for and destroy various kinds of nests.

All field personnel who would be involved in the hunt were provided with the thick, impenetrable suits that were used in confrontations with the giant hornets. These included thick headgear that had thick, clear plastic areas to see through. Per federal and state regulations, these suits had to be thoroughly evaluated, tested, and certified for official use once all the necessary tests were passed. These were the only suits that would protect against this subspecies of vespa. Anyone without this kind of suit would be banned from the hunt.

Once John got his instructions and received the fax from Maria, he began to get the team together. All the other leaders at the other substations were doing the same. Each of the team leaders had to make sure that they had all the chemicals they needed plus some to combat and destroy all the nests. The chemicals were strengthened prior to their being shipped to them. This would be an all-out war and it would not end until all nests were destroyed.

It was quite a daunting task and would take a significant amount of time because the area of focus was the entire state. Each of the substation teams would cover their particular areas which would border other team areas. In effect, each area of every county would be covered by all the teams. The cost to the state would be in the millions of dollars, but that would pale when compared to the cost of all the lives that would be lost if this was not done. No expense was to be spared nor the life of one giant hornet. Without fanfare, the war had now begun.

17

By the time teams had been assembled and readied for the hunt and all the equipment and materials had been obtained, there had been hundreds of other reports of attacks throughout the state. Emergency departments everywhere were getting inundated with hornet sting cases. Some people were lucky enough to survive after intense treatment, while many others weren't so lucky. It seemed they were out to destroy humans.

But it wasn't just humans. Domestic animals, including livestock, were also being attacked, many having died as a result of stinging overkill. Dairy farmers were finding dead cattle in their pastures. The economy of the state was being seriously damaged. Beekeepers everywhere were being either threatened or already had their hives attacked and destroyed. This caused the honey business to rapidly decline. Honeybees everywhere were being killed off while the hornets were thriving and growing in numbers. Nests were now appearing where they'd never been before. Even the stock market was seriously affected.

While the teams began to disperse, Maria consulted with Calvin about the pervasive thought that kept gnawing at her. She had consulted with vespa experts in both Japan and the US regarding the behavior of these insects. Based on what they had told her regarding their normal behavior and what she'd told them regarding their current behavior, it was clear to everyone concerned that the behavior of these had somehow mutated to one which was far more dangerous to all mammals, as well as the general bee population.

She went to Calvin's office. "Got a few minutes? Ooo, sorry."

He was on the phone and put up a finger. She sat down on a nearby chair. Any phone calls now during this crisis would likely be related to what was going on. She didn't want to interrupt.

After a few minutes, he hung up and looked at her. His expression revealed he'd just received some news and it was not good.

"I just took a call from the Visalia Police. They responded to a 9-1-1 call from a woman, somewhat hysterical, that she had found her husband dead at his beekeeping area."

Maria sat forward as it immediately caught her attention. She knew there was more coming and knew that wasn't all. A question flashed in her mind: if hornets were involved, were they attracted primarily to the bees or to the victim? Or both?

"Apparently," he continued, "the death didn't seem natural to her. It took her a while to calm down enough to talk to police and the ambulance people. Even then, the horror of what she had seen of her husband was enough to make even the most hardened first responders cringe."

Maria got impatient. "Cal, please tell me what she saw." She could feel her tension suddenly rise without knowing her hands had formed fists at the same time. That was her way of showing tension, and not a reveal she could easily control.

Calvin looked down with a serious frown, took a deep breath and began. "He was found on the ground in front of his hives. There were three of them. He was not wearing a suit or headguard. But there were no bees. Not one flying around. She didn't look in the hives. But being a beekeeper's wife for so many years, she also knew that it wasn't his precious bees that killed him."

"How did she know it wasn't the bees?" asked Maria.

"Well, because she knew he didn't have to wear a suit. Even without a suit they wouldn't have attacked him."

"Really? Why's that?"

"From what she said, her husband always wore gloves and used a smoker when he went to the hives for whatever reason. The smoke kept them calm and at bay. Most of the time he was out there to check for honey. When she found him, the vacuum cleaner was out there and running."

"Vacuum cleaner?" Maria was surprised. "What in the world did he have *that* out there for?"

"Don't know," Cal replied. "All she said was it was out there and running. Apparently he'd been using it for something. The woman didn't know what. She rarely ever went out there 'cause she didn't particularly care for bees. But she didn't mind that being his business as long as she didn't have to participate. And it was far enough from the house that she didn't have to worry about them getting in."

"Ok," Maria said. "What *about* her hubby? What did she see?"

Calvin went on to describe her husband. The swollen purplish face, the bulging eyes, the open mouth and a tongue so swollen it could no longer fit in his mouth. In effect, his face had a postmortem rictus to it. In fact, most of the rest of his body had a swollen look also, even under some of the clothing. Charlie had died a horrific, agonizing death. He looked like a body in severe decomposition, yet had been dead for maybe an hour, but she wasn't sure at the time. Sounded familiar to her based on other deaths she had found out about.

Silence filled the room as Maria was still processing and taking this all in. They looked at each other as if they were thinking the same thing.

"So," she started to say after a minute or two, "it was them again. It had to be them. They found the bees and killed them all. Sometime after that is when they killed, what was his name?"

"Charlie," he replied.

"Ok. So there must be a nest in that area. Charlie wouldn't have known about that."

Cal looked at her, somewhat perplexed. "Wait a minute. How do you figure they killed him after the bees? Why not before?"

"Remember the vacuum? Why else would he have had something like that out there?"

"Oh yeah, that's right. Ok, got it. Forgot about that. Well, now you know where to send one of the teams."

"Cal, let me see your walkie talkie." They always had walkie talkies to communicate with people out in the field. They weren't used all the time, but this was one of those times she needed them.

Contacting her team closest to Visalia, she advised them of the situation there, the location of the victim's house, and to get there asap and start their search with a maximum radius of half a mile in all directions.

"Something isn't right here. Something has mutated these hornets. I know it. What I need to know is, *what*?"

"Perhaps the question should first be, what could mutate something?" Calvin asked in reply. "What, when, and how? If we think of cancer cells as a form of mutated cells…"

"Chemicals!" Maria exclaimed. She looked at him as if she'd just made an important first discovery. In a way, she had.

"Chemicals," she repeated. "We have to look up where the first attack was reported. Maybe around the San Diego area? Or around here? We have to find out, because that's the area where we may find the answer. Cal, do me a favor. Find out where there are chemical plants."

"Wasn't the first reported attack on that Billy Jansen boy near San Diego?"

She considered all the reports of attacks they had received so far. That one stood out because she remembered visiting him and his mother.

"Yep. He's the first one that was reported. See if you can find out if there are any chemical plants in that area. I'll check around the LA area for the same. There shouldn't be many of them. Then I'll take a look at it and see what we can do from there. We have to find out the source of the mutations."

"Are you going to inform the powers that be?" he asked her.

"Not yet. This is just a hunch. We have to find out for sure before passing this information on. The last thing we need right now is to cause an unnecessary jumping to conclusions. But we have to work quickly on this."

Leaving the walkie talkie, Maria returned to her office to start researching the new issue and concern. Her mind was going a mile a second as she tried to think of where the chemical in question was. It was possible the hornets, even newly hatched, somehow had access to it. Maybe it was passed on to them. Even when or if the source was found, what could be done about it? She decided to pull back a little and not get too far ahead of herself. Yet, it was difficult to do that considering millions of lives were at stake.

Despite that, she realized she had better stay organized. On her laptop, she went to her reports section and found those from two months ago when it all started. Then she checked the internet for all the chemical plants in California north of San Diego and their locations. It was just the beginning for her.

She examined every report from every area starting with those of Billy Jansen in Lemon Grove. Finding none just south of LA, she went back to the previous screen. Deciding to first comprise a list of all the cases she knew about so far and their locations, she went to work on that.

Fifteen minutes later, she had her list. She called Cal and asked if he had gotten a list. He had and was about to call her. The first known case was reported in Lemon Grove. He gave her that case name, then followed it with three others from locations further south and southeast.

"Cal, let me know the names of the chemical plants in that area when you find out. Stockton is the furthest north of reported attacks. I'll check for any near those other two you mentioned. Soon as you find out, let me know."

"Gotcha. Ok, I'm on it."

Maria then got to work on those other two. Not surprisingly, there were no plants in most search areas. Plants like that tended to be in locations not close to populated areas because of the dangers associated with them. About ten minutes later the phone rang. It was Cal.

"First of all, what I found out is that there was a chemical plant that was about fifty miles northeast of San Diego. It closed down about ten years ago due to multiple federal and state violations. There had been leaks which had been contained but not before some of it was absorbed into the ground. Now I don't know how that would have anything to do with what's going on with these things 'cause the contamination was already absorbed by the ground. But it's all woodsy area. The building is abandoned and still standing."

Then he told her his discovery by chance about a plant in the Magnolia section of Stockton called Stanton Chemical Company. But he went a step further and called them to find out what kinds of chemicals they made.

"Agricultural and industrial," he told Maria. "When I asked, they told me there had been no reports of any leaks and whatever waste they had would be dumped a distance away in a location far from urban and farm sites."

He also told her that when he tried to dig a little deeper by asking where the location was, he was stonewalled.

"*We're not at liberty to say, sir. That information is confidential. Are you from the USDA or DEP?*"

"*No ma'am. I'm from the state Department of Fish and Wildlife, entomology section. Just trying to solve a statewide insect problem.*"

Cal said there had been momentary silence on the other end. Then, "*Just a moment, sir.*"

"She put me on hold again," Cal continued. "I wasn't sure what was going on. I waited a couple of minutes, wondering if she was going to get a supervisor. Turns out, she did. He then came on the line."

"Sir, this is Bob Ferguson. I'm the shift supervisor here at Stanton. You said you are from the State Wildlife Department?"

"That's right. My name is Doctor Calvin Kablinsky. Entomology."

Cal knew that if he played his cards right with this guy, he might be able to obtain the information to help them. But that could be a big "might". He decided to explain his call.

It took a few minutes to convince the supervisor that the state wasn't out to "get the company" for some sort of illegal dumping of chemical wastes or anything else pertaining to company protocols. All his department wanted to know was if there was a possible connection between the hornet mutations, which he had mentioned to Mr. Ferguson, and any kind of chemicals the insects may have inadvertently come in contact with. He had to ask him if there were any current or past leaks that he knew about which insects or other things may have come in contact with. He was careful not to be too specific.

Ferguson was finally willing to talk, but with a minor catch. Because the information was not for the public to know, he needed absolute assurance that he was talking to a person he could trust. He requested his official state phone number that he could call right back before he gave the information. Calvin readily agreed and gave it to him. A minute after they hung up, the call came and the information Cal requested followed with an additional bit of information that surprised and concerned him.

"So," Maria started to say," he admitted to us of a small leakage years ago that they took care of and contained as soon as they discovered it. And that there have been no further reports of leakages. Did he say what the chemical was that leaked?"

Cal looked down at his notes. "Well, I couldn't get the first word. It was long and not something I could even pronounce. The second word was 'disulfanate'. He also mentioned that they dump their wastes in a secure burial location fifty miles away from any areas of civilization. It's quite a remote area that no one goes out to and they bury the wastes quite deep in secure leak-proof containers that are impervious to breakdown over time."

Maria was thinking fast. There could be a connection only if traces of the element that leaked were exposed enough for insects or anything else to come in contact with. The waste location was no longer an issue.

"Ok," she replied. "Going back to my office. Got something to do but I'll be back. In the meantime, see if you can get a hold of one of the teams closest to that plant and have them go there. They need to check outside the perimeter fence where that leak might have gotten away somehow. Have them check for drainage ditches, culverts, streams of water, whatever. Have a second team check for nests, starting near the plant and working away from it in the wooded areas. Should be on the same side of the plant as where the leak might have gone. See what they can find."

"Ok, Maria. On it now." Cal picked up the walkie-talkie.

The head scientist went back to her office and checked for plants

just south or east of LA and surrounding areas. She found one and called them up. After identifying herself and the reason she called, they were able to tell her that they had never had any leakages. Although they had some waste products, they would store a certain amount there in highly secure areas in leak-proof and rot-proof containers. When enough was accumulated, they would transport them in special container trucks to a remote area seventy five miles away for deep burial. Its location, as with the other plant, was highly secretive and its whereabouts given out only on a highly need to know basis to appropriate, authorized persons.

Although the plant appeared to have a clean record regarding leak occurrences and waste storage, Maria couldn't be too careful. She had to check it out. Picking up her walkie-talkie, she contacted the teams closest to Garden Grove, a city southeast of LA, where the plant was located. She instructed them to go there to check around the outside perimeter and again as with the other team up north, check around for any way leaks could be dispersed into the community as well as check for any vespa nests in the area.

Going to the large wall map of California, she found some pin markers with different colors. Taking her combined list of attack areas of Cal's and hers, she stuck these pin markers in the map in those areas. Red was for reported attacks, black was for reported deaths, and yellow for suspected or likely areas for attacks.

In the meantime, she knew her teams were well underway in their searches. It would take a significant amount of time for these searches because of the incredible number of areas to cover. Because they had to be conducted on foot, there was no quick way to do it. They did have special equipment to use to help them in their search, as well as the chemical weapons to subdue and kill the hornets on first contact. Although the chemicals used were basically the same as killing regular wasps or hornets, the mixture was three times the potency per half liter. Better to be too strong than not strong enough.

When a team discovered the nest, they were advised to wait until dusk or dark to attack. Most daytime flying insects stay close to or in their nests at night. Vespa hornets were expected to be no different in that respect.

It had been two hours now since the teams were sent out and midafternoon had arrived. No one nest had been reported yet. Not surprisingly and considering the areas to be searched, hundreds of team workers authorized by the governor had been assigned to the tasks at hand. There were one hundred teams, with three people per team, to cover the entire state. Sounding like a lot doesn't mean it is. California is a very big state. In actuality, it might not have been enough. For now, she had to be selective in where they would conduct their searches. She was their shot caller and had to be as accurate as she could, even under the stressful circumstances.

She wanted to do some research on any chemicals that could cause mutations in living organisms. Having studied at UCLA, she remembered a chemistry professor she once had and decided to reach out to him. No time like the present, she told herself, and picked up the phone

***

Just outside the Sacramento city limits, the team made their way through the trees and underbrush. They had received reports of a nest possibly in this area. Despite being late afternoon, they needed to check it out. With their tanks of highly toxic chemicals ready for immediate use on confrontation with the insects, they slowly searched in the most likely areas, both at the bottoms of trees, in suspicious holes in tree trunks, and even up on low lying branches.

"Hey, over here!" The searcher named Joe yelled out to the other members. He had spotted something. The others came to him as Joe pointed down to the ground.

There was a large black hole near the bottom of a tree. Almost as if it were second nature, the searchers automatically checked their sting-proof suits to ensure they were completely sealed. Although they didn't see anything go in or come out of the hole, the ominous-looking hole could actually be a nest. Staying as still and silent as they could, they listened for any sounds of buzzing. There were none. One of the searchers pulled out a flashlight.

"We need to be sure. Let me check it out better." The man got on his knees. He checked his headgear to make sure it was clipped well to his suit so it wouldn't fall off. The others also checked it and reassured him it was on him securely.

He turned the flashlight on and bent over to look inside it. He thought he saw something in the back but couldn't be sure because it turned slightly to the side where the light couldn't reach. Slowly and methodically, he checked every area inside. If this was a nest, he should find something.

As he panned the light across the inside, he thought he saw movement on the other side, on the edge of the darkness.

"See anything, Joe?" asked one of his colleagues.

"Uh, I thought I saw something in here. Still don't hear any buzzing."

Movement again. Just a visual flutter of something. He didn't know what it was, but he did know that there was in fact something inside of it. He informed the others there was something there and they needed to find out what it was. Was it a squirrel, a mouse? Or something else?

"Hey, somebody hand me the pole with that ball thing on the end of it. I need to see if I can draw it out where I can see it."

One of the others removed a stick-like implement. It wasn't one of their official tools, but rather a pole someone had made with a round object on the end of it for use in certain situations when moving something light was too dangerous for direct hand manipulation.

Joe took the pole and carefully, with his thickly gloved hands, stuck it inside to see if he could lure out whatever was in there. Then he heard a loud buzz. *"Oh, shit!"* he mumbled to himself. In a flash he saw it land on the orb at the end of the stick. Shining his flashlight directly on it, his jaw dropped as the largest hornet, the largest *insect* he'd ever seen, turned directly at him. It had the largest, blackest eyes which looked like eyes of evil.

He backed out quickly, and with lightning speed the hornet slammed against the plastic goggles of his headgear. It nearly covered the entire area and he screamed in terror. He saw the large stinger try to penetrate the transparent eye area and its huge mandibles opening and shutting in quick movements of fury. As it moved around, the yellow and black body stripes and its huge body signified its genus and species. He believed that had this thing been large enough, it would have quickly torn him apart, even with protective gear on.

The others quickly doused him with the chemical spray and it fell off of him, still buzzing and convulsing fiercely on the ground as it struggled to rid itself of the toxin and stay alive. Within a minute, it lay still.

One of the suited members grabbed a large, glass container from a pack they had been carrying and removed the lid. With a special tweezer-like implement, the member picked up the hornet by the wing and dropped it into the jar, quickly closing it up as if they were afraid it would come back to life. When the jar was lifted up, they all took a close look at it in shock and fascination. It nearly filled the jar.

They had been prepared verbally for a possible sighting of giant hornets. But actually confronting one, especially one of gargantuan proportions, was a reality shock. It was downright scary looking. It looked every bit as deadly as they had proved themselves to be. "Ok," said Joe, who was the team leader. "Now that we have got it, we have to get it to the lab. Asap."

"You didn't see any more in there?" asked a member.

"No, that was it. There was nothing else in there that I could see or detect."

"I think there is still one thing we have to consider," said someone else.

"Yea," said Joe. "I think I know what you're thinking. Where are the others?"

All of them being in the science field of entomology or related fields knew that finding only one hornet there and disposing of it was not the end of the story. In fact, it was only the beginning. They were in trouble. Despite their suits, they needed to get out of there fast.

Before they left, they sprayed a significant amount of chemical toxin into the hole. This nest was gone. The rest of its inhabitants would soon discover that. Unfortunately, no one knew how many others there could be. However many there might be, hundreds or even thousands, all of them had to be found and destroyed. Like a cancer cell, all it took was one nest to survive and the cancer would spread once again to incur another deadly rampage.

"C'mon. It's getting dark. Too late for more searching. Let's get out of here." Soon the area was deserted once again. Until the death swarm returned.

18

Yosemite National Park

The day after their accident, after making a couple of phone calls, the Sondheims had their car towed back to their hotel cabin. There had been no serious damage to the car itself. The only thing that needed repair was a relatively minor front end alignment and a replacement for the back tire.

The report about the hole where their tire got caught in would not have caught anyone's attention, except for the hornet attack. That caught not only the park staff's attention, but the state as well. As soon as word got to Maria Hernandez, she wasted no time in directing a team there to investigate.

So far there had been no other reports of hornet activity there. But that didn't mean there wasn't any. It was a tremendously huge park covering nearly 1,200 square mile of pure wilderness. So she knew that it was more than likely there would be other holes or potential nests that could be "hornet heavens".

Two days later, a team arrived. Park officials directed them to the site where the Sondheims had gotten stuck and then attacked, as the family continued their week adventure in other areas far from where they had initially been.

When they found the hole, they wasted no time in looking. Instead, they took the chemical cannister and sprayed the toxin into the hole until they were sure it was saturated. Based on what had happened to a team near Sacramento three days earlier, they were determined not to take any chances. Although there was no buzzing to be heard, it didn't really matter. That didn't guarantee that it was not an active nest.

Based on the spread of them and the increase in the number of nests, they knew it was more than likely that there were plenty of others in the park. For now, they had killed this one.

About fifty yards down the road, the black cloud remained hidden within the shadows of a tree. The close-knit swarm could neither be seen nor heard by the team members. One of the team members had an eerie feeling of being watched and looked around as if to reassure himself that there was no one around except them.

Bears almost always steered clear of humans. If one had been around, he wouldn't have stuck around and would quickly disappear into the woods. A pack of wolves, seen less around here than bears, would have also done the same. But this was something else.

"You ok, Jack?" asked one of the other members after he noticed his teammate look around for a minute or so. "See something?"

Jack turned around and looked at him. "Uh, no. No, nothing. I'm ok. Just had a strange feeling of having eyes on us. Didn't see anything."

Then something came over the radio. "Y-team, this is base, over."

Base, code name for Maria's office, was calling them. Jane, the team leader picked it up.

"Got a report of a possible nest in zone twelve over there. Can you go check it out asap?"

"Roger, base. Just eliminated a nest over in nine. Any specifics for exact location?"

Zone 12 covered an area not far from where they were now. That area included El Capitan, the famous high rock that only the most experienced and daring mountain climbers ever challenged.

"From what we were told, it was spotted at ..." She then gave the exact geographic coordinates, which would home them in close to the exact spot.

"Ok, on our way." The team gathered up their equipment and cannisters and packed their vehicles. El Capitan was just a couple of miles away deeper into the park. The road they were on now led down to the river below so they would have to turn around and head back to the fork. They would then take a sharp right and take the road that the Sondheims would have needed to take to get further into the tourist area of the park.

None of the team members had seen the hidden black cloud as they drove past the tree it was hovering over. The leader and its followers had seen what the creatures had done to their nest. They would remember.

***

Back at her office, it was the end of the work day. Although Maria wanted to continue working on the ongoing problem, she was exhausted and decided she better get home and eat and get some rest. Tomorrow would be a full day and she needed to be ready for that. Her teams were all at work and would report any significant findings to her on her work cell.

After saying goodnight to Calvin who himself was getting ready to leave, she was soon in the car on her way home. At the house twenty-five minutes later, she met her husband Earl. He had come home a little early today.

She noted that to him.

"Well," he said. "Things took a little turn for the better. I made the sale on that huge house I told you about the other day. A nice commission, I have to say."

Earl was her husband of fifteen years and turned out to be quite a successful real estate agent. This was the twenty-fifth house he had sold within the past eleven months and it was the biggest. She was proud of him and told him so. They had no children because of her history of having had a hysterectomy. Although they had been thinking of adoption, they had to put that on temporary hold because of the current situation in the state and her major involvement.

"That's so wonderful," she said, with more energy than she thought she had. "Congratulations!" She went up to him and gave him a big hug and kiss.

"Why don't we celebrate tonight? Go out to dinner maybe. My treat." She was excited for him.

He looked at her in a demure way. "Hmm. I don't know about that, sweet pea. I don't know if you can afford that. Especially with your six-figure salary. We better be very frugal." He smirked, trying to keep from smiling which would lead to laughing. Once he got started with his joking, he tended to have difficulty stopping.

Her reaction was to smirk right back at him, but she was unable to hold back a smile. "Know what? You're a funny guy. In fact, you're so funny you oughta be on TV."

That's when he laughed. "No kidding, seriously? Well I'm afraid, my young bug chickadee, that I can't ever do that. And you know WHY?"

Her smile grew bigger and she began to merge it with a laugh. She had a feeling she knew what was coming. "No, I have no idea. Why?" At times they loved joking into each other's faces.

"Because our TV is a flat screen, that's why!"

She decided to play along. The punch line was coming soon.

She took a step back and looked down at his shoes. "But you don'thave flat feet." He laughed. She knew what the line was and she gave it to him before he could say it.

"Because," she said, "you can't stand on top of the TV. Hardy Har Har! Ha ha, I beat you to it." It was corny as hell but they loved corny.

They were like a couple of kids for a few moments enjoying a little levity after a long hard day on the job. For both of them.

"I guess you did," he acknowledged. "Ok. Let's leave in an hour. Tanglewood Restaurant?"

After agreeing, she headed upstairs to the bathroom and then to freshen up a bit, while he loosened his tie and grabbed a small liquor. Sitting down on the lounge chair tended to put him to sleep if he put the footrest up, so he made sure to keep it down.

The sound of her voice startled him and he nearly jumped in his sleep.

"Sweetheart, are you sleeping?"

"Uh, I uh... Guess so. Must have dozed off."

"You want to raincheck this dinner for another night? I can come up with something here.'

He sat up quickly. "No, no, no! I'm ok. Really. It's just that this chair is too damn comfortable. Every time I sit in it I get sleepy."

She looked at him, tilting her head. "Well then, what does that tell you?"

He got up. "Ok. Well I'm fine and totally awake. Anyway, time to see a man about a horse. We leave in fifty minutes, or thereabouts."

While he was in the bathroom, she went back downstairs. The phone rang. She yelled out, "I'll get it" as if he could hear it in the bathroom. She doubted that but it was automatic on her part.

"Hello?"

"Maria?"

"Yes?"

"Maria Hernandez?"

"Yes! Who is this?"

"Sorry to bother you, Doctor Hernandez. This is Jerry Bernstein from the State Department of Fish and Wildlife."

"Commissioner Bernstein?" She had no idea why he would be calling her, unless there was a serious enough problem to challenge his department. She found out that it was.

"Yes, that's me. Again, I apologize very much for calling you at home but I wouldn't ever do this unless the problem warranted it. It's something you need to know. I've already talked with Dr. Bingham and she suggested I call you since you're in charge of the vespa operation. He gave me your number."

Maria was about to be informed of yet another vespa problem.

"This concerns a number of incidents in Yosemite." He then went on to explain what occurred with the Sondheim family and how they managed to get out of their predicament.

"Yes, Commissioner, I had heard about that. They were really lucky considering what they went through."

"They turned out ok, thank God," Bernstein said. "But on their walk back, they claimed to have heard loud buzzing noises coming from seemingly everywhere around them. Even on their dangerous walk back to safety at night, they heard buzzing. The father claimed the noises seemed to surround them. It made their walk every bit more terrifying than it already was. Not to mention running into a mother bear and her cubs in the dark."

"What? Are you serious? *That* I hadn't heard about."

"Mm hmm. That's what was reported. We had to take this seriously because of what's going on all over the state. But it sounds like we may have a serious hornet problem in the park. All over, in fact. There were additional run-ins. Some tourists who were outside their vehicles were attacked suddenly by giant hornets that seemed to come out of nowhere. Fortunately, most were able to get back in their vehicles. Others were in the vehicles and these things attacked the car. Good grief! I never heard of such a thing. Two people got stung and had to be taken to the nearest clinic for treatment. But there is a late report of a large nest in the area of El Capitan."

Maria was taking this all in while trying to formulate some kind of plan for what she was going to do. Considering the time it was now, there was no way she could do anything until tomorrow.

"Commissioner…"

"Jerry, please."

Maria briefly smiled. "Ok. Jerry, I will work on this for a plan first thing in the morning. I'm glad you called me because now that Yosemite is infested, and God knows how many other parks might be also, I'm going to need your full support and possibly the help of some of your officers or park rangers."

"You got it. Want to call me when you come up with a plan?" he asked.

"Yes, please. Time is not on our side so I will get back to you as soon as I can. Any idea how many officers you have patrolling the park? And are rangers under your jurisdiction?"

"Not sure, to your first question. I can find out and let you know. As to your second question, no. Rangers come under the Department of Parks and Recreation. But I'm frequently in contact with their director. Her name is Julie Lambert. Want her home number?"

"Sure," she replied. After taking down her number, she needed to tell him one more thing.

"Jerry, this may sound crazy to you but what I'm going to tell you has been corroborated and confirmed. This is not for public dissemination. Only for those on a need to know basis. You're one of them."

"Ok," he replied.

"These vespas, these giant hornets, I'm almost one hundred percent certain, are mutants. Something they have run into has changed their normal nature, both physically and behaviorally. They are significantly larger than normal. If they were normal-sized for their species, they would be naturally aggressive and more so than regular hornets. Their prey would have been only honeybees. But these…these we have here are far more aggressive than their normal-sized cousins. In fact, their increased aggression has turned them more predatory. Their prey includes more than just bees."

Maria took a breath. The silence on the other end of the phone revealed Bernstein's response at the shocking news. She knew this information would be difficult for anyone to swallow.

"Predatory?" he finally replied. "As in intentionally going after things?"

"Oh, they are already predatory, including their normal-sized cousins. They hunt down and destroy all honeybees and their hives. They bring the dead back to their young to feed them. When I said they are increasingly predatory, I mean, as I said; they are going after more than just honeybees. They are going after animals of all kinds. And us. Intentionally."

"But why, for God's sake? Have you known any other insects to do that?" Bernstein was actually now more concerned than he let on.

"Well, in fact there are others who go after us and animals. Remember flies and mosquitoes? Gnats?"

"Ok. You're right," he responded. "But at least they don't kill like these things can. Except for maybe mosquitoes."

"The thing is, Jerry, these hornets are highly intelligent. That makes them more dangerous to every living creature around them. Tomorrow I will try to get back to you late in the day. I strongly recommend that your officers, if they go into any state park, not get out of their vehicles unless they absolutely have to. They should have special suits to wear with special headgear if they have to. That might be a little difficult to accomplish in a short time."

She then explained to him why normal beekeeper suites wouldn't work, unless they wore thick clothing underneath. All park tourists needed to be advised not to get out of their vehicles. They should have their windows closed while driving through. Although it might be good advice, it sounded far too impractical for anyone to heed. It was human nature to want to get out and enjoy the fine offerings of mother nature. How many people would comply? But she had to advise it anyway. She knew that Bernstein would find the Parks and Recreation Department pretty upset about the whole business. Something like this could seriously damage tourism. But even more so with park deaths occurring. It was a difficult sell, but they had to try.

Bernstein agreed and told her he would be willing to talk with Julie tomorrow and get her on board with this. Maria readily agreed to that and thanked him for his understanding and help. Perhaps she could get in touch with Ms. Lambert tomorrow so the three of them could work on the park's problem and get more teams disseminated. Tomorrow would certainly be a busy day.

Her husband finally came downstairs spruced up and cologned, ready for a nice dinner out. She was ready. She always dressed nicely anyway, even for work. She would need this because tomorrow would be another trying day which might not end the way she would like.

19

San Luis Obispo

"I called the governor's office to give him an update with our boss' blessing. He already had the info. I was really surprised when he told me that our man in the White House had given him a call."

That caught Calvin's undivided attention. "The White House? President Thompson?"

Maria gave him a demure look. "The one and only. Apparently they have been buddies for many years. There was a question of whether a disaster area would be declared. Thompson was the one that brought it up."

What did our gov say?"

"He doesn't think we're quite there yet. Wants to see if all our efforts are paying off. But, if things worsen and we lose control, that possibility could be put on the table."

Cal nodded in understanding. "Well, let's hope and pray that we do this right and get rid of these things. As much as I'd like to study them, right now that will have to wait. In the meantime, I found out something you'll want to know."

"Oh good. What've you got for me?"

"It's a relatively new chemical, recently developed. I finally got the first name for it." Calvin looked down at his notes and said it slowly. "*ethylene glycolate disulfide*. That's a mouthful and a half. Good heavens. Why don't they just spell it in Chinese? Might be easier to say."

With her chin resting on her hand, Maria understood. "Yea, I hear ya. I think those chemical companies can only name things that have two mil-lion letters in them and are unpronounceable. Anyway, go on."

"According to what they told me, it's a carcinogen and mutagen. Can cause cancer and other cell mutations in animals."

"So what is it used for?"

Calvin flipped his pages of notes. "Let's see. Oh yes. Here it is. It is used for, um, looks like helping to stimulate plant growth." He looked up at her over the tops of his glasses. "Now that's a good one. Helps to stimulate plant growth, yet it causes all kinds of cell mutations. Makes about as much sense to me as a lot of other things in this world. None."

"Well, Cal, probably 'cause those bad things in things that are not supposed to come in contact with it."

"Like hornets?"

She nodded her head. "Like hornets. Who knows? Maybe other things as well. But we have to look into that and fast. Still have that specimen?"

Calvin nodded. "Yep. Got it still in a jar back in the office. I know what you're going to say. I'm on it. I'll call toxicology."

"Wait a minute, Cal. Their exam for that chemical might destroy the specimen itself. I need at least half of it to perform my own analysis. There might be other issues with it that I might be able to find. And I'm going to call up to Oregon's entomology department to see if I could obtain a dead regular Vespa specimen they may have they can spare. I need to do a comparison."

"Ok, boss. Let me call toxicology while you call Oregon. We gotta get going on this."

"Yea, we sure do. Let's do it." Maria hung up and was back on the line again.

***

Three days later, a call came in from state toxicology up in Sacramento. The results were not surprising but at the same time it let them know that the problem was as serious as they feared.

The hornets were contaminated with a chemical they'd come in contact with. There was also some other chemical involved they couldn't identify because it was so old and degraded. All they could do was detect it. Although reports had come in disclosing a few chemical suspects from other companies, none of those had panned out due to lack of nearby vespa nests in those areas and any possibilities of leaks.

For the next couple of days, Maria and Calvin worked on the list of chemical suspects. Gradually they ruled out all suspected contaminants until the short list came down to only one left. Ethylene glycolate disulfonate. Whatever that unidentified other chemical was, they couldn't do anything with that, except consider it an unknown suspect.

Maria immediately got on the walkie talkie and contacted the Stockton area team. They were west of the city and were ordered to go to the area of the Stanton Chemical Plant on the south side outskirts. Although the pond was now known to be in that vicinity, they needed to get there and start looking for a hornet nest, starting at the pond and working themselves in an expanding circular search.

She believed this might be the epicenter of the hornet mutations, although she couldn't be sure. They had originally escaped from Los Angeles and that was a distance away. But the problem was twofold: one, if hornets were in the Stockton area, they could have, over time, migrated down from Washington or Oregon; and two, they could have flown up from the LA area. Again, over time. There was no way to be sure.

The team would canvas the area thoroughly. More people would be sent to assist and expand the search area. They had to find the nest in the area of that contaminated pond. Insects, even these huge things, don't fly hundreds of miles from their nest just to predate. They almost always stay in the geographical area where they first find themselves, albeit in zones where they consider it safe.

A little over an hour after they received the instructions from Maria, the team arrived at Stanton Chemicals and wasted little time. They started scouring around the area and noticed the small brook outside the fence perimeter. Expanding outward, most of the ten member team began their search in the surrounding area of woods. Two of them followed the brook for a distance to find out where it led as well as search for any nests nearby.

Thoroughly checking all possible areas or holes where a nest could be, they spared no time in their search while eliminating all areas where they knew a nest could *not* be. This is what all the teams were trained to do in any search and destroy operations. So far, reports of three nests were discovered further south and were subsequently destroyed with the chemicals. They hoped they would find the one in this area. They knew it was around here somewhere. Unfortunately, finding it was similar to looking for the proverbial needle in the haystack. Their hunt would consume most of the afternoon.

***

Sacramento

Williams Senior High School was an older school dating back to the mid to late 1950s. It had a student body of over twelve hundred, comprised of those from all walks of life and socio-economic backgrounds. It was a large school in a relatively large city. Unfortunately, due to a staff shortage, not all things could be addressed when they needed to be. But maintenance personnel did the best they could with who and what they had to use to keep the building clean and safe. No one could fault them for being a little behind.

It was one thirty in the afternoon and classes were in session. In fifteen minutes, classes would change and students would be filling the halls en route to other classrooms for their next subjects.

In the music teaching area, the room was set up a bit differently than the regular classrooms. Along the walls were posters of musical elements and papers related to music. A piano was in the corner of the room. Beside it was a long chalkboard. About fifteen chairs were set up to face the chalkboard. Toward the back of the room, there was a small, enclosed office in the corner that was reserved for the music director, who was also the school's marching band and special chorus director. The orchestra director used the other desk that was in there.

Further back, the classroom connected to the band instrument storage room, mainly for those in the marching band who stored their own personal instruments there, and for the larger ones that couldn't be taken home.

The small number of fifteen chairs were enough to accommodate the small number of music students. Most of them had intentions, or at least thoughts of, continuing their musical aspirations toward obtaining collegiate music degrees and careers.

Like any other day, this was no different for those who used these areas. Students came and went. There was no band practice until later that day so no students lingered in the instrument storage room.

On the roof, the warm temperatures resulted from the sun beating down on it in the late spring time of year. It was a breezy day. One tile, then a second one came loose and was soon making their way down to the edge where they laid silent and unnoticed.

It had been at least thirty, if not more, years since the roof had been assessed. Although plans were already made to have it checked again as soon as possible, none were in place for the near future. The hole that had been made by decades of weather wear and wetness was unseen.

Rainwater had seeped under the already loose tiles and rotted the underlying wood, remaining unnoticed and unaddressed. From above, it appeared as an unsightly flaw that needed immediate repairs, except to things which embraced its inviting space and darkness.

As the school year approached its ending, and summer vacation was just around the corner, students seemed to be more energetic and excited at the prospect of vacation coming up soon. None would complain of no school for three months.

Most students here had heard and knew about the giant hornet invasion in their state. Today, however, they were oblivious to it. Why would they think about that here and now when they had too many other things to worry about?

For Kevin and Ted, they were preparing for music theory class. It would be a very welcome relief from their boring and tedious advanced math class. Numbers were boring and so was the class, although they did well in it academically with mostly A and B+ grades. They were in the honors program because of their overall high grade-point average. "Here comes the music," said one to the other.

In the music classroom, they were soon joined by six other students, who readied themselves for the class, which was taught by their music director, Alfred Landam, a scholar with a Master's in music. He was an excellent teacher who strived to ensure his students learnt what they needed to know. That in itself kept their attention.

Back in the instrument room, unknown to anyone, there was movement in a corner of the ceiling furthest from the doorway entrance. The dark hole there was fairly small and inconspicuous. The movement inside of it was accompanied by its unheard sounds. If any students went into the room, they likely would not notice the small hole. They also would never notice the barely perceptible increase in its size.

Forty minutes later, the class ended, as did most other classes. Most of them started at approximately the same time. All of the theory students, including others who would come here at a later time today, were part of the school's music club, with some in the marching band and some in the orchestra and chorus. Many of them were in two or all of them. As this particular class ended, Tommy went into the band instrument room to get his trumpet out. He was soon followed by two other students.

"Hey, Tommy, you going to challenge Randy for first spot?" asked Seth, one of the clarinetists who walked to where his instrument was.

"I'm set for Friday on that," he replied. "That will give me a couple more days to practice."

In the high school band or orchestra, different players were at different levels of positions, with number one being the lead instrument player and number three or four being at the bottom rank-wise. It was like any other hierarchy: the number one spot was occupied by the best player for that instrument. Tommy was number two, challenging Randy for the number one spot. As the one being challenged, he was obligated to either take on the challenge or forfeit his seat. Most of the time it was a no-brainer as to which choice would be made by whoever was challenged, no matter what the instrument was.

"Well, good luck on that, dude. Hey, did Landam say if we're going out on the field today?" Often Landam had the band transported to the football field for practice. They needed to hone the movement routines that had been created by the director. These routines were performed at half-time at each of the games to entertain the spectators. During inclement weather, the director would have them just practice play inside the school auditorium.

"I think we're going outside today. Next period. I better get going," he said as he closed his trumpet case. "Got biology class coming up. See ya later."

Two of the students left the room, while another one came in. As time passed, more students came in to get their instruments and be ready with them to transport to the field.

Two female students then entered for the same reason. One of them went to the corner to get her flute out of the case. There was no reason for her to notice it coming out of the ceiling because there was no reason for her to look up. No one could have expected something like that.

As she removed her flute from its case, she felt something land on her head. Thinking it was something that dropped from the ceiling, she quickly swatted at it but then felt pain on her hand. It was lightning quick. Whatever it was crawled down from the top of her head and she felt it on the middle of her left cheek. Her screams caused students right outside the band room to run in. The shock of what they saw stopped them in their tracks. She then felt something sharp and painful pierce her cheek and she screamed even louder.

The girl was suddenly surrounded by a swarm of large insects. The students were horrified when they saw that more of these things were pouring out from the ceiling. Their eyes made contact with the enlarged hole up in the corner. They didn't know what to do. The girl was screaming from a combination of terror and pain. One of the boys witnessing this called for the band instructor or some other help outside in the main hallway. Another person got on the phone and called 9-1-1.

Two of the students suddenly took action and took a couple of jackets that were lying around and started swatting at the furiously attacking swarm. Some of the insects were diverted and started attacking them.

"Close the door," one of the boys shouted. "Close the damn door before they get out!"

Now the room was filled with the attacking hornets. The three students left in the room now knew they weren't bees and correctly figured them to be hornets. But they didn't know why *these* hornets were attacking them so viciously and how they managed to make a hole in the ceiling. They suspected yet had no clue as to what they actually were.

The girl had now collapsed as they covered her. Though the boys tried to rescue her, it was like trying to fight an oncoming tidal wave. She was on the floor, moving less than before with her screams becoming less in frequency and volume. She was dying before their eyes. When they realized they couldn't get to her because the insects attacking them prevented that, they did their best to cover themselves with the jackets.

They wanted to open the door and get out of there but were afraid the things would fly out and invade other areas. Meanwhile, knocks were all over the door and screams from outside the room were heard. The boys were also being repeatedly stung and now they were screaming from the terror and pain the girl had endured. When one of them caught a brief glance of the girl's face, he peed in his pants.

Her face was blue and extremely swollen, including her eyes. She didn't look like the same person. Now she lay still. When he realized she might be dead, he yelled out. His terror, as well as the other boy's, likely caused so much adrenaline to rush out that they didn't feel the pain from the toxic venom now coursing through *their* veins.

People outside the door heard screams from the other side of the closed door and yells of "huge hornets" mingling with the screams.

"Tom, Billy, are you ok? What's happening? The fire department is on their way." It was Jim Langley, the assistant band director. He heard screams from them but no verbal responses. Then a minute later, "She's dead. Oh God...ahhh!Carla is dead! God, please get us out of here."

Jim, from outside the door, heard the buzzing. He couldn't hear it at first because of the screaming. The thickness of the door tended to drown out a lot of sound. But the screaming was loud enough to hear through it and between bouts of screaming, so was the loud continuous buzzing.

A couple of minutes later, firefighters and paramedics came in. By this time, student onlookers were everywhere on the perimeter of the scene as fire personnel kept them back from the active area. Called in also were professional vermin exterminators who had the necessary chemicals to deal with the situation.

One of them asked out loud, "Did anyone see any of the insects fly out of that room?" He pointed to the band room. Everyone shook their heads and they started looking around them and up to the ceiling as if to validate what they said.

"The door was opened about ten minutes ago just for about five seconds, so some were able to get out of there." He was one of those who had escaped.

One of the paramedics asked the several students in the music room, "Does anyone know how many students are in there?"

Most of them shook their heads, not sure. But one said, "I think there might be three. I know two dudes are in there. Might be a girl also."

Jim Langley spoke up. "Yes, there is a girl in there. Her name is Carla. She's one of the bandmembers. I heard one of the boys say that he thinks she's dead. I heard them screaming but not her."

The three paramedics looked at each other and realized they had more of a serious problem than they thought. Without some kind of protective suits, it would be a challenge to try and rescue them at this point. Those things were all over the room.

When the exterminator was escorted into the room by the assistant principal and band director who'd been conferring with him at the time of the incident, paramedics and fire personnel related what information they had regarding what was occurring behind that closed door. The man had a couple of insecticide tanks with him and some other equipment. He was wearing a one-piece exterminator suit and carried a chemical mask he wore when spraying vermin. He introduced himself as Jack. Jack asked if anyone knew what species of insects they were dealing with. Someone blurted out the word "hornets". The boy said he believed they were huge because the buzzing was so loud and low pitched. He then knew what they were probably dealing with here. It was the stuff of nightmares that he had received reports about as well as heard on the news. Unfortunately, he did not have the special suit to protect against *these* invaders.

They all wanted to get the students out of there and save the girl as quickly as possible. Yet, their dilemma was almost as terrifying as the incident itself. Furthermore, the exterminator just couldn't go barging in there with "blazing" chemical tanks. Opening the door, for now, was not a good idea. The last thing the school needed was an invasion of the entire school building. He had to have the right PPE and a plan to minimize the dangers to others.

There was also the very real possibility of serious chemical injury to the students inside. The chemicals could cause skin injury as well as respiratory problems. The fumes were toxic to the naked nose and could injure the lungs. Although that was serious and the students could be quickly treated and hospitalized if necessary, that wasn't the fact that caused him to hesitate. It was the opening of the door that posed the more serious threat. They could not let even one of those things, whatever they were, escape. He suspected *now* what they were but wanted to know for sure. He hadn't had all the facts before he got here. Now that he had, he knew he still couldn't go right in. Unfortunately, time was not on their side. And he had to work fast.

He turned toward the center of the room and spoke with the assistant principal and band director.

"I think I know what those are in there. I'm not sure but have to play on the side of safety and caution. For that, I need all students in and around this area of the school to vacate as quickly as possible. This entire half of the school is in the danger zone. All staff also must vacate. Only emergency personnel wearing special suits are to be allowed in this area."

"I'll get right on it now." Sid Johnson was a no-nonsense, quick-to-act kind of guy. "Ok, everyone, students, please. Let's go to the auditorium now. Everyone off this floor. I'll check for anyone else on this floor but get up there now."

Landham directed some of the students out of the music area and told them to go to the auditorium and wait there until they were told it was safe. The auditorium was on the second floor and well away from the danger zone.

The students left without hesitation as Johnson headed down the basement hallway to check for anyone in the four other classrooms in that area.

The first responder EMTs were clearly upset on this call. They were helpless to do anything. One of them spoke up in frustration.

"Good lord, what are we going to do about those poor students in there? And that girl? She may be dead for all we know. Can't we do something now? What the hell are those things that is causing all this chaos?" The female paramedic was clearly emotionally distressed and frustrated that she couldn't do her job at this moment. Yet, what she outwardly expressed was actually felt by everyone around her. And it was distressingly frustrating.

"I'll tell ya," said Jack. "I think they are hornets. I have to make a quick phone call." He picked up his cell phone and made his call to someone unknown to the rest.

After the call, he told everyone there not to open the band room door for any reason. Only he and his assistant would go in when they were ready. But they had to wait for other specialized suits to be delivered there.

Jack continued his take on the situation to those around him. "What's in there might threaten the entire school if we open that door. I know we need to save those students. But far more will be in grave danger if we act and disregard the consequences. That's a hard thing to swallow. But what we are dealing with is an invasion of some sorts and not one that could be easily stopped. If that poor girl is in fact deceased, then we are dealing with killers that act quickly and ask no questions. Has anybody asked again if those boys are still ok?"

Langley quickly went to the door and asked the big question. He heard a voice saying, what sounded like, "ok". But it was weaker than before.

"Are *both* of you still ok?" he asked again.

Some groaning and then a loud, "ahh".

"Tom, Billy? You still with us? We're going to get you out of there as soon as we can. We're in the process of making it safe enough to open the door. Stay with us, guys. Cover yourselves as best as you can. Got it?" He heard in response only slight groaning. *Oh my God, this is an absolute nightmare,* he thought to himself. The fact that the boys were barely talking or making sounds anymore was a clear indication to everyone there that the situation seemed to be becoming more deadly.

"What the hell is possibly killing them, Mr. Jones?" Landam asked the exterminator after noticing his name tag.

"Hornets, sir. As I had told the EMTs. And not your run-of-the-mill ones either. Better I say what I think when the assistant principal gets back here. You ok with that?"

"Fine with me. You think they are the ones…"

"I think so," Jack answered. "That means real danger. Need to make one more call. Will you excuse me for a minute?"

"Want to use the phone in my office?" Landam asked, tilting his head toward the back of the room where it was. "If it's this important, you don't want to lose a cell phone signal in here."

The exterminator readily agreed and soon was on the phone to some-one he happened to know who worked for the government of California. The assistant principal returned during the phone call.

20

Stockton, Stanton Chemical Grounds

Trudging through the thick brush wearing those suits and with all that equipment was no doubt challenging for all of them. They had no idea where this pond allegedly was or if they were even heading in the right direction. On the other side of the plant was another smaller team that was searching that area, heading away from them.

It was a tremendously large amount of area to cover and would no doubt take them hours, which meant all day. They would have to stop when it got dark, mark where they had stopped and continue to search the next day from that point if they didn't find it today.

The larger team noticed an incline so they had to watch their footing. Many of the dead leaves on the ground were damp and slippery. They thought that strange considering the ground itself was dry. Brushing that aside, they focused on searching and hopefully finding what they were looking for.

As they proceeded through the forest, the incline became a little steeper. The leader of the group thought he saw what looked like a clearing up ahead and he put up his hand to stop.

"Think I see something down there," he said. "Let's see what it is."

Pressing forward, the group followed with one of the members exclaiming, "Yea. Hey, that's the pond! Could we be so lucky to find it?" Although Steve sometimes showed slight over-eagerness, he tended to be the first to verbalize what they were all thinking. At times. This was one of them.

"Think you're right, Steve," said Don. Don Henson had worked for the state for ten years as a wildlife biologist, with a special interest in small mammals and insects. He wasn't an entomologist but knew enough to get by to assist one. He had assisted many times in field searches like this as well as extra research, so he knew what he was doing. His experience and knowledge trumped the others, which was why they were following him here.

At the bottom of the incline, they examined the large pond visually at first to assess its potential for contamination and then looked around the area for any kind of clues.

One of the team members spoke up and said he was going to examine the ground all around the area with special devices and equipment he had carried along. Basically, he was looking for any kinds of liquid that might be seeping down to the pond that he could see.

While he started doing that, Don suggested testing the water. Two others broke out their equipment from their packs. They removed some vials to obtain water samples. These samples would have to be sent to the state's toxicology lab to perform a qualitative analysis. That analysis would determine what, if anything, was in the water. Further analysis would help determine how much per parts per million of whatever was in it. If ethylene glycolate disulfide was found, then they would know they may have found the epicenter of the mutant invasion.

The first member was already halfway around the perimeter of the pond but hadn't yet found anything. As he continued, the collected water samples were put into larger containers and sealed before being inserted into the backpacks. Another member of the team proceeded to help the first member look at the ground for seepages until they converged. Both headed back to the rest of the group.

"We didn't see any seepages or any kind of slight streams flowing down."

"Sounds like maybe it's in the ground," Steve suggested.

"You're probably right. We all set here?" asked Don. It was more of a rhetorical question. They were done here but not done with their searching. They had found the pond. Now came the hard part. They all knew what that was.

Although they kept their headgear on just as a precaution when searching for the pond, now they *had* to keep them on to stay alive should they discover the nest. It was a chilling thought that they all did their best not to think about. Searching for a potential toxic pond was one thing. Searching for something that could easily come at you and kill you was quite another.

Although they had no idea if this was *the* pond Maria had been talking about, they had to assume it was. Better to play on the side of caution. If it was, they were in the immediate danger zone and they knew it. That meant the initial nest which launched the first of the mutant invaders would be right around here somewhere. Again, it would be like looking for a needle in a haystack: an absolutely daunting task that they were obliged to perform.

To cut back on the amount of time it would take to search the entire immediate area, Don had the team split in two, starting at opposite ends of the pond, and working outward into the forest. Heading out, they hit the thick, woodsy trails and the intensive search began. First, he contacted Maria on her radio to inform her of what they'd found.

***

Upon the return of John Gilliam, the assistant principal, one of the faculty members who was in the music room informed him that the exterminator had a connection to someone working for the state who could help expedite help for them.

When the exterminator and the band director exited the office, they met up with Gilliam who he was quickly introduced to.

"Sir, I just spoke with someone in state entomology who happens to personally know the chief entomologist running the show in this state regarding these insects."

"Insects?" Gilliam suddenly blurted out. "My God! Are you telling me that those things in there…?" His arm shot up, pointing his finger toward the closed room.

Jones nodded. "I'm afraid so, Mr. Gilliam. I have every reason to believe those are the giant hornets. Apparently there was a hole in the roof above that room. They, like some wood wasps, can bore through wood. Although these aren't them, they are more than big and strong enough to do that. Looks like they have. And now they are inside."

Landam quickly interjected with his own question. "Wait a minute. How do you know they aren't wood wasps? What makes you think they are those hornets when you haven't been in there?"

"Good question. For safety reasons, we should assume that they are. First, let me tell you that I have men going up on the roof now to find that hole and try and attack them from above." He looked at both men. "Mr. Gilliam, one of my calls in the office was to call in reinforcements to do that. Hope you don't mind."

"No, of course not. Thank you for doing that."

"Have to get a head start," said Jones. "Now, I know those are the hornets because neither regular hornets nor their wasp cousins intentionally attack people unless they are directly threatened or provoked. Although they are a type of predator in their own right, they are not overly aggressive. In fact, they prefer to stay away from people.

"But *these* in there. Apparently from what I understand, after they got through the ceiling, they wasted no time in attacking whoever was in there. The students were never a threat to them yet they attacked anyway. No other insects are known to do that. So we have to work fast."

Just as he finished the sentence, more exterminators came into the room. Jones immediately spoke up.

"Alright, everyone. My guys are here. Before we do anything, everyone in this area has to be evacuated. Mr. Gilliam, is everyone off the floor except us?"

"Yes. No one is in any of the classrooms down the hall. As far as I could see, there is no one on the floor."

"Ok, Mr. Gilliam and Mr. Landam, I need you to please go upstairs and stay there. Please make sure no students or staff come down those stairs. It's imperative that absolutely no one come down here. If any of these insects escape when we open that door, we're all in trouble. Then the entire school building would have to be evacuated."

Gilliam started to think, "*Now how the hell are we going to…*" then he erased that thought. It would be done because it had to be, knowing lives were at stake. "Ok, I'll get up there now and gather up a few available faculty. We'll keep them up there and make sure all the hallway doors are and remain closed." In seconds, he was out of the room, followed by Landam.

Now he turned to the only people left. His men. With quick but precise instructions, they headed to the closed door of the instrument storage room. Close to the door they could hear the buzzing. But unfortunately, they still couldn't go inside. Although thanks to his earlier call, the special thickened suits were on the way. Until they arrived and were donned, that door had to remain closed. He reluctantly reminded them of that. It was heartbreaking and they wanted so badly to go inside and save those kids.

But doing so without the proper protection and planning could be a virtual death sentence for them. If the room was filled with them while going in under-protected, the result could be worse than now. It was a catch-22 situation and a waiting game. Any one of them would have gladly risked their lives to save even one of the children. But dead or dying men can't save anyone. They headed back to the main music room area and took seats.

The tension in the room was so thick you could almost cut it with a knife. It wasn't so much tension but more from the fear, although there was both in the air. Waiting to act was the hardest part for them. Trying hard to not look at the clock or the closed door of the storage room, they engaged in whatever small talk they could to keep themselves occupied.

Jones returned to the closed door. "Anyone ok in there?" He knew deep down that they were not and was not surprised that no one responded. He asked the question again just to be sure. His heart was undoubtedly at an all-time low. He knew, deep down, that they were likely no longer alive, if not in a coma.

It was the most frustrating feeling he'd ever felt in his life and one he wouldn't wish on his worst enemy. Over the years he had experienced all kinds of things in his line of work, from the smallest insects to nuisance animals that sometimes required more than he could handle. He even had a call one time to rid a household of a skunk that had somehow made its way inside. But this was the worst situation he'd ever experienced, by far.

All he had heard through the door was the loud incessant buzzing, which sparked his anger. He had to get away from that door before his anger toward the situation and toward those insects increased so much it would turn his rational thinking into dangerous behavior. He was the leader, the most responsible. He had to think clearly and not worsen an already bad situation.

Upstairs in the principal's office, Gilliam and Landam conferred with Randall Munson, who for six years had run the school with no significant problems. This was his first, which made him a very unhappy camper.

"So do we have staff watching all the hallway doors?" he asked Gilliam.

"Yes. In fact, I had a couple of the teachers who just had study class report to the auditorium to keep them in there. I had a couple of other school staff go to all the classrooms that have classes in session and talk with the teachers in private about the situation and to keep them there until things are safe."

Munson was disturbed with good reason. "Wait a second. That's fine so far. Did they have the teachers tell the students of the actual situation and why they have to hunker down for now and stay away from the first floor?"

Gilliam started getting nervous. "They said they didn't want to panic the students. The teachers were told of the actual situation but were willing to tell the students of a toxic leakage on the first floor and not to go down there until the all clear was given."

His nervousness abated when Munson breathed a low sigh of relief. Munson tended to be very strict on many issues, much more so than Gilliam. But even he too realized that they all knew that it was one thing to tell young students to report a toxic leakage limited to one area. It was quite another, however, when you're told that deadly insects are in the area, that they can quickly travel from area to area, and they will come after you and kill you.

What are the chances that the students, after hearing that, wouldn't panic and not participate in a stampede? In their fear of the terrifying threat, some of them would likely run over each other trying to get out of the building. That's the last thing school officials would want to happen.

Because there weren't enough faculty and staff to cordon off all the areas, Munson assigned his assistant to ensure that all major doorways to the downstairs were cordoned off with some kind of tape or other barriers to unauthorized entries. Gilliam was on it. At the same time, men came in through the front door of the school, close to the administrative offices.

They were carrying several wrapped-up bundles. The special anti-hornet suits had arrived. After signing for them, Munson sent them downstairs to the exterminators.

The exterminators were exuberant to finally get them, especially Jack Jones. Within two minutes, both men were fully donned and ready. Each of them grabbed their chemical sprayer tanks, leaving several extras in the music room. Everyone had left the room. After ensuring that the door to the main hallway was closed securely, they made their way toward the closed storage room door but waited for further instructions from Jones.

"Ok, Sam, let's mask up." After they were on, Jones gave a final instruction.

"We know this is no ordinary job. We move in fast and close the door as quickly as possible. Before I open it, I'll spray around the door edges then push the door open and continue spraying up into the air to keep the hornets away from the doorway. Sam, you're the last to come in. While you spray upward toward the ceiling and the hole, I'll put these masks on the three students."

"I thought they were already gone," said Sam. He preferred not to use the "D" word. Especially because they were just kids.

Jones looked at him. "They might be. We don't know yet. I certainly hope they are not. But the masks are needed on them on the God-given chance that any of them might still be alive. Last thing we need is for them to die from our chemicals. Until I get the masks on, spray like hell towards the buggers and that hole in the ceiling. I'll let you know when they are on, then I'll join you in wiping them out."

Jones turned back to the door. On the count of three, he quickly opened it and they moved in and did what they needed to do as planned. Once the door was closed, Jones put his tank down while Sam took them on and their entranceway.

The sight that met Jones' eyes widened them into saucers. What he saw on all three bodies told him instantly that there would be no need for masks. They could not have survived. There was no breathing seen on any of them and they had turned blue. Tragically, this would be a recovery, not a rescue. This was not the time to regret being too late for them. That would come later.

He yelled out, "Full force, Now!" They blasted into the hole and then covered every inch of the storage room, including the instrument cases and the compartments many of them were stored in. Every inch of the room from floor to ceiling was doused with the chemical. After they completely saturated it and searched for any surviving strays, it was clear the hornets appeared to be gone.

As soon as the men turned around and saw the condition of the students, Sam took off his mask prematurely and promptly vomited onto the floor. "Oh God!" he yelled out, while coughing. "Those poor kids. Oh my God!" He then ran out of the room. Jones looked at the unrecognizable, bloated, purple faces of all three bodies in total shock. Small penetrating holes covered many of the purplish areas. The eyes had even been stung enough to make some vitreous fluid visible if one looked carefully enough. He, too, felt sick to his stomach.

These poor kids, Jones thought, never had a chance. It was unfathomable that such creatures could exist. What purpose did they serve other than to kill and destroy? Murderers! There are enough human monsters in the world to do that. Jones was angrier than he'd ever been before.

He believed that there must have been many more hornets in the room than what they saw. For them to cause this much damage, there had to be hundreds of them. Hundreds of these things could equivalate to thousands of regular-sized hornets or wasps. It took only one sting to kill a person with the venom they carried.

Before leaving, he looked closely at one of the many dead hornet bodies on the floor. It looked terrifyingly huge. He didn't know of any other insect that looked more menacing. Thank God for the stronger mixed chemicals they had, for the reason of 'just in case.'

He finally left the room after ensuring that it was truly clear. The hole had already been filled on the roof by an emergency maintenance crew. If any insects had been left, there would be no way now for them to get out. The task had been successful. But at what terrible cost!

He removed his suit and watched Sam looking forlorn in one of the seats. Jones knew he was trying to pull himself together after seeing what they both saw. Now it was up to Jones to relay the good and bad news to the powers that be upstairs.

As for notifying the parents of the deceased students, he didn't even want to think about that. Whoever had that job he would never envy. Slowly he made his way upstairs, knowing that the coroner's people would soon be on their way after he informed the principal.

21

Maria had informed her director what was discovered, who then notified the governor's office. It was up to the state now to inform Stanton Chemicals that they were solely and directly responsible for the contamination of the pond. They were eventually fined heavily and ordered to clean up the area and do something about that pond. How they would go about that was up to them and was their responsibility. But they were given a time limit to complete it; otherwise, the state could shut them down.

Unfortunately for the chemical plant, that would likely only be the beginning. Once word got out to the public, especially to those who had family members that were affected or killed by these hornets, the legal processes of lawsuits could skyrocket into the tens of millions of dollars.

Although the state believed that the mutant condition of the hornets was most likely associated or caused by the chemicals in the pond, they couldn't prove it. At least not yet. So they kept that information on hold for now until Maria's office determined if that was the case.

Maria had just received a phone call from a state wildlife office near Sacramento. The news of the three student deaths at a local high school up there had been broadcast, which shocked all that heard it. It spread quickly, both nationally and internationally. The school was closed for the next three days and counselors had been provided to help those in need with the mourning and grieving process for their fellow students who had passed.

It was not surprising that states bordering those from Washington to California were on high alert and were taking steps and extra precautions to warn *their* citizens of the potential danger and invasion of the giant hornets. Special suits were even ordered by some of their agencies to provide their scientists with the necessary protection in case the insects crossed into their territories.

In all three of the westernmost states, beekeepers with hives that hadn't yet been affected or invaded weren't entirely sure what they could do to protect their hives. Until they figured out something quickly, their hives were in serious peril. Attacks from the killer hornets could come without warning, from anywhere at any time. Regardless of whether they were beekeepers or not, all citizens were at high risk from attack. It was like the entire state was under siege from these things.

Back at the entomology office, Maria called all staff in, including those off-duty. Phones were ringing off the hook as calls flooded in from everywhere, reporting attacks now occurring all over the state. The governor had now declared a state of emergency. Hospital EDs were also being flooded with sting victims. Treatment results were bittersweet. Although many did survive thanks to quick treatments, many others succumbed to the venom. Deaths occurred at the scenes, en route to the hospital, and at the hospital. It seemed to be a never-ending crisis, almost like a statewide pandemic.

The hornets seemed to be everywhere now, including the cities. Pedestrians just walking on the sidewalks would be fine one minute, and then the next would be attacked out of nowhere from swarms that seemed to come from everywhere. It was like a horror movie with the main characters completely out of control and engaging in absolute chaos. Hospital emergency rooms were being overwhelmed with sting victims

People were panicking. In Stockton, which seemed to become California's epicenter, some victims ran out into the streets and got hit by moving vehicles. Even some of those moving vehicles were attacked by the flying killers, which terrified and panicked many of the drivers. The number of vehicular crashes was escalating, and so was the number of stinging victims. No one, not even the state's main entomologists, were aware of the unnatural speed of the spread of these invasive insects.

"Maria, Governor Capulette is on the phone."

"Thanks, Marty." She quickly picked it up. "Good afternoon, sir, this is Maria."

"Good afternoon, Maria. I wish it really was a good afternoon. Well, I guess you heard what's happening."

"I sure have. I have all my teams out there in all directions, including down to near the Mexico border."

"That's good so far," replied the governor. "I've been in touch with the governors of all our eastern neighbor states and they are making preparations for a potential spread of these things eastward. And now Mexico's president has contacted *our* president who has contacted me regarding the situation. He's afraid these things are going to fly into their country as well. Not surprisingly, the feds are very much involved now. That I am quite glad of because we sure can use all the help we can get. They are going to send front line scientists and workers to help us prevent any more spreading and eradicate this problem once and for all."

"I hope these things don't go into Mexico," said Maria. "If that happens, there's no stopping them. Just like when the killer bees left South America and now here they are. How's Oregon and Washington doing with them?"

"No comparison. They don't have our mutation problems. Because of that, they seem to have far less difficulty dealing with them. Both states are underway in keeping them contained and eradicating them at the same time. They are not having the attack problems we are having. Still sending out field teams to search for more nests, though. They have destroyed a number of them. A couple of stings here and there. But nothing like here. We are the area of catastrophe. They've offered to send us help."

Maria realized that California was the state that the entire nation and *world* were looking at. And she was near, if not at, the center of it all. More help was certainly what they could use. And she told the governor that.

"I've already accepted whatever help they can provide. In the meantime, I've already ordered aircraft to fly over and drop the chemicals needed in remote areas where nests are known or strongly suspected. I don't think your teams will be enough to get all these nests, especially since they seem to be spreading so rapidly."

"What about the state and national parks?" Maria asked.

"I've contacted the state ranger service commissioner. He's going to close the parks for the time period for the drops to be made. We don't want any tourists to be caught in the middle. I've also contacted the feds. They're going to temporarily close their parks here for the next week.

"So within the next three days, the planes or helicopters will start flying over the parks. Do you have any teams in any of them?"

"Yes sir," she replied. "I have two teams in Yosemite where two nests were discovered."

"Where exactly are they?"

She told him after looking at the map. Capulette then told her he'd contact the aircraft service which was assigned to perform the job and ask them to hit those areas first after he assured them the park was clear of all visitors and the presence of any rangers or other staff who were not wearing appropriate PPE.

After their conversation, Maria sat for a few moments contemplating the entire situation. It seemed so overwhelming considering the entire state was involved here and an awful lot of people. But she didn't have time to waste and so began contacting her teams again to assess their progress.

Her mind was going full speed and there didn't seem to be any letup. All these teams were out all over the state. Planes and choppers would be flying overhead in rural and park areas and making their chemical drops. It was an undertaking that never before had been done in the history of California. But was it enough?

And there was still a problem which she just now had thought of. The hornets were invading and attacking the cities. It seemed no one was safe anywhere. From what she had understood, the governor had ordered the chemical airdrops over rural and park areas, away from people.

What was happening in the cities, however, could not be ignored. These insects were ferocious and aggressive and did not discriminate against what or who they attacked. The fight against them had to be taken to the cities as well and not by ground forces. But how could air drops be done in those areas without harming people? It seemed an impossible task. California and its cities truly seemed to be under siege. Maria picked up the phone and dialed the governor's office, wishing she had thought of this before hanging up with him.

"Hello, this is Maria Hernandez from entomology. I have an urgent matter that needs to be brought to the attention of the governor. Can you patch me through to him please?"

After a couple of minutes of soft elevator music and then a couple of clicks, Governor Capulette got on the phone.

"Governor, I'm sorry to bother you and I should have brought this up on our previous talk. I just thought of this now." Then she briefly reiterated about the airdrops over the parks and rural areas, following that with the problem of attacks over cities. The attacks in them were too numerous and widespread for ground forces and there weren't enough of them anyway.

"I thought of that already, Maria, after we got off the phone. I'm guilty of not bringing it up before too. That's going to take a little more planning because of the population. Are there any chemicals that can kill these things without doing any harm to people?"

"Afraid not, Governor. Although they usually don't kill people, they can still make people very sick or possibly cause cancer if they breathe enough of it in. If anyone is allergic to any of the kills, they can go into some serious anaphylactic reactions."

The governor rubbed his chin as he was thinking.

Maria added more information. "Governor, believe it or not, chemicals that are used against regular-sized flying insects can kill these things. You wouldn't think so, but they can. Because of the size of these things, more has to be used. Either that, or the companies that make them for everyone's use will provide more potent mixtures just for this purpose. So supply shouldn't be a problem."

"Ok. Well, it likely would be literally impossible to cover every square inch of the state with this chemical. That would be like watering the Sahara Desert with a garden hose. And it's obvious that cities will have to be air dropped. However, only those where these things have attacked. For now. And their immediate surrounding areas. It would certainly be quite impractical and unimaginably costly to spray every city in the state."

"Ok," replied Maria. She wanted to let him know she was listening and to what he would say next.

"I will have logistics place bulk orders for chemicals to be dispersed by air over all selected areas of the state. I will set a date and time for the drops to be made and notify all the locations by media broadcast. While I have people working on this to set this all up and make the notifications to all the local TV and radio stations, you will ensure that your teams are searching in all the areas that they can and destroy whenever they can."

"Yes sir. Sounds like a plan. Please give the locations and people time enough to prepare and be inside somewhere before these drops are made."

"Of course! That can't be ignored. But we have to move on this quickly. Going to try and make this happen within the next three days. So I need to get going and if anything else comes up, please let me or someone in my office know."

After they hung up again, Maria contacted her teams and then let everyone know in the office of what the plan was. Three days was not a lot of time for the state to do everything it needed to do before implementing it. She thought it should have been a little bit more, but then in this situation how much was too little or too much? The only thing that everyone could agree on was that things had to be done fast in order to prevent more deaths. So if the governor could get everything ready within three days and then get the planes up in the air, that would be a plus in their favor. As it stood now, this really was war. Time continued to not be on their side.

***

It was not until the next morning that Maria had heard from state toxicology on an urgent call directly to her. It was clear the governor's urgent call about the situation and plans had already been announced to all government agencies. Toxicology had worked overnight and quite expeditiously to get at least preliminary results.

The good news was that they were able to salvage part of the insect for Maria, which should be enough for her to do her exam. The bad news was that the chemical they now dubbed "ed" was definitely in the specimen. Although they could not determine specifically that it caused the hornet's mutation, they did concede that it was possible because of its toxicity and its side effects.

It was now up to Maria and her assistants to determine any occurrence of mutation. Toxicology had already packed and shipped the specimen part back to her. She should receive it either later that afternoon or early the next morning at the latest.

Oregon fortunately did have several dead specimens of the vespa and could spare one. Because they knew of the crisis in her state, they packed and shipped it that morning. That, too, should arrive sometime the next day. The game would be on to beat the clock and hopefully stop this venomous epidemic. Although reports were coming in of hundreds of nests being found and destroyed, there was no way to tell how many or what percentage of the hornets were also destroyed.

She couldn't wait until the next day came. But there was nothing more she could do until then. For now, she would monitor the many more search and destroy teams that were out there. The governor had kept his word and quickly ordered hundreds more team workers, even volunteers, to assist while at the same time assuring enough appropriate anti-sting suits to accompany the worker increase. The cost to the state was now in the millions of dollars. But the cost of more lives would be infinitely greater.

22

Platteville is a small town east of Sacramento and about an hour's drive to the Nevada border. It is a small, fairly nondescript town with its own pleasantries and small town charm. Unlike the large towns or cities, it is quiet with inhabitants that are cheerful and welcoming to any who happen to be passing through.

On the morning of the day Maria was to receive the vespa sample from Oregon's state lab, the town was beginning to wake up at its usual 6:00am time. A few morning risers would go into the town's café and have their beloved scrambled eggs and ham breakfast, with coffee of course. Others would begin to rustle about at home getting ready for their official workdays at the office or store or wherever they had to be at their scheduled time. In other words, it was no more than any other typical day in any other American town or city.

In Dottie's *Eggs Roundup Cafe*, Dottie herself was wiping off the counter that had just been vacated by a previous customer. There were two other customers sitting at one of the tables near the front windows. The food here was considered by most town residents as the best in the entire area, let alone the town. Here customers could order home fries that had their own seasoned flavor which seemed to outdo everyone else's. Dottie had her own recipe that she refused to give out to anyone. However, she would make helpful suggestions to those who wanted to at least assimilate some of her cooking without being too exact. They were fine with that.

The normal small restaurant sounds were interrupted once again by the bells announcing the entrance of another customer. This time it was Ted, the local deputy sheriff with the El Dorado Sheriff's Department coming in for his morning coffee. Sometimes he would order a small breakfast and would engage in a brief chat with Dottie or customers that he knew.

He took a stool seat at the counter and greeted the waitress that helped Dottie there. After ordering his coffee, he decided he would order his usual breakfast because he had a little time before he started his eight to four shift. It was still early yet.

Dottie came over to him with her matronly appearance and charm. "So what's cooking for ya today, Teddy bear? How ya doing this beautiful morning?" She called him that occasionally as a tease. He didn't mind. They'd known each other for years.

"Well, babe, I gotta tell you, it's ok for now. The sun is shining out there and not a cloud in the sky. Seems like it'll be a terrific day. Not always the case for us so-called people monitors."

Dottie laughed. "Hell, that's a new one on me. Never heard you guys being called that before. People monitors." She giggled.

He joined in with that. "Think about it. That's what we do, among a million other things. However, today I plan on starting the day off right. I will eat my breakfast, including your delicious home fries, have my coffee. And then…" he said with a mockingly sinister tone, "I will leave here and go out and look for some bad guys. How's Tony, by the way?"

Tony was her son who was still in college. "Oh, he's doing pretty good. In his second year now. A sophomore, I think they call them. Getting good grades the last I heard."

"Studying accounting is he?"

"Yea. Guess that's what he wants to do. Good for him, I say. I could never do that. Just like the world will always need old café owners and cooks like me, the world will also need more accountants."

The bell rang as another customer came in and took a seat at one of the tables. Her waitress, Minnie, went to take his order.

Then the cook's bell rang out from the back kitchen. He called for Dottie and he didn't sound so happy. "Excuse me, Ted. Duty calls."

As she turned and went to the back, Ted got his breakfast from another waitress. While taking a sip of his coffee and starting in on his eggs, he thought he heard a muffled voice. It was Dottie and it sounded like she said, "Oh my God." That caught his attention and made him look up. He was not overly concerned because it could be anything from an overdose of a recipe ingredient to a spilled large container of pepper or liquid.

He didn't hear anything more and continued to eat his food. The business of being served and eating continued out in the front area and the sun continued to shine on calm streets, with only the occasional passing car reminding those who noticed that life was moving forward as it always did.

About ten minutes had passed before Dottie came out from the kitchen. Ted was gobbling up the last of his eggs. When he looked up to her, she looked a bit paler than before. She looked at him with obvious fear in her eyes and at first didn't say anything. He knew immediately that something was wrong and that what she had seen or heard was no spill or recipe overdose.

Walking up to him and leaning over, she quietly asked him close to his ear to come back to the kitchen. She wanted to show him something.

"Sure. Is it that bad?" he asked while wiping his mouth. His expression was a mixture of curiosity and concern.

"I can't talk about it here. You need to see this." It was now clear to him that whatever it was, she didn't want anyone else in the restaurant knowing about it.

Without making a big to-do about it, Dottie calmly brought him into the back kitchen area where he saw the cook standing in front of a huge pot. His face looked like he'd seen a ghost.

The smells of cooked and cooking food filled the air around him. Normally those smells would have made his stomach grumble and immediately brought up more of an appetite. For now, any more eating out front would have to wait.

"What ya got, Aaron?" he asked the cook.

"Look in that pot," he said.

The deputy looked down and now saw the reason for the alarm in Dottie and the cook's faces. It would have been bad enough to see any kind of bug or other vermin in soup that was ready to be eaten. This brought that up to a whole new level. He looked up at the owner and her employee, trying to minimize the shock on his face. He knew what it was and what it meant. The town was in imminent danger. He'd heard the news on TV.

"You just noticed this now, Aaron?"

"Yep. I don't like bugs, Ted. But this thing ain't no regular bug. Is this…"

"Yea. I'm afraid it is," Ted answered before Aaron could finish.

It was clear some kind of action needed to start immediately. "I strongly suggest that this kitchen be thoroughly searched for any others. You're lucky you found it dead rather than alive," Ted told the cook.

"No shit, Sherlock. Damn!" he responded.

Ted continued, "Check the back doors here and make sure they are closed securely. If there are any windows, check to make sure they are closed."

Aaron nodded and went to the back door and the emergency door, checking all around them.

"Are there any vents that open to the outside?" he asked Dottie.

"The only vents here are above the grill and one up on the ceiling over there. The one above the grill can be closed. We close it before we close the café for the night. The one up there in the corner we can't close."

"What about windows?" Ted continued.

"There's no windows back here," Dottie informed him. "For crying out loud, how the hell did that thing get in here anyway?" she asked, as if someone would know the answer. The question was rhetorical because they were all wondering the same thing.

"I don't know, Dottie," Ted replied. "Maybe that vent on the ceiling. But we have to figure that out. If one could get in here, then others could too."

"Guess maybe I'll have someone put a small screen over that vent just in case. No way anything could get in with that thing on it. I know someone who can do it today."

Ted agreed that was a good idea. Dottie was suddenly on the phone making the call. After she hung up, she nodded her success in getting someone.

"Oh Lordy. Are these things invading *us* now?" Now Dottie was getting scared. Ted could only look at her, not having an answer while hoping it was negative. He couldn't know at this point. He shook his head and shrugged. But he didn't want to ignore the possibility as horrifying as it might be.

Ted and the cook checked around for any holes or wall breaches that might have been unseen or overlooked. While the two were checking around, Dottie went back to the front area to check on things. There were still two customers and Minnie was cleaning the counter. Fortunately, it was not one of the days that was busy. She pulled Minnie aside and whispered to her that after the last customer left, she was going to close up for the day and the reason why. She would call her the next day to come in if the place was cleared and safe. The waitress nodded.

In the back area, nothing suspicious had been spotted that could have been an entranceway. And neither of the men saw any more of the insects. Ted was perplexed as to how that thing got in here. So far it could only have been that vent.

According to what he'd learned on news reports, they wasted no time in attacking people or animals. It wouldn't be like letting a fly in. Flies just go right in. This thing was no fly. Why it flew into the soup was beyond him. He figured it was just one of those things that can't be explained. But they were truly fortunate it did that.

"Ok, all doors checked. Nothing that big could get in here through the doors, under, around, or over." No one could say Sid the cook wasn't thorough, even in his cooking. Dottie said she didn't see anything about the vents that would suggest allowing anything in. Nothing flew in while she was looking. She said only when the front door opened by a customer might something fly in. Happened all the time, especially in the summer. It's unlikely, yet possible, that the hornet could have flown in when the door opened without the customer noticing despite its size. Even though it couldn't be ruled out, that wasn't too likely.

Meanwhile, Sid got a pair of huge tongs that looked nearly half his size and went over to the pot with the dead hornet in it. He lifted it out and carried it stiff-armed to the back door where he opened the door and threw it out. All the while making a funny face. It didn't go unnoticed by Ted and he had to let out a laugh. But in a way he couldn't blame the guy. Even dead it could make one cringe.

"Sid, you can't be serious," he said to Sid, with a lingering smile. He just had to tease him about that.

The cook looked at him. Then he looked at the monstrous tongs, then back at Ted.

"Hey, ya think I'm going to waste my time trying to find the right size of this? That dead son of a bitch still looks like it could kill."

As he put the tongs in the sink, screams erupted from the customer area. Ted turned his head and started running toward the front. He and Dottie nearly had a head on collision.

He'd never seen her in hysterics before because she always had the ability to maintain her composure, even in the direst circumstances.

"The front windows," she rapidly yelled at Ted. "Look out there. God almighty, it looks like a scene from that killer bee movie from years ago."

Out front, the three customers were cringing in fear with mouths agape. They were so shocked they could barely make a sound. Ted's jaw dropped.

Outside, there was chaos. It looked like a gigantic swarm of locusts of biblical proportions. The cloud was thick enough to barely see through it. He saw the few pedestrians running and swatting at the hundreds or thousands of attackers that were pelting them. Their screams were bloodcurdling as many of them were completely covered by the flying creatures. They quickly collapsed. In front of the cafe, those inside could see that their faces were completely covered. No one in the cafe could recognize who they were. They were as terrified for themselves as they were for the victims outside.

Ted yelled at Dottie to have Sid check the back door to make sure it was securely closed and not to open it for any reason. She wasted no time heading toward the back. Ted got on his shoulder mike and contacted Dispatch about the situation and location, identifying himself by his badge number.

"We are aware and are dispatching more officers to the scene, one-ninety-one. Advise stay inside and everyone else there until further notice. State Fish and Wildlife has been contacted and they are sending over people to assist."

Ted realized this was worse than the scariest horror movie because it was real. What made it even worse was that he felt so helpless. He saw people attacked and being killed in an incredibly horrendous fashion right in front of his eyes and there was nothing he could do.

Suddenly he heard a woman scream in the back. It was Dottie. He turned quickly and ran to the kitchen. At first he didn't see her, then looked to his right and realized what he feared was now real. By the time she reached Sid, it was too late. He had already opened the back door again and stepped out to have a cigarette. After stepping a few steps away from the building, he had been attacked.

Just a brief glimpse through a crack in the almost closed door told them all they needed. Sid's body was covered by the huge insects. They slammed the door shut.

"We need to hunker down for a while, Dottie," he said. He was as mortified as Dottie but recovered faster. The café owner's face had paled as the shock of her employee's death right outside her door momentarily froze her in place.

It was only after her brain had processed what she'd seen did she break down and cry. It was not only a loud cry for the death of her cook, but also for the terror that was engulfing everyone there. It was the worst of nightmares that one could only pray waking up from.

Outside, more people were on the ground than those running. It looked like a war zone, except without the guns and bombs. The town was under siege by the hornets and they were flying everywhere and all over the place. Moving vehicles had crashed into other moving and parked vehicles, as well as signs and other inanimate objects. Front store windows had been crashed into. It was a scene of utter chaos, destruction, and death. Ted and Dottie were realizing the predicament of something unnatural happening to the town that appeared apocalyptic and of biblical proportions. They saw nothing but a disaster zone and prayed nothing would crash into the front windows of the cafe.

The two customers in the café were just as terrified and shocked. It was a young married couple in one of the booths. Ted could have sworn there had been a third person there. He remembered seeing a man in his thirties with long hair sitting at the far end of the counter.

"Wasn't there another fellow here?" he asked them.

Although his wife was crying from fright, the man was able to answer. "Yea. He ran out the door. I tried to yell at him not to go out there but he wouldn't listen."

Well, thought Ted, that was that. Nothing anyone could do about it. He only hoped the man made it to where he was going.

Several minutes later, they all looked out the windows to see a sheriff's car coming slowly down the road. The deputy inside was yelling on the car's loudspeaker. The sight was chilling because of the bodies lying on the ground. Yet he had to make the announcement for the benefit of survivors or those who hadn't yet come out from where they were. Ted and the others saw large hornets landing on the deputy's windshield. This attack seemed to go on forever.

"Attention. Attention everyone. This is the El Dorado Sheriff's Department. Anyone inside, please stay where you are.

It is not safe to go outside at this time. We need to clear the area so please stay put in an area of safety. We will let you know when it's safe to go out." Then he repeated it as he continued to drive down the main street.

Ted thought he knew who the deputy was. He got on his mike and let Donnie know he was in the café and to stay safe and inside his car, even if he had to park it.

"I'll be ok, Ted…um, 191. Thanks for checking. You stay inside as well. Maybe this will clear out soon. Talk to ya later," he said, signing off. He then continued his loudspeaker announcements.

After he drove by the café, a couple of ambulances followed by a fire truck slowly came into view and stopped a block away from the restaurant. It looked like the hornets were leaving. There were no more people or animals they could get to attack. In their wake were bodies and a swath of destruction. Ted and the others saw some firefighters in full suits with headgear and masks exiting the truck. Although there didn't seem to be any of the insects around now, they didn't want to take any chances.

At each of the areas where there were one or more bodies or unconscious survivors, they picked up however many they could fit into the two ambulances to be transported to the nearest hospital.

"What are they doing?" asked the male customer.

"Looks like they are picking up bodies or possible survivors."

"One-ninety-one, Dispatch." Ted answered his call.

"Be advised, area appears clear. Exit, but advise the other people there to remain inside until we give the all clear. Do a ten seventy-five of the town's perimeter and advise of any sightings."

"One-ninety-one, ten-four. Be advised there is a ten ninety-nine behind this location." Code for possible deceased victim.

He would do a complete sweep around the town and see if there were any more of the attackers around or of any injured or deceased victims. That would take a while but he wouldn't have to get out of his patrol car.

After advising Dottie and the customers, he left to finally continue his duties which had now changed because of the situation. He wanted to get out of there anyway. But it was not so much because of the hornets: it was now because of the media which he knew were already on their way. The buzz patrol, he thought with a smirk. The smirk faded quickly as he started a search which would forever be etched in his memory.

23

Back in San Luis Obispo, Maria was receiving reports from all over the state about more nests being found and destroyed. This resulted in the extermination of thousands of the hornets and the queen of each nest. Yet she knew it would be impossible to know for sure if every single nest and hornet was eradicated.

Calvin was up in Sacramento investigating the high school incident and attacks on the three students. He would bring back a specimen of one of the dead hornets found in the band room. At the lab they would examine it for mutation properties to determine if it was one of theirs or if it had migrated down from Oregon. It was just one more example from a different area of mutagen validation and expansion.

Although reports of attacks had been coming in almost on a daily basis, their numbers seemed to be on the decrease from the extermination efforts. Maria hoped this would continue until there were no more attacks reported. That would be the closest way she would be able to tell if the statewide extermination efforts were successful.

The attacks at the high school were quite disturbing to her but paled in comparison to the attacks on the entire town of Platteville. That attack was considerably more serious because of the numbers involved but not compared to the attacks at the ball park a couple of months earlier. Maria was quite sure there were far more fatalities than she knew about. People had died at almost every area of attacks. Billy Jansen either had been very lucky or had come through it through divine intervention.

The phone rang and she picked up. It was Earl.

"Hi, honey. Everything alright there?" She had to ask because Earl rarely ever called her at work.

"Yea, everything's fine. Just got very busy here and trying to take care of some urgent issues before I call it a day here. Sorry I didn't call you."

"That's ok. Just wanted to make sure you're ok. It's suppertime and you weren't home yet, so…"

Her eyes climbed up to the wall clock. It was 5:30. She was usually home by 4:30 the latest. "Oh my gosh, I hadn't realized it was so late. Got caught up in my work here. I'm sorry, sweetie!"

"That's alright. It's OK. You must be working hard on this hornet thing, huh?"

"Yea. Going crazy here with that. There was another recent attack, this time on an entire town."

"What?! Oh my…"

"Yea, that's what I say. Listen, I've got to do just a couple more things here then I'll be heading home. Won't be but a few minutes."

After hanging up, she called the El Dorado Sheriff's Office to find out what the current situation was there. If necessary, she'd go out there to investigate. For now, she needed to find out what she could on the phone before determining whether or not that necessity called for her presence.

Sacramento

At the high school, Calvin stood in the music classroom to first take in the adjoining area to the band room before entering that area. By this time, the bodies had been removed by the coroner's office and both areas remained cordoned off by the police. Although it wasn't a crime scene, people from the state and police weren't quite done with their investigations yet. This gave Cal a final chance to go over the scene and collect one of the dead insects. That was one of the first things he did after assessing the areas.

He couldn't help noticing how claustrophobic that band storage room could be. There were no windows. Although there was a very wide doorway which led into the hallway outside the music area, that was always kept closed and locked except for taking out the largest band instruments, such as sousaphones. So the only door that was kept unlocked was the one everyone went through. He wondered at first how much of a fire hazard this was.

These poor victims had been trapped inside this closed up room with deadly insects they couldn't get away from. He didn't want to think about the tragedy too long or the emotional pain the parents must be feeling right now, even hours after they first heard about it. Their entrapment with the insects was, in effect, the same as if those insects had been a fire instead. Except that this was worse. A fire wouldn't have quickly followed them out the door with escape nearly as quickly as the hornets would.

Having collected his specimen and given a final assessment of the area, including the patched up ceiling hole, he left the room. After thanking the school officials there and the principal, he turned and was soon in the car, heading back on the long drive to L. A.

***

San Luis Obispo

The next morning, Maria got a call from the lieutenant governor's office. It was Sheila Birmingham herself calling on behalf of Governor Capulette. He had to attend the western regional governor's conference in Nevada and wouldn't be back until the next morning. But he'd given instructions to Birmingham to relay to Maria regarding the current state plan to battle the hornets.

She identified herself and after a brief courteous greeting, she explained the current plan now underway for eradication of any nests in Yosemite Park. The task would be daunting and required a minimum of two days. The entire park was now closed to the public for at least that amount of time.

Starting the next day, the intense aerial assaults would begin. Special airdrop-type planes and helicopters would fly over the entire park dropping the deadly chemicals. The state had consulted with chemists and other professional scientists beforehand. After determining that these chemicals would not be deadly to the wildlife but only to most flying insects, including the hornets, the plan moved forward into the execution stage which would begin at 6:00am.

From the earlier reports made by a tourist and park ranger, the epicenter at Yosemite was believed to be around the area of El Capitan. The assaults would begin there and gradually spread out in all directions until the park's perimeters were reached.

Originally, the plan, before it was implemented, was to select only the most viable areas where the insects might nest. But that plan was scrapped when they all realized it would be unrealistic to believe that even the best experts would be able to predict where new nests would be built. Right now, time was ticking and they had to move fast.

Maria and Calvin agreed. Chances are the animals would go down to the lake to get away from the smell of the insecticide. There would be no need for the spray drop there.

Over the radio which Cal was listening to, there was a news flash. Although he had listened to it at low volume just for some background noise while he worked, the interruption of the soft music by the news made him stop.

As the radio newsperson broadcast, he turned up the volume. What he heard sounded like a higher level version of that old killer bees movie. He listened to all of it before he let Maria know. This time there was a much wider spread of attack, more savage in the way the attacks were carried out, and many more deaths than seen in previous incidences. Platteville.

He needed to find where this was. He'd never heard of it. It didn't take him long Googling it. He then called Maria.

"Oh my Lord," she responded to the news. Without hesitation, she called the Platteville PD and asked to speak to the chief.

When she was finally connected, she identified herself and informed him she had just heard the news on the radio and requested information from him that could help her help them.

"Well, Doctor, it apparently started suddenly and without prior warning. One minute it was quiet and peaceful here, the next minute it was sheer chaos. I've never seen anything like it. I looked out the window and the air was so full of them you could hardly see through them. It was like a cloud, I tell ya. They literally came out of nowhere!"

"This happened earlier today?" she asked.

"Early this morning."

Her mind was racing. She'd have to get them help fast. There was a nest in the area. More likely two or more, and they had to be found and destroyed. Not to mention the insects themselves.

"How're things there right now?"

"Well, people here are scared and still traumatized. I have officers going around, ambulances all over transporting the living and the dead, tow trucks trying to clear roads of crashed vehicles. It's terrible but not like this morning."

"Ok, Chief. I got to tell you something but please don't broadcast it. It could start a panic."

"You have my word on that, Doctor."

"Ok, good. Now I believe, from the sounds of it, that there are likely two or more nests in your area. I think you know what they are."

"Yes I do, ma'am."

"Because they are deadly, they are mutations of the original species and far more aggressive than they ever should be. That means they pose a dangerous threat to all living creatures, especially people. I'm going to request an air drop of insecticide to cover the town and its surrounding areas. You need to keep your citizens inside when this happens. Think you can do that?"

Both of them knew how daunting a task that would be. The chief would have to call in off-duty officers who could be reached for assistance in getting the news out. He knew he couldn't rely just on his men on-duty alone. There was also a faster way: the media.

"I will do that. When do you think this will happen?"

"Don't know yet. But I'm going to make a call now and get this going. They are already spraying over Yosemite and surrounding areas."

The chief didn't know what to say to *that,* he was so taken aback. Apparently his town wasn't the only large spot to be under siege.

"Please let me know when this will happen. By the way, is this insecticide deadly to people?" he asked.

Maria answered with a brief rundown on the chemical and its dangers. She would let him know the approximate time well ahead of that to give people time to take cover. Although she couldn't be everywhere at once, she decided to take a look at the town there and have a couple of teams accompany her. If this happened once there, it could happen again. They had to find the nests.

Before she could go up there, she had to find out about whether or not the state could spray the town. It wouldn't be practical for her and some teams to go up there without the area having been airdropped first with the chemical. They had to work fast on this because lives were at stake. So she called the governor's office directly to inquire to save time. Normally, she preferred to go up the chain of command but there really wasn't enough time. Besides, she was told that her boss was out of the office for the week.

After several clicks, she was passed to the governor himself. She quickly explained the situation over in Platteville and what her plans were. Agreeing that she should do that after the town was sprayed first, he made the commitment to divert some of the spraying over to that town as other planes continued to spray the rest of Yosemite. It would basically be a two-fold attack on the nests in the northern areas of the state. Although it would become even more costly, it would still be far less than the cost of human lives, which is the main reason Capulette quickly agreed to it. Until now, he hadn't been aware of the Platteville situation. He would put his plan into action as soon as possible.

As soon as she hung up, she let her partner, Cal, know who then asked to go along. "Of course. I'll need your help anyway to help coordinate the teams and obtain all the necessary equipment," Maria replied.

"So what's the plan?"

"Well, the governor said he'll contact Director Bingham and then me with the blueprints. Things have to happen quickly so he's wasting no time putting this together. He'll let me know when the action will begin and then we will make our plans to get up there. Since we have our teams ready for call-up and you'll arrange to get all the necessary equipment ready to go, it's now just a matter of waiting for a callback from the gov's office."

Taking the team lists and members of each, they each took half and contacted members of the "hornet task force" as Cal so graciously called them. Their calls included members that were reserves or standbys. In this situation, it was now a call for 'all hands on deck."

After about forty-five minutes, they had called all the people they could get a hold of. Some were unavailable.

"Cal, find out anything new up at the school in Sacramento?"

Maria was curious but didn't expect to hear about anything else that was earth-shattering other than what had happened. That in itself was bad enough.

"No," he said with a sigh. "Not really. I did see the layout of the area and where those things had come in. It's one thing to hear about it on the news. It's another thing to actually see all that in person and where the victims had lain. It did make me very sad for the victims. Then I tell myself, 'if only'. If only that hole in the ceiling and the roof weren't there. If only no one had been in that room."

"There can be all the 'if onlys' in the world, Calvin. But you can't beat yourself over the head about it. No one could have known that it would occur. Hell, no one even knew about the hole in the roof or that the damn things were in the area. That's another thing that makes them so dangerous. Their insidiousness."

She looked at him and he knew he couldn't argue that.

"Well, no time like the present to start getting ready." He needed to get that thought out of his mind now and get cracking on preparations. "If you like, I can start arranging for all the equipment if you want to get the personnel. How many do you think we'll need?" He got up from his chair and did a quick stretch.

Maria was thinking. This was not easy. How many indeed? How many people did she have or could spare?

"Give me a few minutes," she said. "I'll get back to you on that. Will you be in your office?"

"Yep; heading there now."

As he headed there, she turned around in her chair and pulled out the manifest which included names of all those active in the field right now. Periodically she had been getting reports of nests found and destroyed in various areas of the state. Each team had identified itself which told her their location. When each of those teams in their specific assigned areas had reported no further discoveries, they would report that to her. So far, of the twenty-five teams that were out there, ten of them reported total extermination.

Even so, the reports of total exterminations, in her mind, could never be a guarantee. Unlike humans or large animals, insects even as large as these hornets, could still easily hide behind anything. They, in effect, could easily hide in plain sight unseen. To her, it was nearly like a creep show with someone having the feeling of being watched without a tangible sight of anyone or anything.

After an hour of studying the manifests and determining who was available and how many she could use, she made the calls. Because there were several dozen on standby, she called them. It basically took the rest of the afternoon to round up the fifty she chose from the lists they had compiled earlier. But there was no need to use all of them. Besides, there were a few that were unavailable for various emergency reasons. Still there was more than enough for her to select.

By midafternoon she let Cal know she had the people and wanted to find out how he had got on so far.

"I believe I've got everything. I got a hundred special suits and accompanying gear for the job."

"That's great, Cal. But we'll need only fifty. Make that fifty-three, which includes for you and me, and then an extra just in case."

That being said, they agreed on the plan once again and that before they disembarked at their destination, she would brief everyone again about the operation. It would be organized, thorough, and methodical. Specific teams would already be established en route. Team assignments would be made in Platteville. But she would first quickly meet with the police chief to advise him of their plans.

They would leave with all necessary equipment on a state bus she was able to obtain from the state's Transportation Department motor vehicle section. Departure time on Thursday was set for 6:00am sharp. The trip would take about three hours so they had two days to get everything ready and set for departure.

By 4:00pm, before they said their goodnights, Cal had another question, which was a good one.

"Hey, Maria, um, who's going to drive the bus?"

Maria turned and looked at him, with a somewhat Mona Lisa smile before turning into an expression of surprise, as if she hadn't thought of that.

"Oh my goodness, Cal. Why, I…" she started to say with hesitation. "Guess *you* will."

Apparently, Cal for a moment hadn't caught on. He looked at her like he had just stuck his finger into an electric socket. She nearly laughed. She knew neither of them had public service licenses. "Got that covered buddy. See ya tomorrow."

He kept looking at her as she turned and walked out, shaking his head and mumbling with an unseen smile, "I should've known." Soon he too left. Tomorrow would likely be another long day.

24

The next morning, ten teams south of Los Angeles reported in, stating they had found and destroyed fifty-eight nests. After weeks of searching and going over previously uncovered areas, they were unable to find any more. Everyone knew that it would be literally impossible to guarantee that every nest that existed would be found and destroyed. But for now, all areas of southern California were covered as best as humanly possible.

She decided to leave five teams down there to canvass whatever areas were left to do. They would maintain communications with her wherever she was and advise her when their mission was complete or if they discovered more nests. The other five teams were pulled and told to go home and wait for a call-up again, which could happen anytime today or tomorrow. Platteville would be their next assignment. And it would be very soon.

There was nothing Maria could do out there right now. They had to stick close to the office and wait for the call that would set things into motion.

Cal decided to check things on the equipment which had been delivered already to their building. It was important that they be as patent and protective as they could be, so he asked one of his assistants to check on them and make sure the fifty-three that were ordered were there. He could check for patency as he was counting each one. All that needed to be done was done quickly in case of a callup today.

In the meantime, Maria was doing her own little checking up. She looked at one of the two vespa specimens they had obtained for further examination. Even dead, they looked devilish. Yet the scientist in her was still in awe at both their simpleness and complexity. She could well understand the terror something like this could instill. However, scientist or not, running into something like this while it's alive could cause anyone to have a very bad day.

With just her eyes, she examined every area of its body. The thorax was thick and long, and the head seemed to be slightly disproportionately large, even for its size. The venom glands were large and obviously held considerably more venom than those of the vespa's smaller cousins. In addition, she knew that it wasn't just quantity that made the venom deadlier, but its potency as well. These vespas had venom that was one and a half times more potent than normal-sized ones, and three times the potency of regular American hornets. Their aggressiveness seemed to be a match in intensity to their menacing appearance. This thing had once been a very dangerous killing "machine." And there were still plenty of them still out there.

Maria hated waiting for phone calls. She'd always been that way. But then, who didn't? To pass the time throughout the day, she played catch-up on much of the paperwork and organized some things that she had put on the backburner for a while. This was her chance to do this while she had it. Most of the time, especially now, the only chance for her to even get close to it was to look at the to-do list while passing by. That's what occurred on most normal days.

Several hours had passed and it was now 3:34pm. She was glad she had not watched the clock. In her lab and field, there was always something to do.

Then ten minutes later she jumped in her seat, startled by the phone call which seemed to rip through the silence, almost like an unexpected explosion. It was the governor's office.

Speaking with his assistant, she was informed that the governor was authorizing the chemical airdrop over Platteville once all residents and all other persons who were not wearing protective gear were inside buildings somewhere.

Maria had three days to gather up her personnel and equipment and get up there. The airdrop spraying would be conducted in two days.

"So how long before it would be safe for people to go back outside?" she asked the caller. Maria needed to know this to let the police chief there know.

She heard papers shuffling on the other end. "Let's see…" the assistant said. "According to what's on the official paper here, two hours minimum. If I were there, I'd wait three."

"Thank you, ma'am," replied Maria. "I would too. Thank you so much. Tell Governor Capulette I'll keep him posted after we are all done."

Now the "race" was on. She wasted no time in contacting the teams and the bus driver, then let Cal know. The equipment was already there in storage, so his part had already been completed. Rendezvous would be in three days, which would now be Friday instead of Thursday. They were to meet at the office building at 5:45 am. Departure would be at 6:00am sharp. An early start was necessary to arrive there at a decent time because it was a three-hour trip and they might be there all day. In fact, she wasn't sure how long exactly they would be there. But she *was* sure that they could not leave until it was certain they had gotten the nest or all the nests if there was more than one. It was not knowing how many there were that was the hard part.

A half hour later, her phone calls were done and everyone coming in understood what she had told them. While en route, she would instruct them on the strategic planning that had to go into this. The mission had to be well-organized for it to succeed. They could not afford to miss any areas. Her plan had to be precise in team area assignments. All equipment had to be checked again before they proceeded out, and their suits and headgear checked again also, to ensure that none were compromised. This was a one-shot deal and they had to get it right.

Up to now there was still no further reports of attacks. It seemed that the statewide problem was nearing a resolution. After nearly five months, the number of known attack victims had dwindled down to nearly zero. Thanks to the quick actions of the California's entomology scientists and the governor's office, the public was beginning to relax from all the fears of going outside. Yet for many still-having seen, witnessed, experienced or simply heard about the attacks and the horrible suffering they caused-it was difficult to completely relax. People were still looking up in the air and all around them, even briefly, whenever they went outside. As it was now, things were quiet. None of the giant insects had been seen anywhere. For most people, that was perfectly fine for them. But then in life, nothing was ever guaranteed.

***

Platteville, one day before the attacks
Unknown to anyone, a homeless man had found something huge on the ground in a grassy area behind some stores. It looked to him like a giant hornet, something he'd never seen

before. He didn't like bugs of any kind, especially the stinging kinds. This one scared the bejesus out of him because it was nearly as long as his shoe. He could have just run away. But out of fear and reflex, he didn't hesitate to stomp on it as fast as possible. Unfortunately, it took numerous stomps before he could kill it. He couldn't understand how a bug could be so gargantuan.

"Die, you son-of-a-bitch, die!" he yelled at it as he continued to pummel it with his shoes. The huge insect tried to get away as the soft ground gave way under the man's shoe.

Finally, after at least a minute or two of continuous stomping, the insect finally died. The man breathed a sigh of relief. "Serves you right," he said to it with a couple more expletives. "Hope you go to insect hell where you belong."

He looked at it for several moments but it didn't move. Once he was sure it was dead, he moved on. He had to look for something to eat, so the next dumpster wasn't far away. Right behind a restaurant. Good. The incident was immediately out of his sight and mind. He still felt a nice buzz from his last drink.

He didn't know it, but the queen he had unwittingly killed had sent out her pheromones during her death throes. When the queen sent those out, subjects everywhere who could smell them immediately took to the skies to home in on the source with furious determination.

The man found something to eat and pulled it out of the dumpster, not giving what happened a second thought. He chomped on the thrown out burger. There were more important things to think about anyway. Like food.

25

San Luis Obispo, Friday

Departure was only about five minutes later than planned but was not late enough to affect their plans for the day. There were about forty persons that could comfortably fit on the bus. Two state vans were appropriated for the rest, which carried the chemical tanks needed for their task.

It was now 5:50 am and after a pleasant "Good morning" and a few more pleasantries, Maria got down to business about their strategies in Platteville. She used a walkie talkie while she was talking to connect with those in the vans behind them who were on it also.

First, she read off the different teams and who would be in each group. There would be five teams of ten people. Their base would be initially at the police station there. By that morning, it would have been twenty-four hours since the last spraying. Hopefully, they would find no hornets or other stinging insects. Unfortunately, if there were any bees, they'd likely become casualties as well if the hornets didn't get them first.

After all was said and done, Maria sat down. It was just a couple of minutes after six. Everyone was present and accounted for and the bus began the journey. For the team, the next three hours would be uneventful. Some of the members settled down to relax, others engaged in conversations about anything and everything. Much of those talks related to the issues at hand and what they would soon face.

***

Platteville

Friday was a cloudy day without rain. It was late afternoon. The

driver was a local resident who delivered food supplies and other things for the restaurants in town. His final delivery of the day would be behind the restaurant at the loading dock.

Although he was only in his late sixties, his pokey driving sometimes aggravated other drivers who were in a rush. But no problem. They could always pass him. Most of the roads around here were rural anyway and he didn't care what they thought of his driving. He was careful and had never had one accident; at least not any that he had caused. Today there was no one behind him as he neared the downtown area, if you could call it that. He always just kept plugging along as if he believed sluggishness meant safety.

As he hummed familiar favored tunes, he often looked out his side window at the sights going by in the opposite direction. It was just a habit he had. It didn't interfere with his driving. He never would let that happen.

He neared the driveway with his box truck and turned into it, slowly making his way toward the restaurant's delivery area. Nearing his delivery stop, he slammed on the brakes when he spotted something near the dumpster.

His eyes scrunched up and narrowed as he slowly neared the suspicious object. It didn't look like it belonged here and it just lay there without moving. In fact, there were two things on the ground. He felt the blood start draining out of his face and his heart pumping rapidly. His brain had a difficult time processing what he was seeing while trying to convince him it was only a broken manikin. He hadn't had a drink for a couple of days.

He saw the head and then the body, separated from each other. "Shit, it has to be a manikin. Sure looks real," he said out loud to himself. He knew immediately what he was looking at, yet his brain still tried to deny it. His eyes opened nearly as wide as his mouth as shock started to wrap itself around him, and then hit him like a brick wall. That made him stop in his tracks. When he left his truck and walked over to them, he realized this was no manikin. He recognized the face of the homeless man. Turning quickly, he vomited on the ground and pulled out his cell.

Seven minutes later, two Platteville police cars pulled up. It didn't take them long to see the torn apart body. A crime scene was established because they as yet didn't know the perpetrator of the man's death. The chief was notified who then contacted the coroner's office. It was the beginning of an investigation that would immediately go statewide, then national and international after identification was confirmed. The victim had no known family in the area or anywhere else that they could determine.

Their initial visible assessment of the body itself revealed what looked like puncture holes all over the clothing. It would be known soon enough because the coroner was now on his way.

***

They arrived a little less than three hours after departure. The riders were all ready to stretch their legs and take bathroom breaks. At the police station, they disembarked, with the SUVs parked behind the bus. The tanks were left in the SUVs for now. They would don their protective suits and gear just before they headed out to their assigned areas. Maria would let them know where each team would be dispersed to. But she would have to quickly assess the area after getting a briefing and description of the area by the town's police chief.

Some of the members went inside to use the facilities, others waited their turns outside. The station was small because the town was. Maria went to the chief before anything else, wanting to get a brief rundown of the area. She drank very little on the bus, so she could wait for the restroom just a little longer.

After introducing themselves followed by polite small talk, they got down to business, with Chief Riley starting out. He immediately told her about the dismembered head and body, which sent shock waves into her. She didn't know what to think at that moment. But she couldn't help wondering if the killing was related in any way to what was going on here.

"Our town isn't very big but it's large enough to support a decent population of five thousand," continued Riley "We never get incidents like this. Not only is this a shock, but it doesn't make any sense. Now we have to wonder who could have done such a thing. First the insects, now this."

Maria nodded as she listened. "I'm wondering if it's a *what* rather than a *who*." Riley looked at her with a 'what-the-hell-are-you-talking about look.'

She then explained what she was thinking yet found it difficult that it would be possible. But rather than speculate, only the coroner and medical examiner autopsy would reveal the true culprit. For now, she had to continue what she came here for.

"How did the spraying go, Chief?" she asked. "Were they able to cover all areas?"

He nodded. "That's what they told me. According to what the pilots reported, they covered all areas they could see from the air. After the spraying was done, the state sent in a couple of drones with cameras to get a closer look at the trees and ground. Although they couldn't specifically ID any nests, they were sure that every spot in the area was covered. In fact, they covered such a large area that one of the pilots suspected he'd gone into another county. That's when he stopped spraying."

"Ok, sounds like they were pretty thorough," she nodded.

"Here," said the chief as he pulled out a large, folded paper from a shelf behind him and unfolded it. "Got a map here where I can show you at a glance the entire geographics of this area."

Bending over, she examined the map to gain some kind of insight for the topography of the area. There were a number of forested areas spotting the landscape along with a few hills and small ravines. This suggested plenty of areas that could support nests.

Meanwhile as she went over this with the chief, the team members kept going in and out until everyone had used the restrooms. Once they started their mission, they might not have another opportunity for a while.

Once satisfied that she had all the information she needed, Maria thanked the chief, promising to keep him posted on their progress when she could. On her request, Chief Riley readily agreed to let as many people know to stay out of the team's working areas until they were done.

As she walked out of the station to prepare the team, a call came in to her cell phone. She stopped to listen as the team stood outside the bus.

"You're not joking, right? I mean, tell me you *are* joking!" she responded. She didn't talk loudly but the team heard her anyway and it caught their attention. If they had been dogs, their ears would've stood straight up.

They saw her jaw drop which instantly alerted them that something incomprehensible must have happened. As many terrible things had happened that they had worked with her on, they had never seen her react with such shock. Whatever it was, whatever was being told to her would probably haunt her for the rest of her life. Maybe them too. All their conversation had stopped on a dime. All they could do was look at her, listen, and wait for her to hang up.

She must have been on the phone for at least seven to ten minutes.

"This was confirmed by the coroner?" they heard her ask. "Ok, thanks Ron."

She looked up to the chief. "That was one of my team members who had heard about observations of the body by the coroner earlier. The body and head were removed to his office. Puncture holes all over the body. Apparently the victim was a homeless man in town."

"Yea, that's what was reported to me earlier." He wasted no time in calling the coroner.

"I'm about to begin the autopsy, Fred," the coroner told the chief. "But as a preliminary thought and seeing as there is a crisis going on in town, I'm letting you know at the start that there are puncture holes everywhere on the torso and legs which I don't think were made by knives or anything else that could be tools. I won't know for sure until I've examined them more thoroughly. Give me about two to three hours.

"Well," he said to Maria, "guess it's a wait and see. He's about to do the autopsy. The victim was a guy nicknamed "Pickles." A homeless guy. Lived here the whole thirty years I've been here. No one knows his real name or why he has that nickname. Guess he just liked to keep it that way. Right now, it doesn't appear to be a crime. Not in our sense of the word. I'll be standing by and waiting for his call. In the meantime, I'll have a couple of my men standby for you in case of anything."

"Ok. Let me know when you find out something, would you, Chief? Especially about the puncture holes."

"Doctor, I don't understand about the decap. There is no animal on this entire planet that I know of that can do that. Except humans."

The scientist looked at him and looked down for a few moments. She was thinking, then looked back at him.

"I have an idea what it could be. But it's so preposterous that I can't say it out loud without sounding like a loony. But when I find out the coroner's assessment of those puncture holes, I'll know whether to can my idea or expand on it. If I have to expand on it, we may have more trouble than we think. We better go. See ya later."

Outside she had everyone gather around and laid out their assignments and which teams would go where. With the town having been sprayed the day before, she hoped that they would find nests but no inhabitants anywhere around them or in the area. They were to spray the nests directly anyway just to be sure.

One of the town officers had talked to the truck delivery driver to find out what he knew or witnessed since he was the one who discovered the head and body. He hadn't seen who did it and did not see anyone leaving the scene or anyone else around at that time. No real leads developed from that information.

There were no eyewitnesses to the actual incident. No weapon was found and no blood trail. Even the county sheriff's office sent a couple of its deputies to check on it and offered to lend assistance to the small police force. With no possible suspects as yet, there wasn't much that could be done for the moment. It was a waiting game, and that was for the autopsy results.

Ten minutes later the teams were being dropped off at their assigned locations throughout the town and perimeter areas. Each had an experienced leader who knew how to conduct a methodical and organized search. The only way they would be able to cover all of their area within a reasonable time was to conduct it that way.

Two hours later the teams were still out there. Chief Riley received a call from the coroner's office. The autopsy was complete, and the news was gruesome and disturbing.

"Fred, in all my thirty plus years of doing this, this is the first time I am truly boggled about the manner of death. From what I saw, examined, analyzed and concluded, it doesn't fall under the first four prime categories. Right now, it can only be classified as undetermined."

Riley just stared ahead at the wall as if he'd heard the sky was falling.

"Let me explain without going into too much detail. From the largest to the tiniest details that I examined as best I could, I concluded that the head was not detached from the body by a human or wild animal. There were no indications of a saw or machete being used, nothing else that a mad person might use. And no teeth marks. It was certainly not pulled off. Sounds like science fiction? Tell me about it." He then continued on.

"The puncture holes on the body itself were not made by bullets, knives, or any other pointy objects that would be tools or any other hand equipment. Nothing I could think of that's man-made would have made those kinds of holes. So the mystery continues.

"The head was not actually cut off. Where it was cut and separated from the neck shows no clean edges but rather serrated edges all around it. Nothing like I've ever seen before. It was almost like it was *sawed* through area by area all the way through the different levels of tissue until it was separated from the body. Whatever did this, it took it a while to complete. A human could have sawn through it in a matter of a couple of minutes. But I don't believe a person did it. If it had been, he or she would have a serious mental illness. Or would be a very deranged psychopath.

"Now for the third and final part of my report to you, but by no means the end of the report itself. Toxicology. Turns out there were very unusual substances found in the blood and tissues and there was a lot of it."

Then he told the chief what it was, that it was one natural body chemical normally in the brain and nowhere else. Yet the body was wracked with it everywhere. "The other two substances I am unfamiliar with but I know are not found in humans."

"Doc, what do we have going on here?" the chief asked. "This sounds like the freaking twilight zone. In a small nutshell, give me your conclusive findings." He didn't know what to think after hearing this. Were they dealing with some kind of supernatural phenomenon or alien issues here?

"Ok," the pathologist said. "This is not something I would be able to hand in to a court of law if it were a criminal case. But there is no crime. Here are my findings: Cause of death: envenomation. Mechanism of death: injection of a chemical neurotransmitter and other toxic substances not common in the body in deadly amounts causing collapse of the major blood vessels, major tissue destruction of the internal organs and collapse of the respiratory system, leading to heart failure and arrest, as well as respiratory arrest. Each of the holes was created by something round and sharp. Manner of death: undetermined. From what I told you, you can see why I could not classify it as any of the other categories. That's it in a nutshell, Chief. As a brief last word, because I know you're wondering, the head was detached *after* death. If there was a manner of death category called *unnatural,* that's what I would have given it."

After he hung up, Riley now feared the worst. It was them. The invaders. But how? Even with their increased size, he just couldn't believe they could possibly do something like that. It was ludicrous. As bizarre as it seemed to be, he now knew his suspects were not human. The coroner had been right. It was no crime, but rather an abomination.

He contacted Maria with his walkie-talkie and filled her in on the report. She didn't seem surprised by what he told her. Now she could expand on that idea she had and follow up on that as soon as possible. But something had changed and it was not for the better. Another mutation and not for the better. They had a bigger problem on their hands. Literally.

***

"Wait a minute," said the chief with his hand up. "You really think the man was killed by…?" He didn't even want to say it, but she knew.

Instead of answering, Maria just looked at him, nodding ever so slightly. He couldn't argue the autopsy findings.

He went and sat down behind his desk, rubbing his face, not knowing what to say to that. "Well, I find that hard to believe. But well… Godzilla hornets, for Jiminy's sake! How the hell would that be possible? I thought these damn things were three inches long? No one has to be a rocket scientist to know that even three inchers can't decapitate people. So now you're suggesting, pardon my fuckin' French, that these things are now big enough to eliminate a person's physical identity from the rest of him?"

"Chief, from what we know of what these things in their natural state do, if large enough, I'm not surprised if this thing that killed the homeless man was trying to take the body away but it was too large and heavy for it to lift. That's what they do to honeybees in order to feed their young."

He was too dumbfounded to respond to that. Despite her science fiction type explanation, the circumstances and all the information combined seemed to point in that direction.

Riley was struggling with it. Yet he knew at the same time that if it was no mammal that did it, then that left a lot of other things that were not mammals. It was difficult for his brain to process. It was crazy.

Maria knew her theory would be a hard sell, because that's all it was: just a theory. But she would challenge anyone to come up with something better and more plausible. She as much as said so to him. Not surprisingly, he couldn't come up with one. He never saw any crime or heard of any one or any offender in his twenty plus years in law enforcement to commit something like this. This was not even typical of satanic rituals, although there hadn't been one in his county for at least twenty-five years. Hell, even Manson hadn't done that, although he would have if he chose to.

"So what's your plan if it turns out we have a hornetzilla on our hands? And what's even more curious, how could it have gotten that way in the first place? From what I heard on the News, they were contaminated with something down around Stockton."

"I don't know how it might have gotten bigger," Maria replied, frustrated at not knowing the answer. She intensely disliked not knowing something she should. "A fluke maybe. It's possible the contaminant caused out-of-control growth. Hell, look what happens in cancer. That's exactly what happens. Unless it was a queen that might have turned out a lot larger than it normally should be. But that can't be verified unless someone saw it. That someone was killed for it."

Moments ticked by along with the wall clock.

She broke the brief silence by explaining the contamination further south and the insects becoming mutated from the chemical. But if there were more chemical leakages elsewhere, say further north around where they were now, that could explain the possible gigantism of the local hornets. But it was only speculation.

There seemed to be more questions than answers, and the chief had another one. "Well if that's the case, why haven't all the other insects become more gigantean mutants? They must have come in contact with whatever caused the problem, especially mosquitoes. They just love water."

"That's a good question, Chief Riley. But one I don't have an answer for. We will definitely look into that as soon as we get this immediate business taken care of."

"Think we have that problem in this town?"

Maria nodded. "Very possible. I know this is a lot to ask but this thing is here. We are all in danger. Even us. We are prepared to fight these things as three, even four inchers. But at least one of them is considerably larger than that. Our thick suits might not protect us. Everyone here might be in mortal danger. That is, if any of those are still around after the spraying. I ask that you do your best to have everyone stay inside until we can confirm."

He looked at her. "Why would your suits not protect you? Aren't they almost thick enough to stop a bullet?"

She shook her head with a sheepish grin. "Not quite. I'll tell you why. They are made of a material that is almost as good as Kevlar. They won't stop a bullet but the suits are strong and thick enough to stop a one-inch stinger, which in itself is still humongous. The only thing we know that has a stinger that big or almost as big is a scorpion. If, for example this hornetzilla, as you call it, is say twenty inches long-God help us if it is-its stinger would be at least two or two and a half inches long. That would penetrate even the strongest protection suits. Kevlar would stop it, but not our suits. And, one of these things that large could probably do what was done to your victim."

Maria thought she saw the chief's face go pale. Even the most veteran law enforcers would find that a challenge to their "show-no emotion-be-professional" mentality. He picked up the mike on his shoulder and made an announcement to all on-duty officers. When he finished, she made a request of him.

"Chief, my teams are out there now. I need to make some phone calls, including to the governor's office. May I use a part of your station here to work?"

"Of course, Ddoctor." He then directed her to a small unused office outside of his she could use across the small hall.

He told Maria he would contact the local media and hope everyone heard about staying indoors somewhere for at least the next couple of hours. She thanked him and let him know of their progress as she was regularly updated. Then she left his office after thanking him, bringing her computer tablet, some documents she had in a case she carried with her, her walkie talkie and phone.

If what she said was true, they were all in a potentially life-threatening situation. Before they had left for their assignments, they were allowed a few minutes to process what they were going up against. They all had constantly heard about these things but none of them had come across any of them. In that sense they were extremely lucky. Like her, they all had families they had to take care of. Endangering their lives to the extent that death became a high probability was not something they had signed up for. Yet somehow she sensed they were strong and determined enough to fight them if they had to. All were initially offered to return home if any of them didn't want to take the risk, with absolutely no repercussions whatsoever. None took her up on it. They were ready to tackle them.

One of them had actually suggested obtaining a flame-thrower to use against the giant "monster", as he put it. Maria smirked at him. Really? She was waiting for him to also suggest a bazooka.

But, after quickly brushing it off, it gave her pause for thought. Now *that* was something she had never considered. The flame-thrower, that is. Sounded ridiculous as if it were in a class B sci-fi movie. Against the three-inchers, no way. But against a true giant, maybe a twenty or so incher like she mentioned before? It was certainly something she had to consider. If the thing turned out to be that big.

She wanted to keep it to herself regarding that last suggestion because she had to find out if that was even doable. Was one available anywhere around here? Or could one be obtained?

At her desk, she became aware of the eerie silence and quiet in the air. There were no sounds of anything, not even birds. The fact that there was no breeze was not necessarily suggestive of anything. In fact, the silence itself didn't necessarily suggest anything wrong. But she had a gut feeling and it made her nervous.

Going to the chief, she apologized for interrupting him, but decided to run the idea by him to see what he thought. He remained courteous, not brushing it off as nonsensical. However, the flame-thrower turned out not to be practical and he shook his head. Being a military vet himself, he knew that was something only the military had. It was not to be used for her purposes. Besides, none was not currently obtainable anyway.

Even if one was, they wouldn't be able to get it in time for their current mission.

"But our fire department has water cannons. Think that could help you?"

His suggestion was the next best thing and not a bad one at that.

"That would be wonderful. We could use them on standby. But Chief, they would have to know the extreme danger they would be placing them in. If the monster is around here, their thick fire suits might not be enough. There also might be lots of places that they couldn't bring a firehose to."

He stood up and came around to the front of his desk. "Now don't you worry about that, little lady. I think those suits they wear are plenty thick enough. If those guys were afraid of any kind of danger, even this, then they wouldn't be firefighters, would they?"

"You have a point. Anyway, we have plenty of chemical tanks we plan on using if the need arises. Likely more than enough."

"Tell you what, I'll contact the fire chief right now and give him a heads up. Want the truck to meet you somewhere?"

"Let me check with the teams and see if any active nests have been spotted before any trucks are sent. Who knows-we may not need them. I have my cell and will get back to you if you can give me your number?"

The chief wrote it down and gave her the paper with it.

"We won't ask for the truck unless we need it. Hopefully, we won't find any nests but if we do, we have our chemicals. If our leviathan hornet shows up or is suspected to be in their area, I will call you for the truck."

Back in her temporary office, she kept in touch with them frequently for an update, wanting to know of any sightings. If she was needed at one of the areas, she would go there immediately with the bus.

After calling Cal, she learned there had been no further reports of significant hornet attacks down there. There had been quite a bit of spraying over the previously affected areas. In fact, much more spraying than was expected. Some people were likely wondering if there was overkill happening. The few search teams that were still out there had seen nests that were no longer inhabited, but plenty of hornet bodies were seen outside most of them. This was good news to her and hopefully the problem was starting to be resolved.

When she checked with the teams down at Yosemite, the spraying was nearly complete and the searches of the affected areas had resulted in finding some nests but no inhabitants. It seemed the prolific spraying of the park in those areas was a success. Although, as with most things in life, nothing is ever truly guaranteed. For now, it was a turning point in the battle no one thought would ever be.

26

Governor Capulette, along with Maria Hernandez, decided that it would be imprudent to declare the war against the hornets a complete success at this time. Premature conclusions often came back around and bit one in the behind. Karma can be a bitch.

She had talked with him on the phone at her operations base in Platteville. So far the teams reported no sightings of any of the creatures, although they had thought they spotted a nest. It turned out to be a false alarm, believed to be a ground squirrel's nest. They hadn't seen any hanging from any trees. Either the creatures had been killed, their nest was farther away than they believed, or they had migrated elsewhere. There was no way to know, except from new reports. So far there were none.

Next call she made was to the El Dorado Sheriff's Department. After identifying herself, she asked to speak to the detective in charge of the Pickles death. Chief Riley had mentioned to her that the Sheriff was assisting the small Platteville PD in the investigation of the homeless man's death.

It was a Detective Williamson that they connected her to.

"Oh yes, hello, Doctor Hernandez. I've heard of you on the news investigating these hornet attacks. I was kind of expecting you to call."

"Oh? Did you have some information for me?" she asked.

"Well I just wanted to give you an update on the death. I talked with the coroner and…"

She interrupted him to let him know that she also talked with him. Her conclusion based on what he told her was that the victim had been killed by a larger form of the vespa and that he was likely the only person to have seen his killer.

Because the death was not from a crime, law enforcement no longer had a case. But he asked her to keep him posted when she and the teams were done. He wanted to be assured that the area was safe again.

After that assurance was made and the call ended, the chief came to her office door.

"Would you like a coffee, Doctor?" The chief's voice startled her and she jumped slightly. "Oh, I'm sorry. I didn't mean to scare you."

She brushed her hair and smiled. "Uh, no that's alright, Chief. I was just thinking. Yes, I would love a cup of coffee."

Riley pointed toward the back. "How do you take it?" She told him and thanked him.

Three boring hours later, she wished she had gone out with one of the teams. It was turning out to be a long day, but she preferred that to having a busy one being attacked by giant six-legged creatures from hell. Although she hated just waiting and not doing anything, sometimes silence can be golden. But then the walkie talkie broke through the silence.

One of the teams had completed its search area but not found any nests or signs of the vespas. Maria advised them to move ahead toward the next adjacent area to help the other team out.

As the searches continued throughout the day, teams continued to find no signs of the insects. One nest was found with dead bodies inside and surrounding it. On the opposite side of town where the last team was let off, another nest was found with the same results. Hundreds of dead hornet bodies were discovered. The chemical drop spraying had worked.Maria breathed a sigh of relief but she had to be sure before she called it completed. All the teams eventually gathered together and she told them to make one final sweep of all accessible areas to be sure. Once they left, they were not expected to return.

After informing the chief, she walked to the front of the station and looked out the window. Her exhaustion suddenly caught up with her. She hoped this was nearly over and just wanted to go home and get some rest. Only the final report from the congregated team would determine if their mission was successful or not. What surprised her was the fact that there had been not one report of a gargantuan hornet in the area or anything else of that nature.

She hoped it had been killed by the spray. But at the same time, in the back of her mind, she hoped a little that it would still be spotted somewhere so its existence could be validated. Right now, that might not be possible. If it was still alive, allergic reactions to it would not be an issue. It would kill anything and anyone. The ideal situation would be to find its dead body, assuming it was the only one that size.

The walkie talkie suddenly erupted thirty minutes later. The team's final report revealed no new discoveries of any insects or other nests.

"Ok, copy." Maria gave them their final command. "Return to base here. I'll send the bus down there now."

As she went to the door, there was a sudden loud bang against the thick glass of the police station. It sounded almost like a gunshot. She jumped back in fright and the chief came running out of his office. "What the hell was that?" he shouted. "Doctor, are you alright?"

"Yea. Look at that!" she yelled back, pointing toward the window.

There it was. What she had feared yet hoped to see anyway. It was as huge as she had believed. Twenty inches maybe, give or take an inch or two. It was not something anyone would ever want to run into.

"That's it!" Maria yelled at the chief. "Chief, please call your firefighter buddies and bring the water cannon. I will call my bus driver on the radio and get the team back here. Advise your officers not to get out of their cars."

Maria then contacted her bus driver on the walkie talkie, hoping he wasn't sleeping. There was no way she was going out to him with that thing just outside the window.

Fortunately, he answered and when he saw what she was referring to, he immediately slammed the bus door shut. In seconds he was on his way down to pick up the team.

After hearing from her, the team got their tanks readied and primed for use. Although there were no more swarms to deal with in this area, it was apparent that the danger wasn't gone yet. There was one more they had to deal with.

On their arrival they looked out their windows but the thing wasn't there on the station window anymore. Maria had seen it fly off but there wasn't anything she could do.

"Doctor, could that have been the queen?" the chief asked.

She turned, shaking her head. "I don't know. Maybe. Although queens are always larger than all the others under normal circumstances, none are close to being this big. It could be an even larger mutant. I wasn't able to see it long enough. We have to find it and kill it before it kills anyone."

Within minutes, the firetruck arrived. The chief and scientist went outside and talked with the firefighters. Several gathered outside the small police building and she immediately made it known that they had to find the mutant and have the water cannon ready for immediate use. It was all they had in addition to the much smaller hoses from the chemical tanks.

As plans were being made to begin the search, one of the firefighters was suddenly hit on the back by something which seemed to come out of nowhere. He screamed in pain as something pierced deep into his back through the thick firefighter coat.

It took only a few seconds for their brains to process what they were seeing. They immediately jumped into action.

One of the other firefighters, without thinking, swiped the large creature off his colleague's back. It fell onto the ground upside down. The adrenaline had kicked in so fast that he didn't have time to become furious. That would come later. He just wanted to save his firefighter brother's life.

The creature was trying to fight back. Its large wings were flapping furiously as it tried to right itself back onto its feet. "Get it," yelled Maria. "Don't let it get back up!" Its loud low buzzing revealed its fury.

One of the others had called the station for an ambulance. The stung firefighter had to be treated at the nearest hospital immediately. In about two minutes the ambulance arrived. In another two minutes, he had been put on a stretcher and was soon on his way.

Another two firefighters had the hose in their hands pointing at the grounded twenty-plus inch hornet. The man who had knocked it off his buddy had stomped on it several times. After one of the others yelled out a warning, he then jumped back and let the now spurting water cannon do its deadly work. Just brief enough to ensure that it would never get back up again.

It seemed to Maria so surreal. Here they were in a very small town, appearing devoid of residents, in front of a police station and shooting a powerful water cannon at an outrageously large hornet, the likes which had never been seen before other than in a science fiction movie. There was no way to tell if it was the last of its kind. But she noticed that there were no "regular-sized" vespas- if one could call them that- around.

No signs of anything else. When all was suddenly quiet, they all stood around as if they were waiting for something else to happen.

The quiet included no buzzing. But then she started hearing some birds chirping in the distance. She hadn't heard that before. The signs of success seemed to be in the air. A sense of normalcy was finally returning.

Reports of no nests being found continued to pour in. When she checked with Cal, he also had no further reports of any more nests or attacks so far further down the state. Although not all of them were in, the likelihood of major eradication was increasing. There were still a number of other teams that had yet to report. This was a situation of no news being good news. But as with most things in life, there were never any guarantees. Though complete eradication might not be possible, the fact that they had it under control was the realistic goal that Maria knew could be obtained.

Thanking the chief and the firefighters for all their help and support, she wished them well and prayers for their firefighter brother to recover. One of them asked her if she wanted the dead sample over on the sidewalk, now flattened pretty much.

She looked at it and for a few moments, the scientist part of her brain was kicking in. But the practical part of it took over.

"No, thank you. I'll pass on this one. I think we have had enough of this creature for the time being."

Within thirty minutes, the entire team was in their bus and vehicles and was en route back home. Although their mission and all the other missions were successful, the chances of this happening again, either here in California or elsewhere, would always be present. For now, she was certain beyond any doubt that they had contained the problem and that it was under control. She would be ready next time should the need arise.

EPILOGUE

One week later

In Platteville, there were no further incidents of attacks against people or animals. But those few residents who had been attacked during the swarm onslaught and survived were permanently and emotionally affected. Although all continued to move forward with their lives, several became phobic of many stinging insects when they hadn't been before. But for all residents, life continued.

The scientists at the lab in San Luis Obispo continued to talk about it for weeks afterwards. Despite the fact that there were no reported attacks anywhere so far, Maria knew she could never believe that they were permanently gone. It was just a gut feeling. After all, they were still up in Washington and Oregon and could migrate down anytime if they left their controlled areas. And that contaminated pond was still there. Thinking about that, she picked up the phone to check on that.

After speaking with Dr. Bingham, she found out that Stanton Chemical Plant had chosen to clean it up and stop the leakage once and for all. It would be cheaper than the alternative.

In Lemon Grove, Billy Jansen, now fully recovered, was back home doing what little boys do. But his experience made him constantly wary every time he went outside, especially when he saw insects. He had learned never to take anything for granted. For him, it was certainly a life-altering experience.

The Bindells had memorialized their two sons in their Garden Acres church and then buried them in the city's cemetery where their parents were buried. A lot of people outside the family had gone to their funeral. It would be a day they would remember for the rest of their lives, along with that terrible day of discovery. Robert and Ruth would go on with their lives as before, except that life would never be the same.

California was settling down, thanks to the efforts of all the people involved in the fight against the invaders. Even so, it would never let its guard down again. The budget was increased for the state Department of Entomology. It was additionally given the task of permanent monitoring for any re-appearances of the murder hornet and have a special unit of assigned people to respond more quickly to a call. Maria would choose those people.

Logistics would include more chemical tanks with the proper strength of chemicals for fighting vespas. In addition to that, they would be provided an additional state van for use in emergencies or other important needs. They would no longer need to request a bus or other equipment. What equipment they received would be stored in one particular area of the building.

For her handling of the situation, Dr. Maria Hernandez was awarded a commendation by the governor. That was a feather in her cap for not only her, but for her department as well. But she didn't think she deserved it because it was her teams and front line members that really deserved the credit. They were the ones that actually faced the dangers. She smiled when she thought of them.

Outside her building, at the end of the day, she looked out at the lights starting to come on in the city. She deeply inhaled the fresh air, briefly appreciating the beautiful sight of the distant city lights in the valley below, before walking to her car to begin her journey home.

Check out other great
Cryptid Novels!

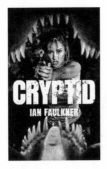

Ian Faulkner
CRYPTID

Be careful what you look for. You might just find it.1996. A group of 14 students walked into the trackless virgin forests of Graham Island, British Columbia for a three-day hike. They were never seen again. 2019. An American TV crew retrace those students' steps to attempt to solve a 23-year-old mystery.A disparate collection of characters arrives on the island. But all is not as it seems. Two of them carry dark secrets. Terrible knowledge that will mean death for some – but a fighting chance of survival for others. In the hidden depths of the forests – man is on the menu. Some mysteries should remain unsolved...

Eric S. Brown
LOCH NESS HORROR

The Order of the Eternal Light, a secret organization have foretold the end of the human race. In order to save all humanity, agents of the Order must locate the Loch Ness Monster and obtain a sample of its blood for within in it is the key to stopping the apocalypse but finding the monster will be no easy task.

Check out other great
Cryptid Novels!

Hunter Shea
THE DOVER DEMON

The Dover Demon is real...and it has returned. In 1977, Sam Brogna and his friends came upon a terrifying, alien creature on a deserted country road. What they witnessed was so bizarre, so chilling, they swore their silence. But their lives were changed forever. Decades later, the town of Dover has been hit by a massive blizzard. Sam's son, Nicky, is drawn to search for the infamous cryptid, only to disappear into the bowels of a secret underground lair. The Dover Demon is far deadlier than anyone could have believed. And there are many of them. Can Sam and his reunited friends rescue Nicky and battle a race of creatures so powerful, so sinister, that history itself has been shaped by their secretive presence? "THE DOVER DEMON is Shea's most delightful and insidiously terrifying monster yet." – Shotgun Logic Reviews "An excellent horror novel and a strong standout in the UFO and cryptid subgenres." –Hellnotes "Non-stop action awaits those brave enough to dive into the small town of Dover, and if you're lucky, you won't see the Demon himself!" – The Scary Reviews PRAISE FOR SWAMP MONSTER MASSACRE "B-horror movie fans rejoice, Hunter Shea is here to bring you the ultimate tale of terror!" – Horror Novel Reviews "A nonstop thrill ride! I couldn't put this book down." – Cedar Hollow Horror Reviews

Armand Rosamilia
THE BEAST

The end of summer, 1986. With only a few days left until the new school year, twins Jeremy and Jack Schaffer are on very different paths. Jeremy is the geek, playing Dungeons & Dragons with friends Kathleen and Randy, while Jack is the jock, getting into trouble with his buddies. And then everything changes when neighbor Mister Higgins is killed by a wild animal in his yard. Was it a bear? There's something big lurking in the woods behind their New Jersey home. Will the police be able to solve the murder before more Middletown residents are ripped apart?

Check out other great

Cryptid Novels!

Edward J. McFadden III

THE CRYPTID CLUB

When cryptozoologist Ash Cohn receives a gold embossed printed invitation inviting him to join The Cryptid Club, he sees the resolution to all his problems.Famous cryptid scientist and biologist, Lester Treemont, one of the world's richest men, and the leader of the Cryptid Club, is dying. What he offers via his invitation is a chance to succeed him. To take over his wealth, laboratory, and discoveries. All Ash has to do is beat eight others like him in a series of tests both mental and physical involving Treemont's collection of cryptids. Seems simple enough, and Ash has nothing to lose.Nine strangers from across the globe, all with reasons for wanting to win. When they start dying one by one, the competition shifts to one of survival. Who among them will rise to the top and reign over The Cryptid Club?

William Meikle

INFESTATION

It was supposed to be a simple mission. A suspected Russian spy boat is in trouble in Canadian waters. Investigate and report are the orders. But when Captain John Banks and his squad arrive, it is to find an empty vessel, and a scene of bloody mayhem. Soon they are in a fight for their lives, for there are things in the icy seas off Baffin Island, scuttling, hungry things with a taste for human flesh. They are swarming. And they are growing. "Scotland's best Horror writer" - Ginger Nuts of Horror "The premier storyteller of our time." - Famous Monsters of Filmland

Made in the USA
Middletown, DE
17 May 2021